THE CRYPTID CLUB

♫ Hum-Dum-Dum-Dum-Dee-Dum ♪

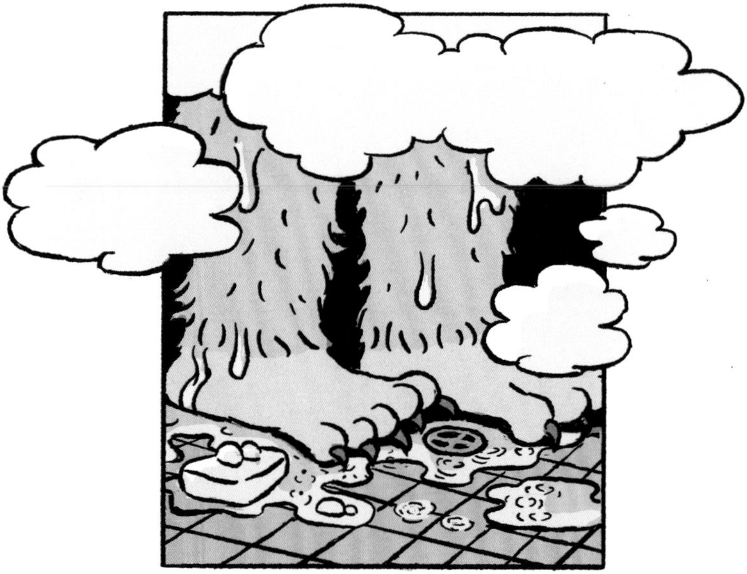

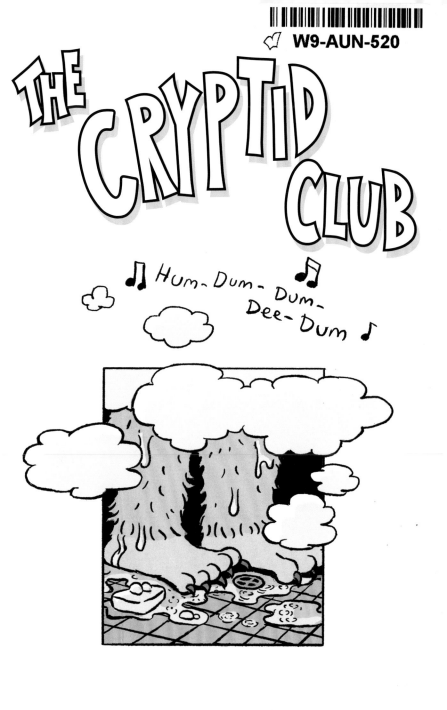

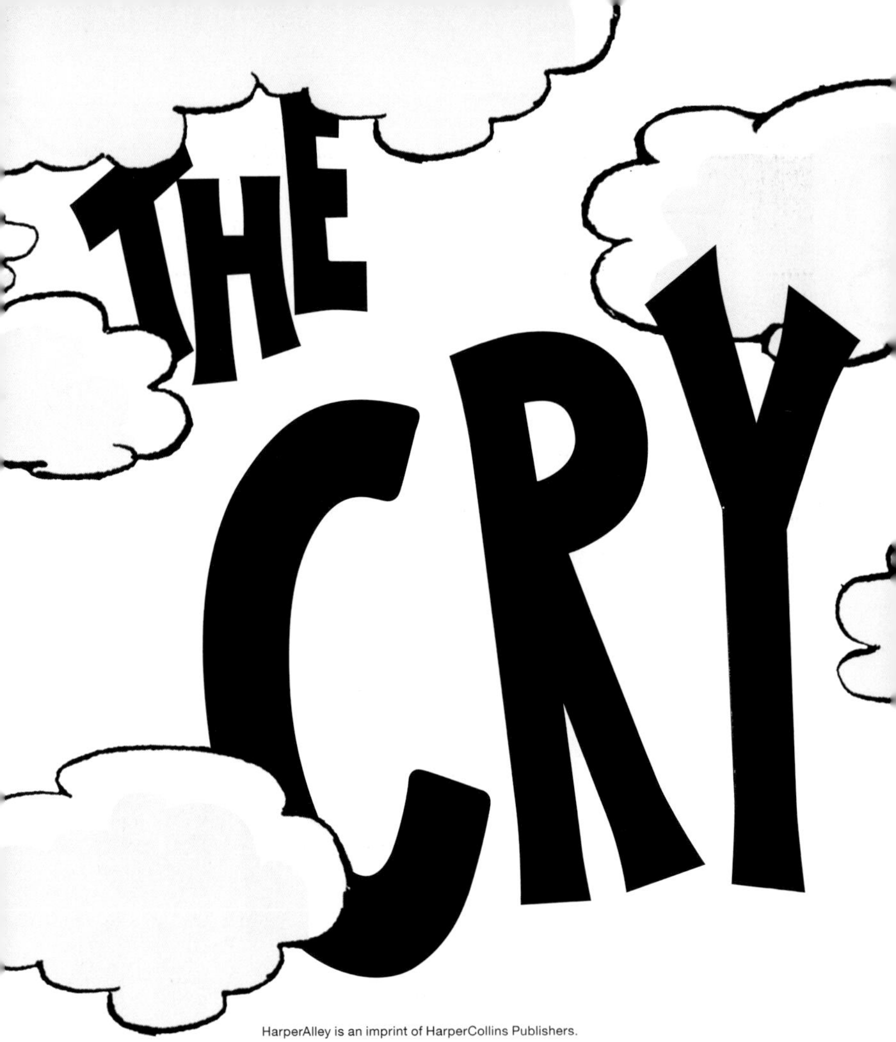
THE CRY

HarperAlley is an imprint of HarperCollins Publishers.

Cryptid Club #1: Bigfoot Takes the Field

Library of Congress Control Number: 2021933200
ISBN 978-0-06-306079-1 — ISBN 978-0-06-306078-4 (pbk.)

Typography by Joe Merkel
22 23 24 25 26 RTLO 10 9 8 7 6 5 4 3 2 1
❖
First Edition

PTID

CLUB

**BIGFOOT
TAKES THE FIELD**

HARPER
alley

An imprint of HarperCollinsPublishers

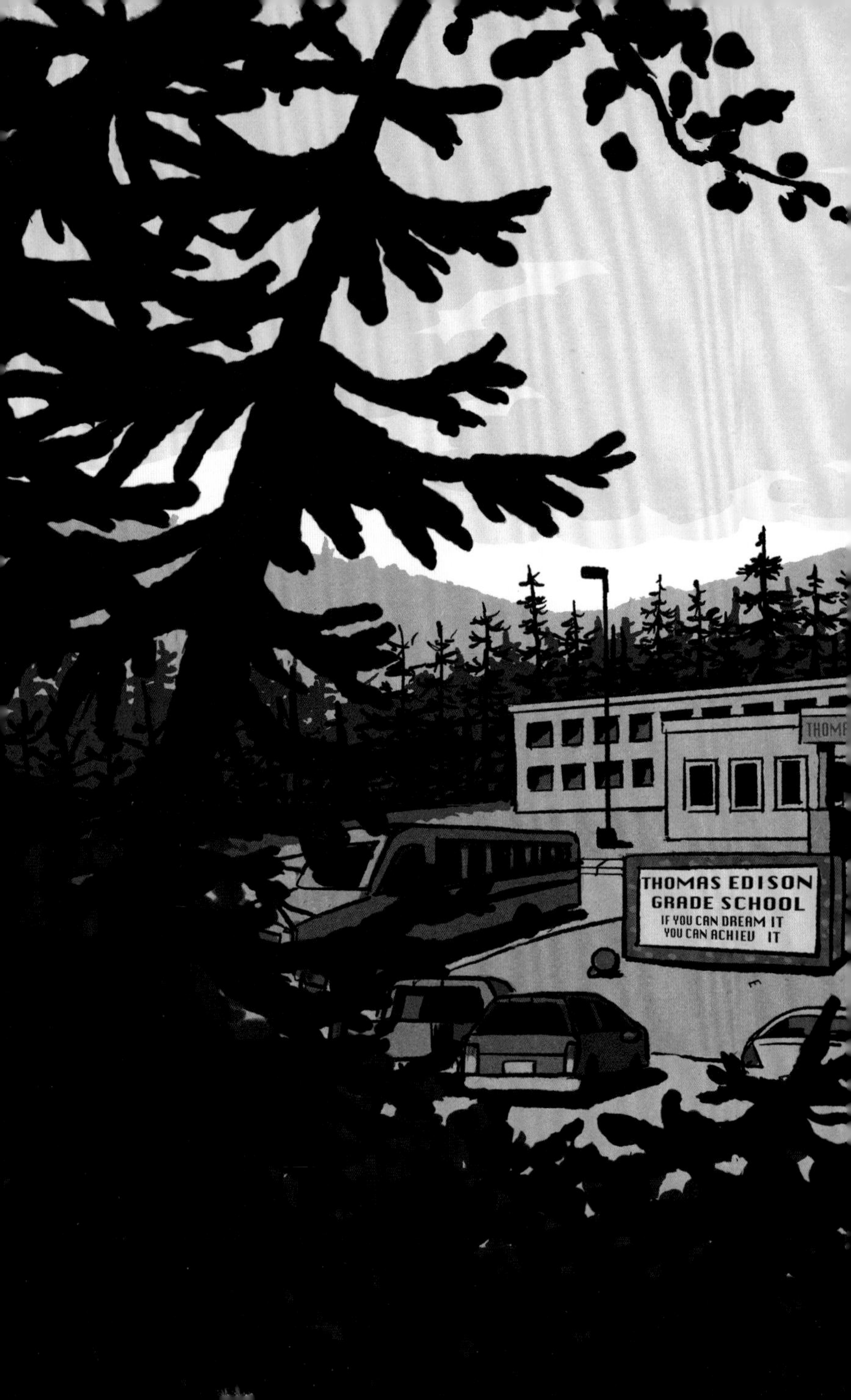
THOMAS EDISON
GRADE SCHOOL
IF YOU CAN DREAM IT
YOU CAN ACHIEV IT

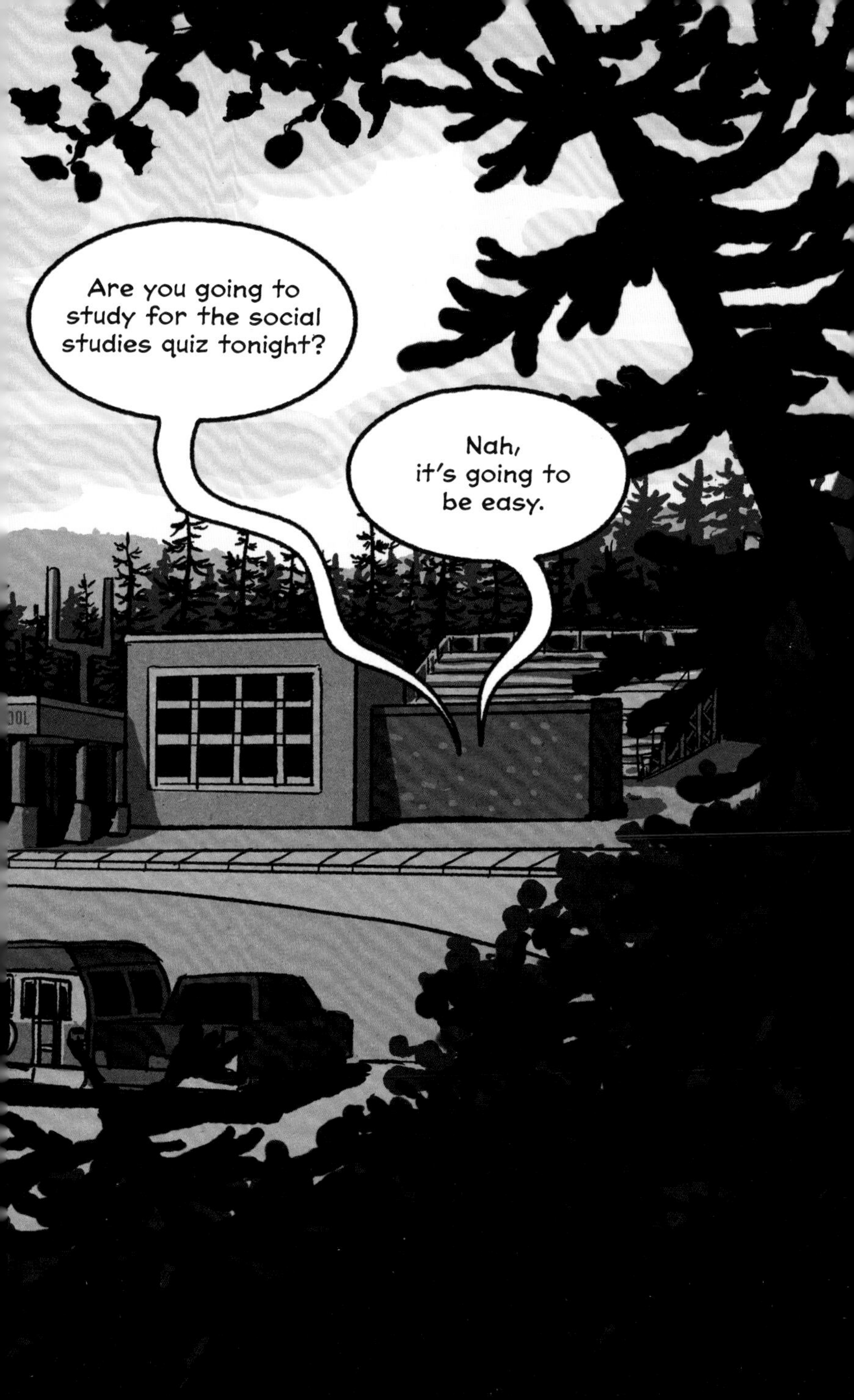
Are you going to study for the social studies quiz tonight?
Nah, it's going to be easy.

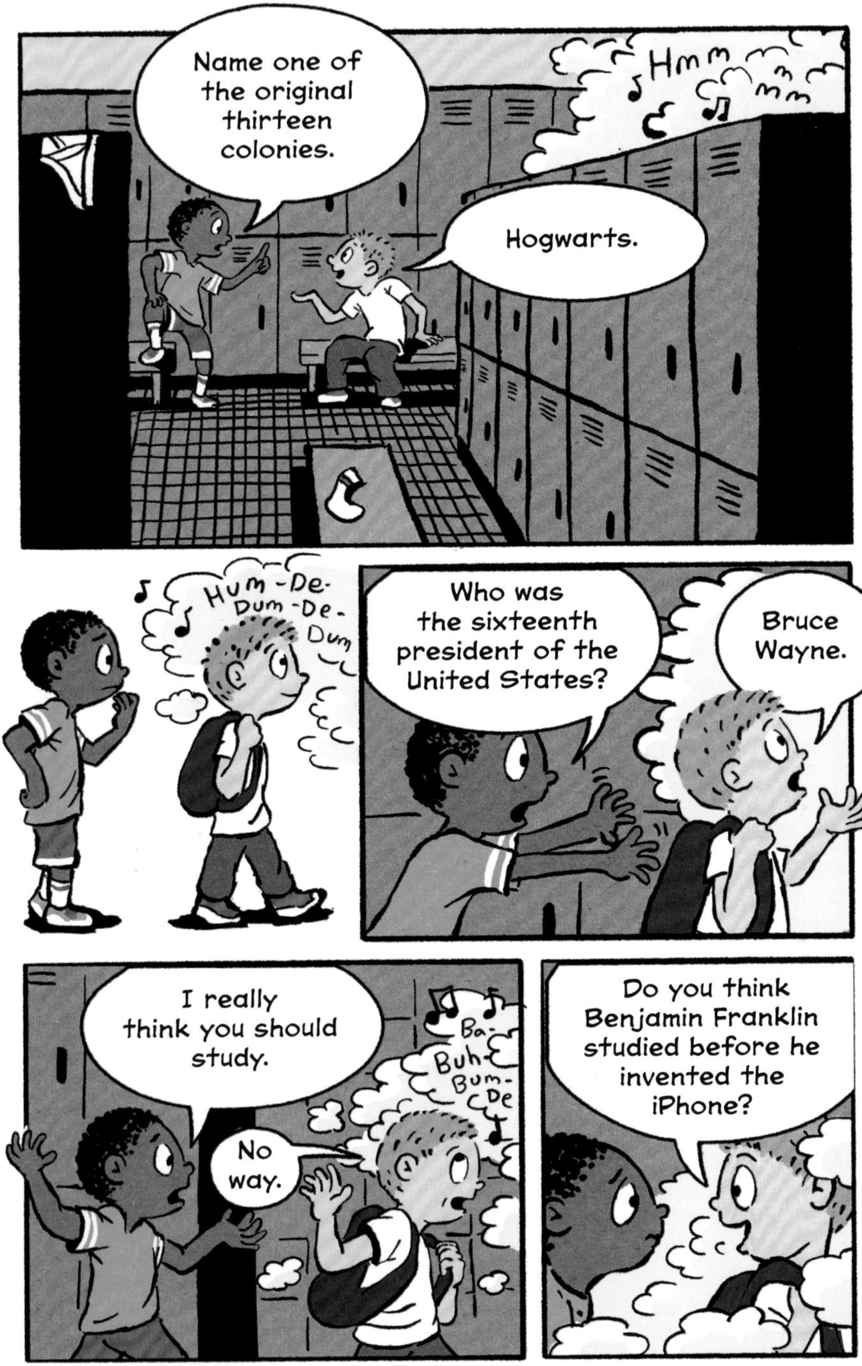

Name one of the original thirteen colonies.
Hmm mm mm
Hogwarts.
Hum-De-Dum-De-Dum
Who was the sixteenth president of the United States?
Bruce Wayne.
I really think you should study.
Ba-Buh-Bum-De
No way.
Do you think Benjamin Franklin studied before he invented the iPhone?

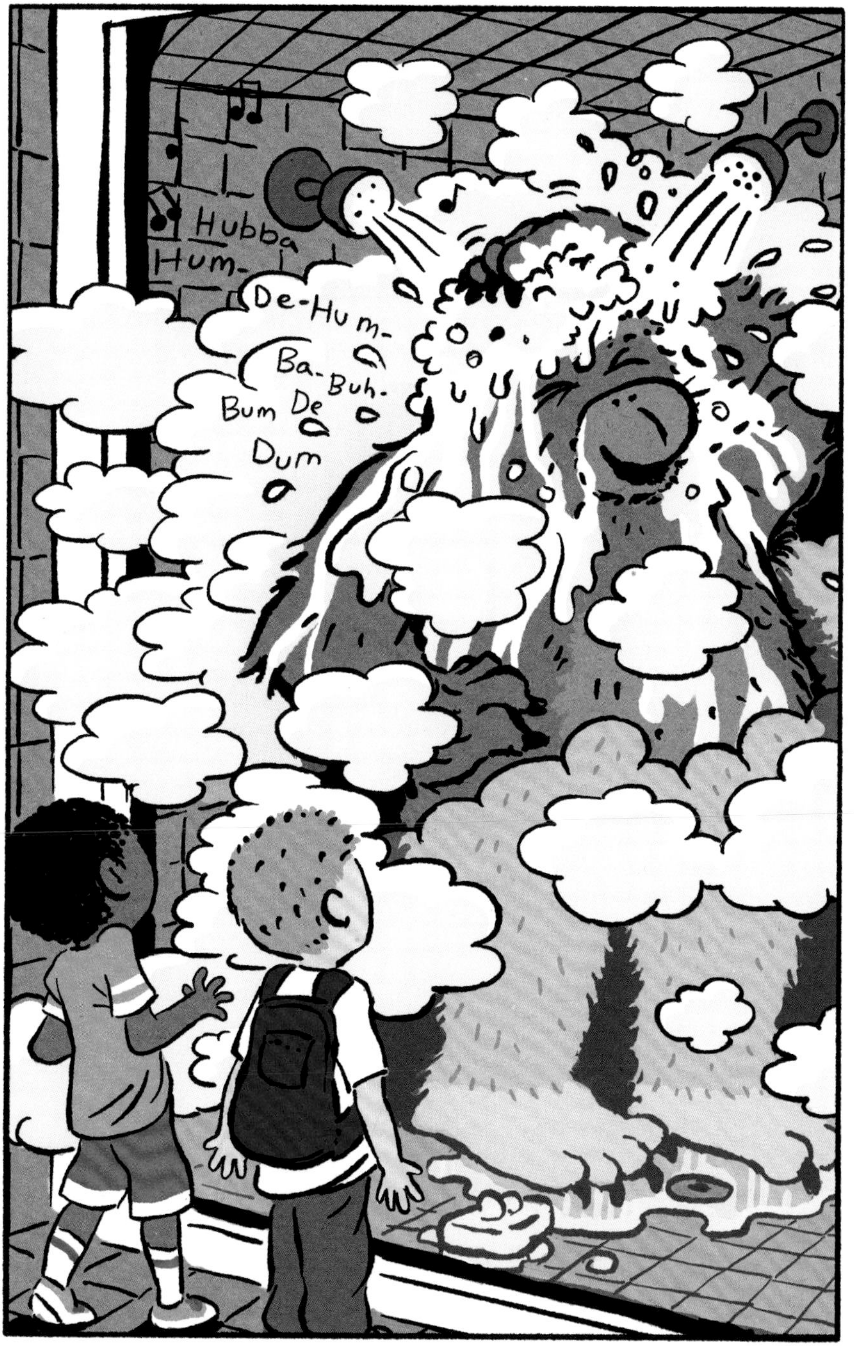
Hubba
Hum-
De-Hum-
Ba-Buh-
Bum De
Dum

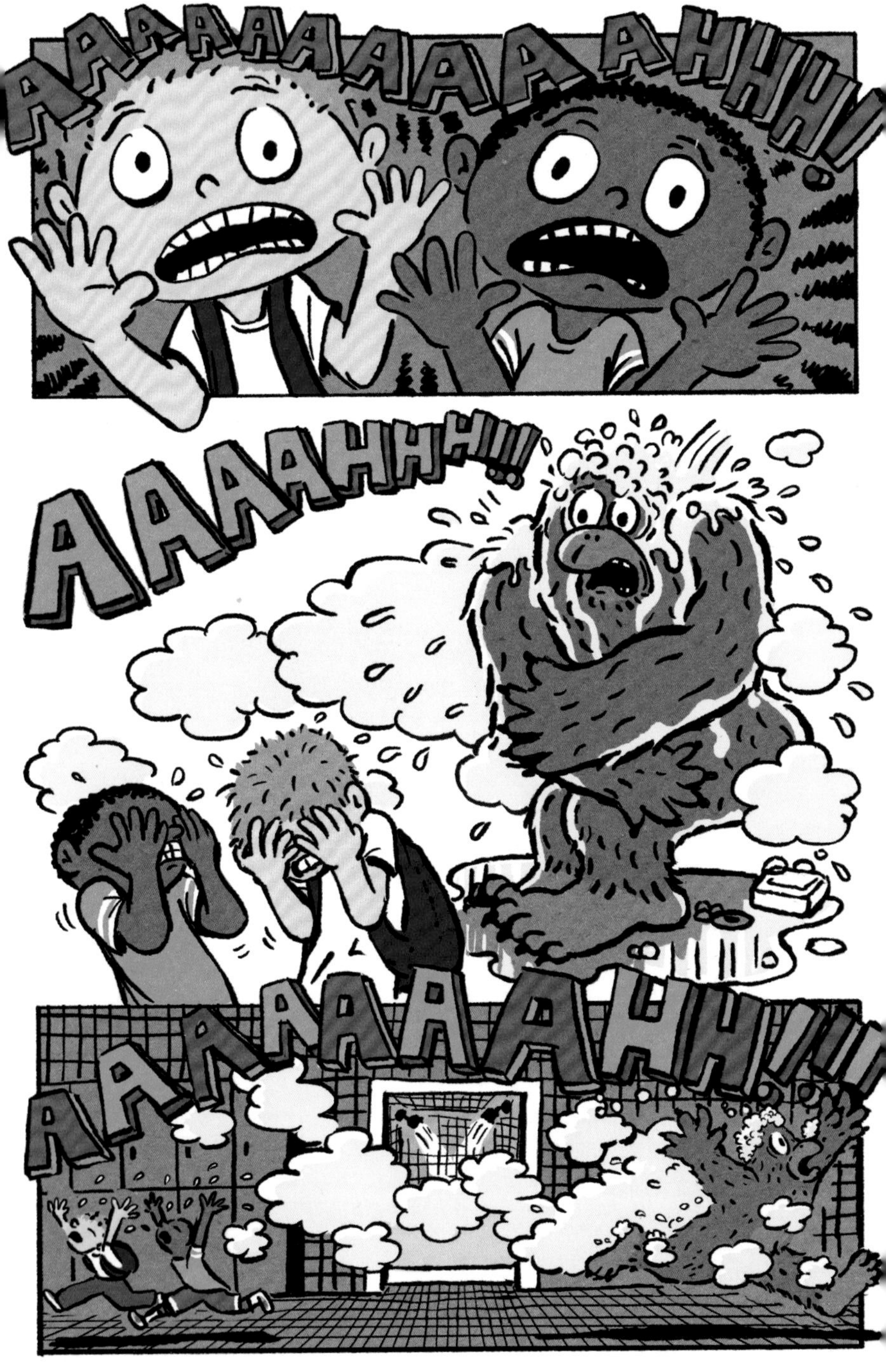
AAAAAAAAAAHHH!!
AAAAAHHH!!!!
AAAAAAAHH!!!

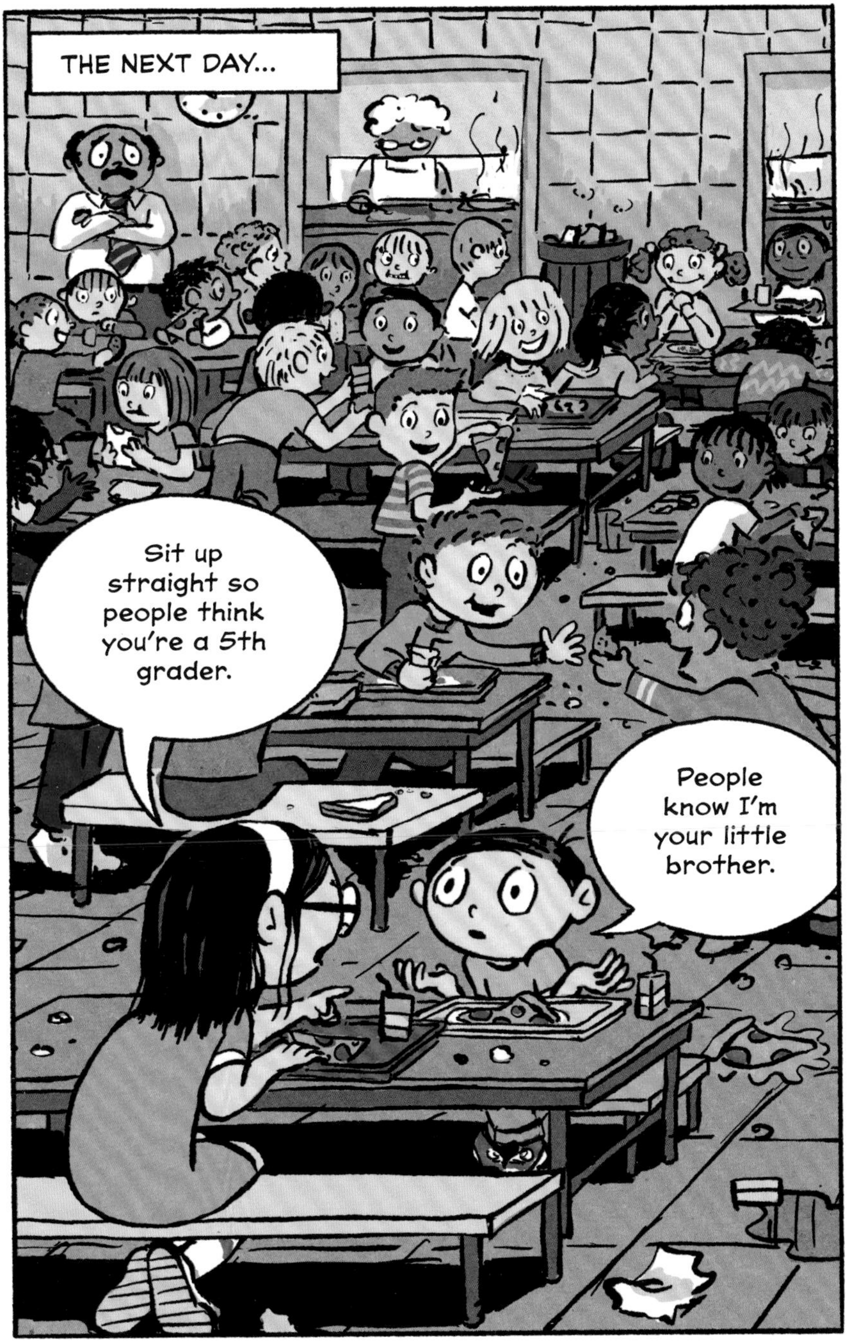
THE NEXT DAY...
Sit up straight so people think you're a 5th grader.
People know I'm your little brother.

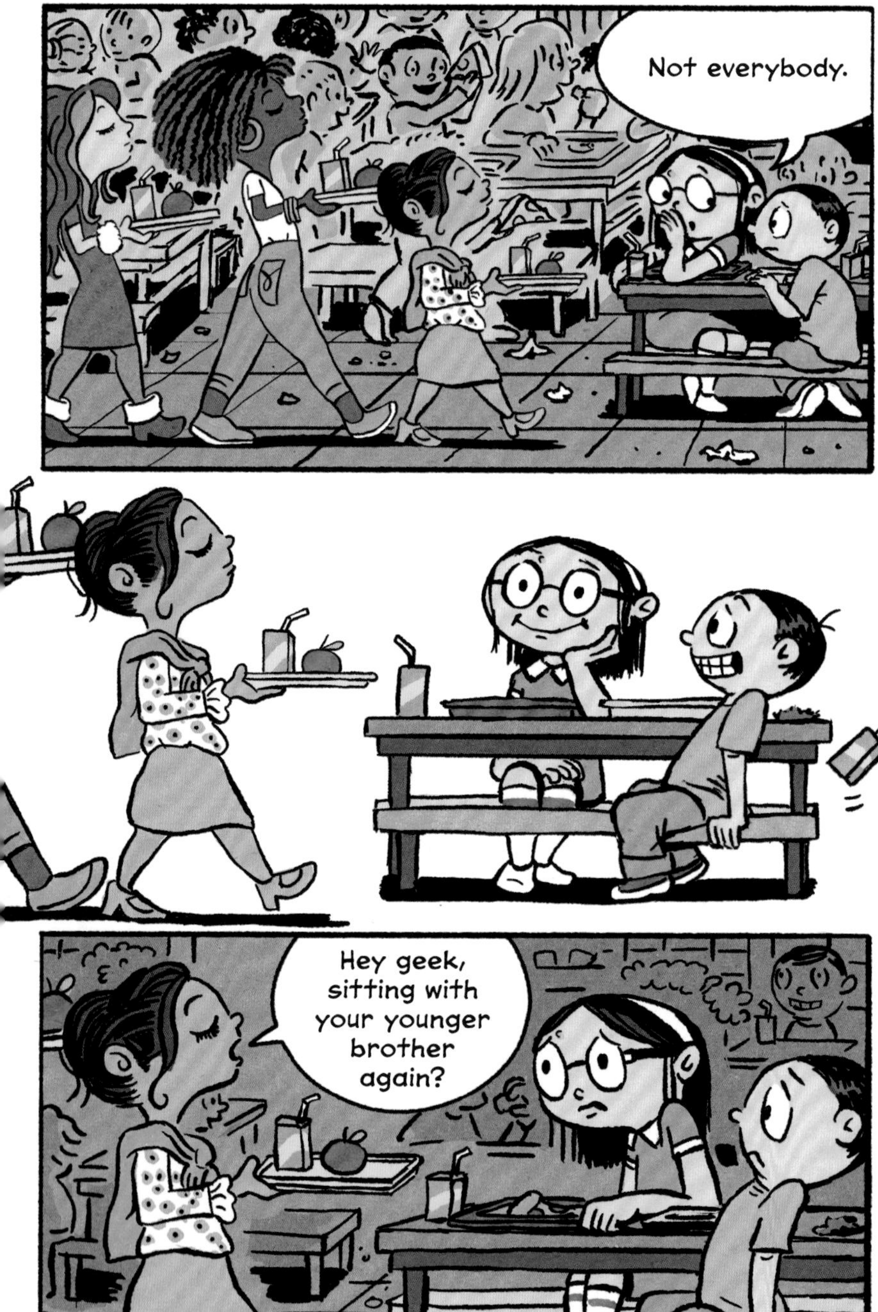
Not everybody.
Hey geek, sitting with your younger brother again?

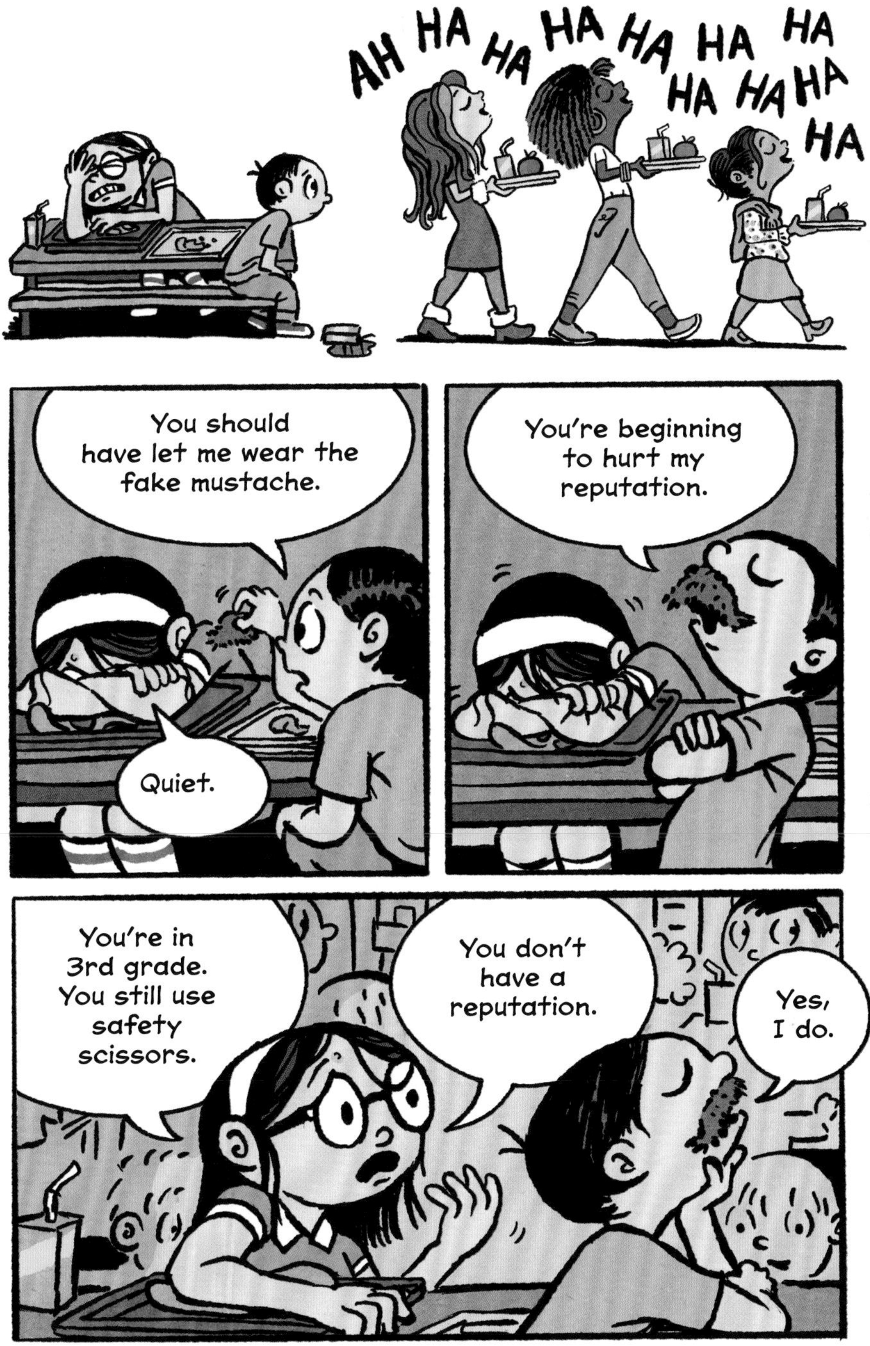
AH HA HA HA HA HA HA HA HA HA HA
You should have let me wear the fake mustache.
Quiet.
You're beginning to hurt my reputation.
You're in 3rd grade. You still use safety scissors.
You don't have a reputation.
Yes, I do.

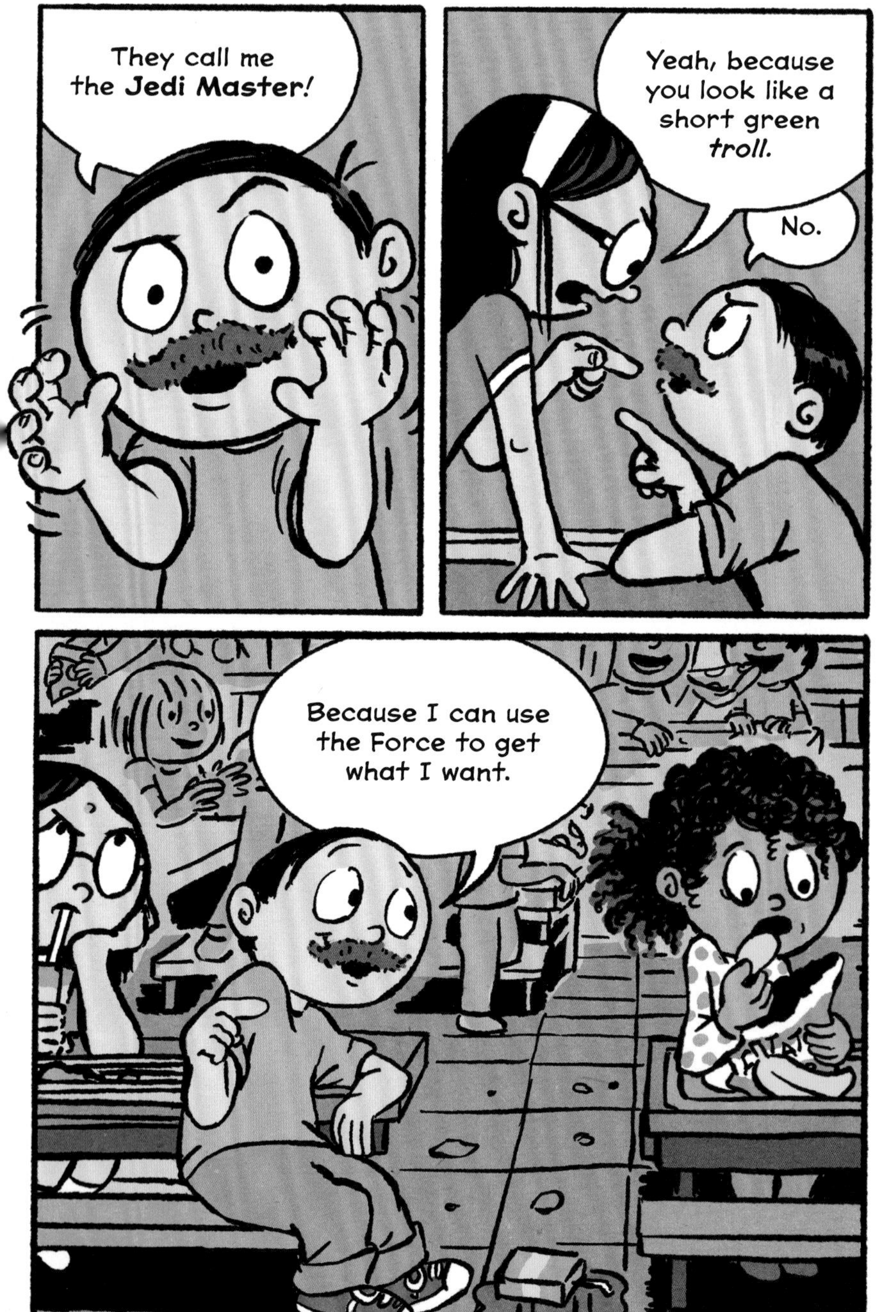
They call me the Jedi Master!
Yeah, because you look like a short green troll.
No.
Because I can use the Force to get what I want.

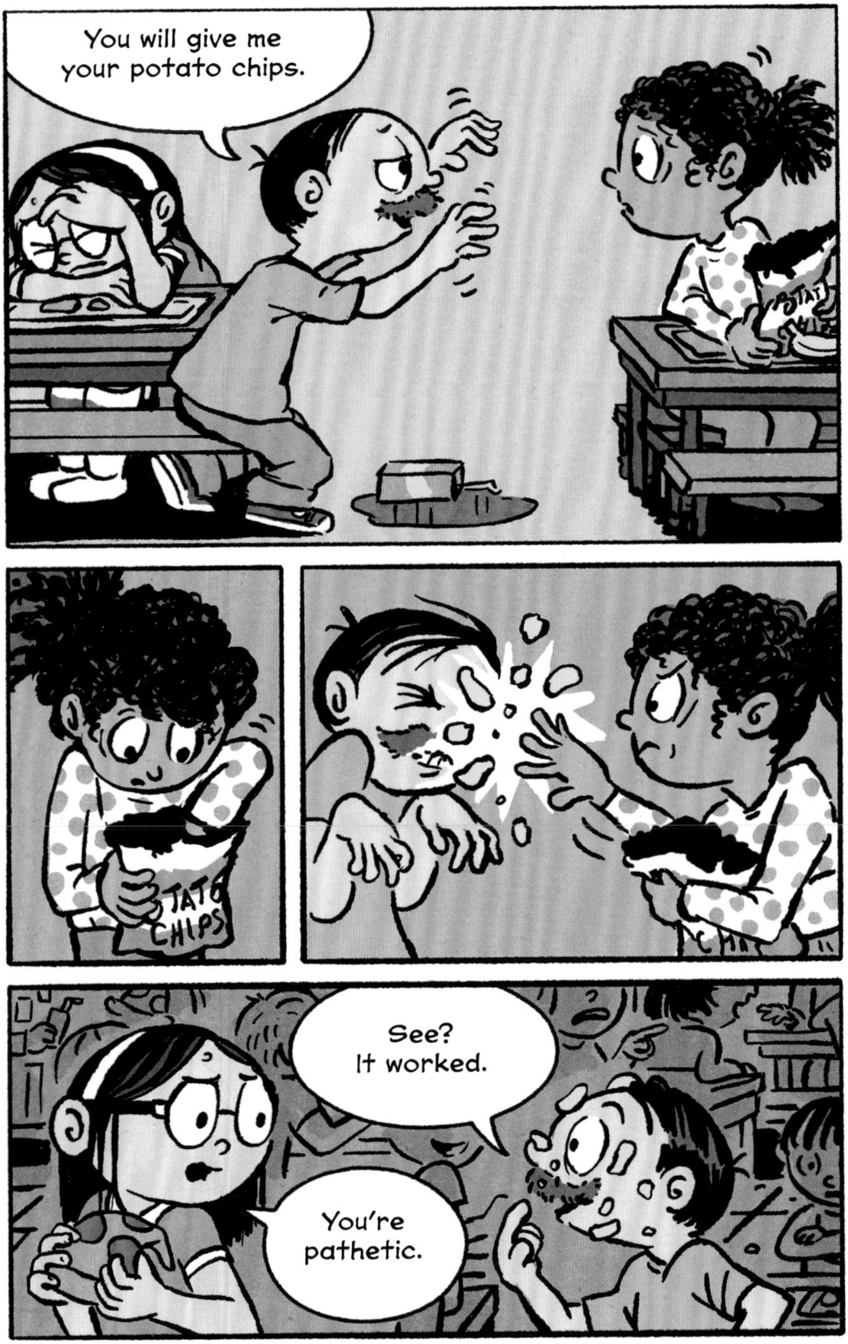
You will give me your potato chips.
TATO CHIPS
See? It worked.
You're pathetic.

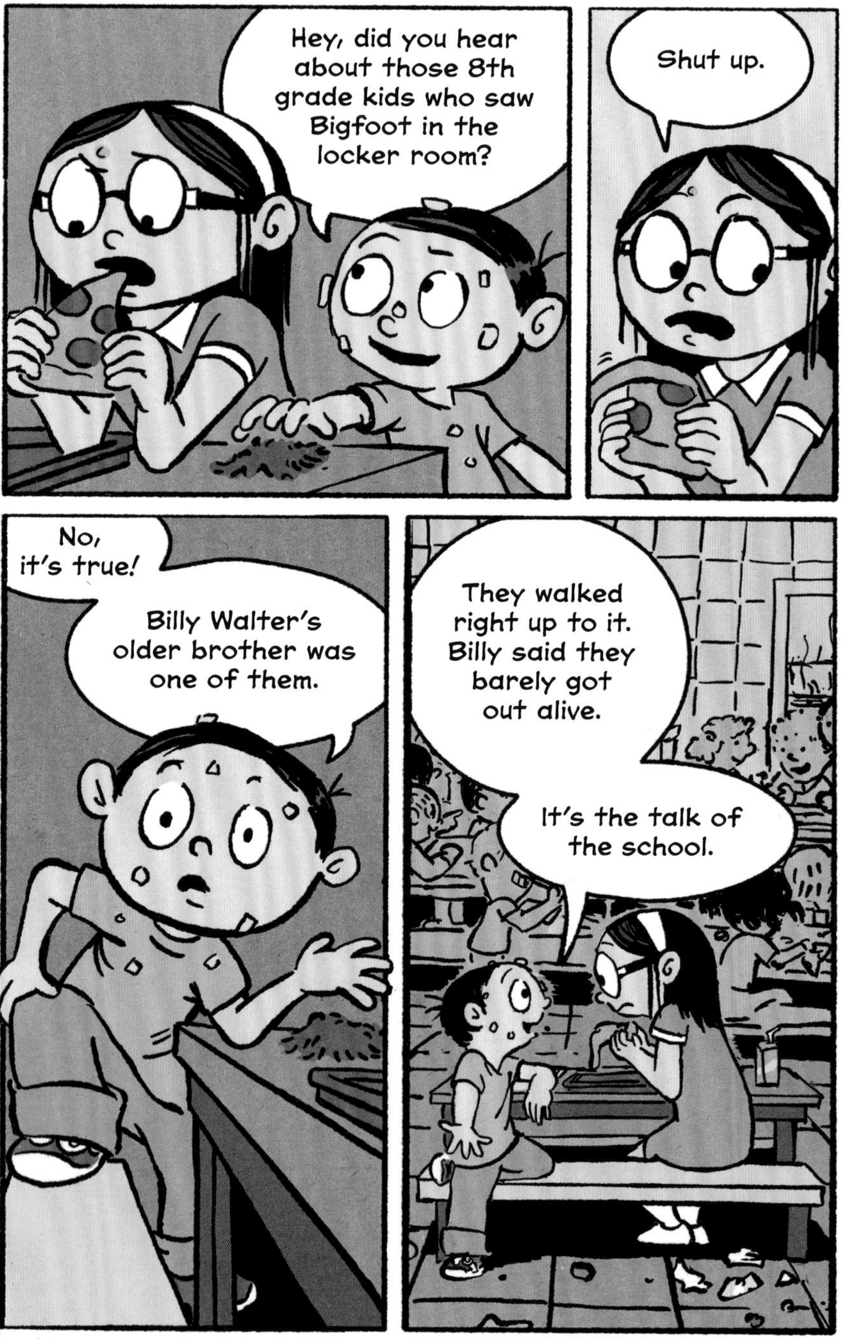
Hey, did you hear about those 8th grade kids who saw Bigfoot in the locker room?
Shut up.
No, it's true!
Billy Walter's older brother was one of them.
They walked right up to it. Billy said they barely got out alive.
It's the talk of the school.

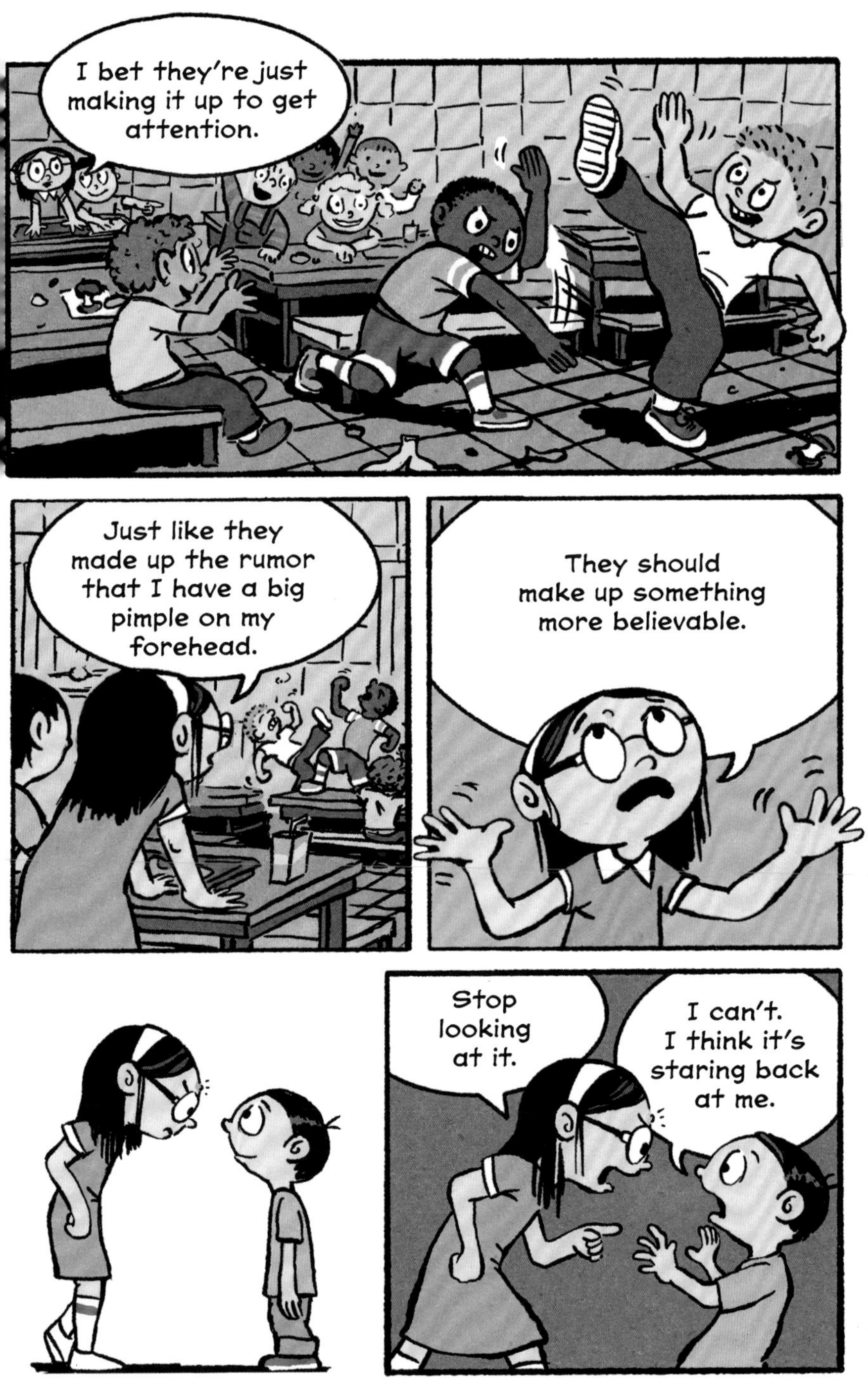
I bet they're just making it up to get attention.
Just like they made up the rumor that I have a big pimple on my forehead.
They should make up something more believable.
Stop looking at it.
I can't. I think it's staring back at me.

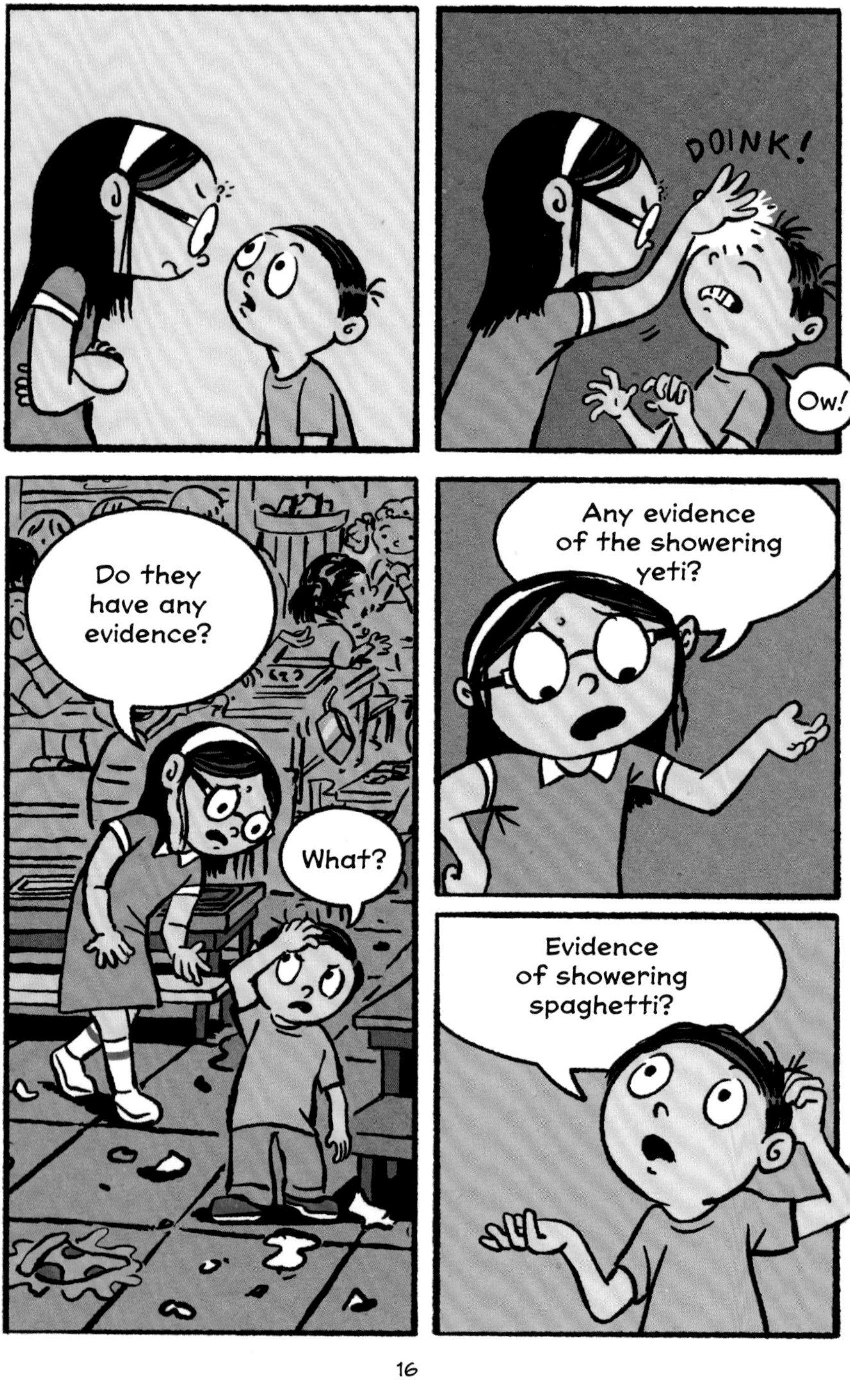
DOINK!
Ow!
Do they have any evidence?
What?
Any evidence of the showering yeti?
Evidence of showering spaghetti?

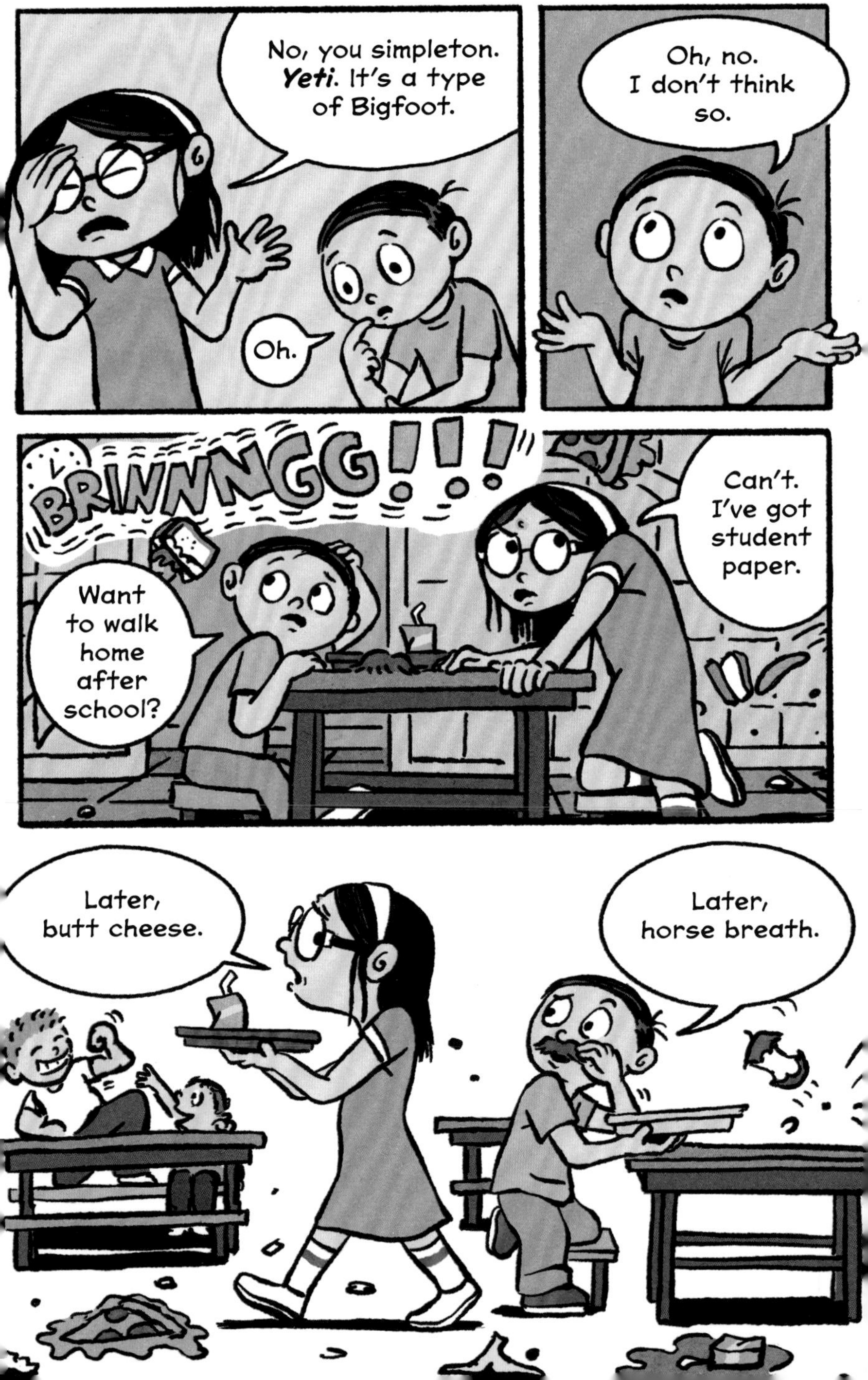
No, you simpleton. *Yeti*. It's a type of Bigfoot.
Oh.
Oh, no. I don't think so.
BRINNNGG!!!
Want to walk home after school?
Can't. I've got student paper.
Later, butt cheese.
Later, horse breath.

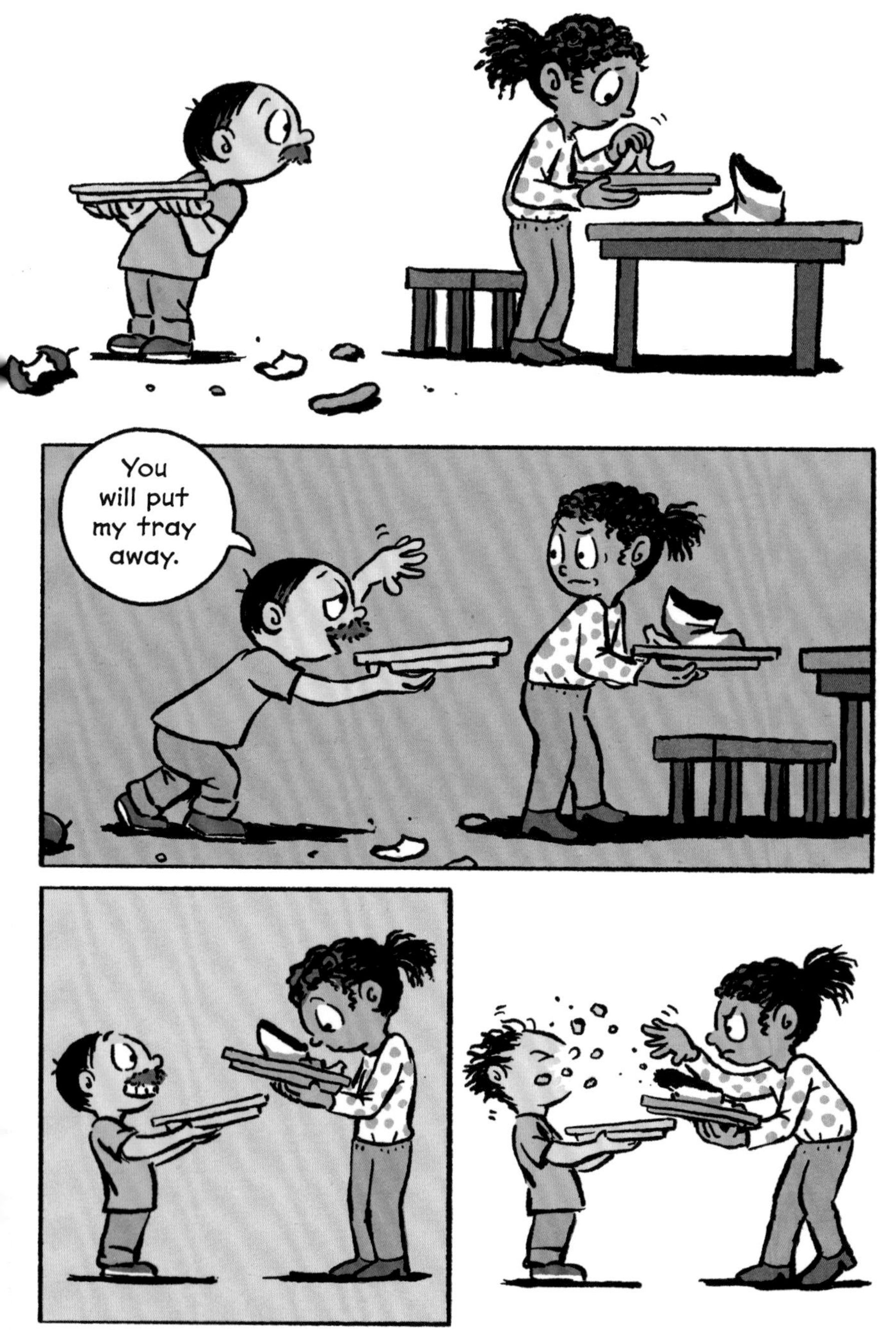
You will put my tray away.

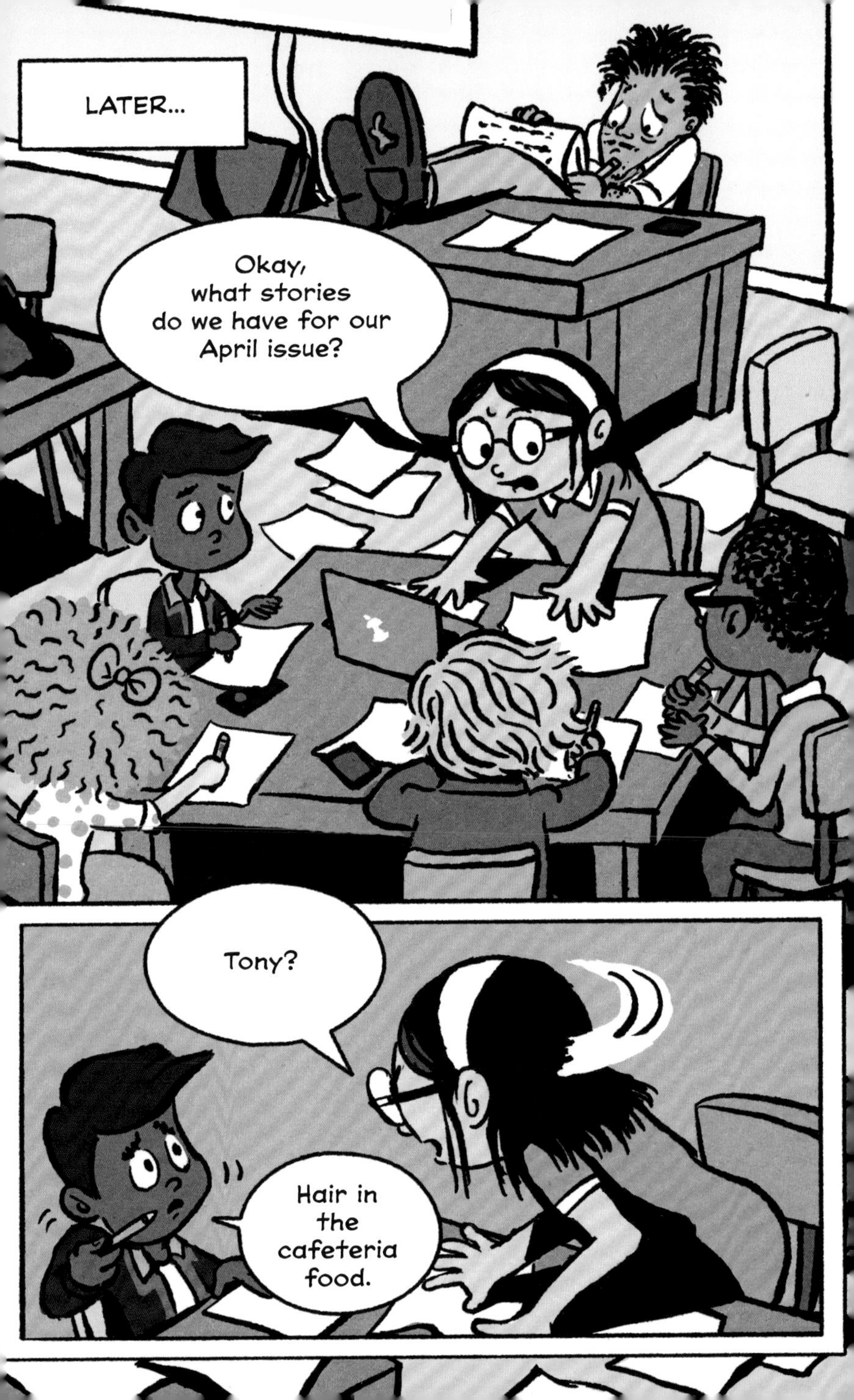
LATER...
Okay, what stories do we have for our April issue?
Tony?
Hair in the cafeteria food.

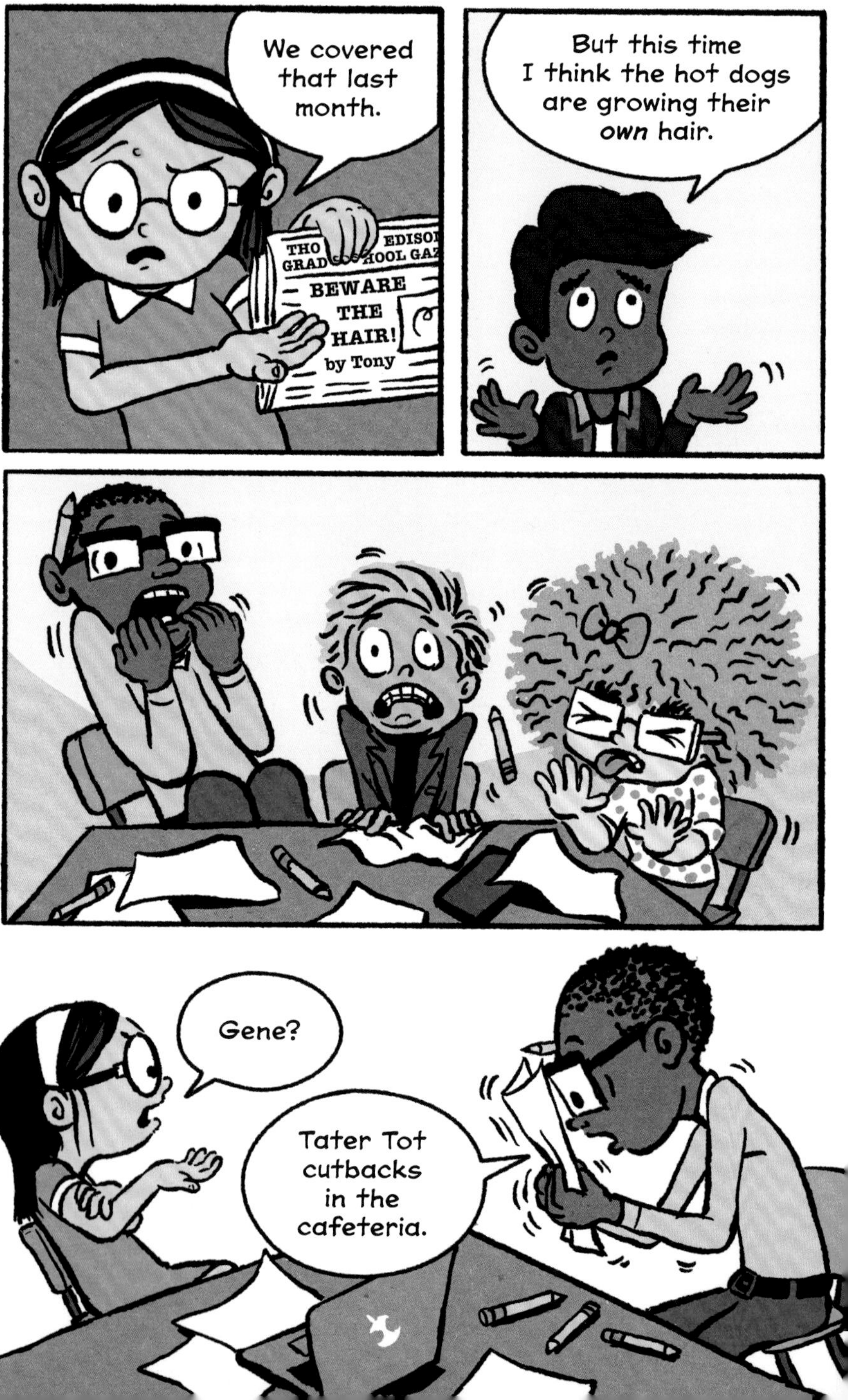
We covered that last month.
BEWARE THE HAIR!
by Tony
But this time I think the hot dogs are growing their *own* hair.
Gene?
Tater Tot cutbacks in the cafeteria.

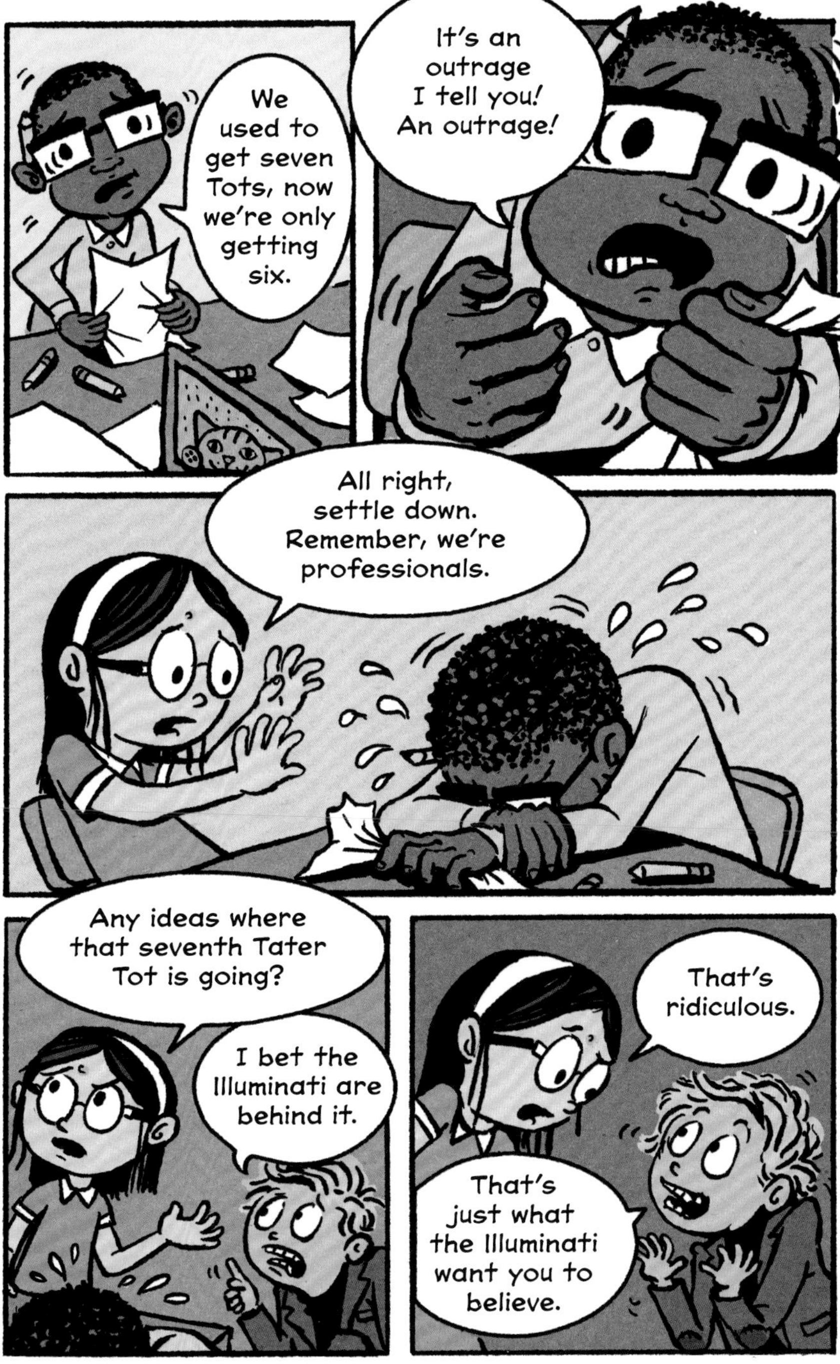
We used to get seven Tots, now we're only getting six.
It's an outrage I tell you! An outrage!
All right, settle down. Remember, we're professionals.
Any ideas where that seventh Tater Tot is going?
I bet the Illuminati are behind it.
That's ridiculous.
That's just what the Illuminati want you to believe.

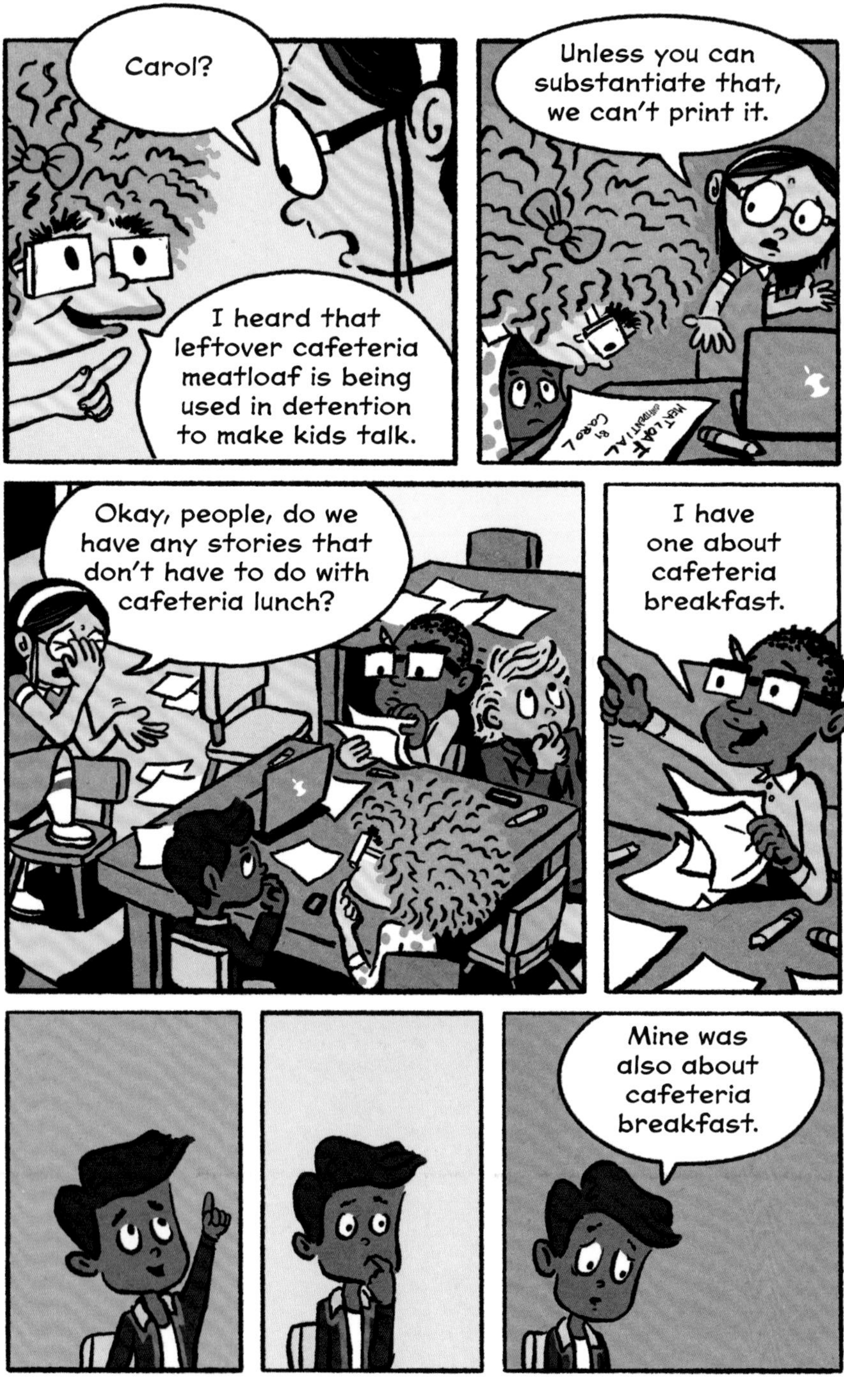
Carol?
I heard that leftover cafeteria meatloaf is being used in detention to make kids talk.
Unless you can substantiate that, we can't print it.
MEATLOAF CONFIDENTIAL BY CAROL
Okay, people, do we have any stories that don't have to do with cafeteria lunch?
I have one about cafeteria breakfast.
Mine was also about cafeteria breakfast.

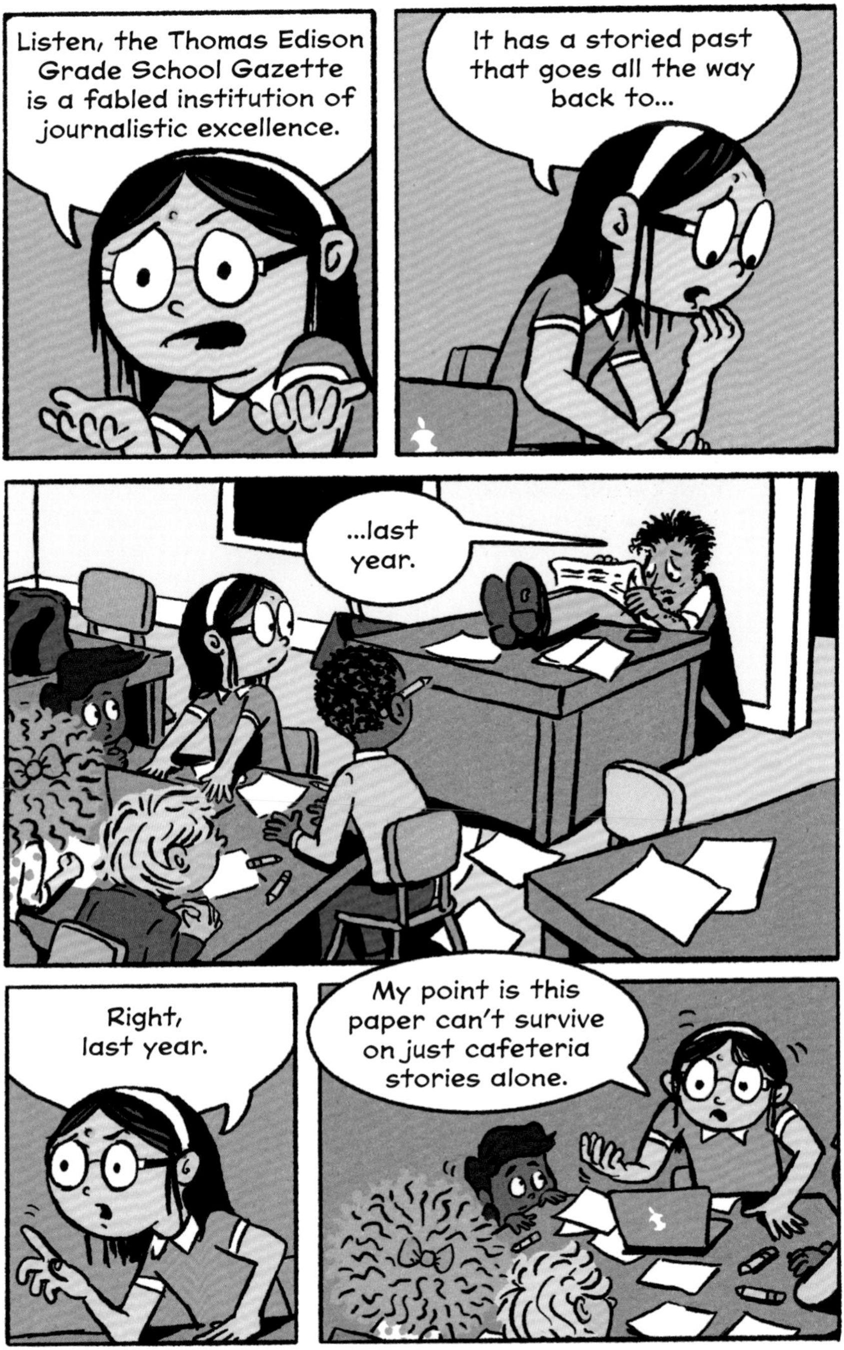
Listen, the Thomas Edison Grade School Gazette is a fabled institution of journalistic excellence.
It has a storied past that goes all the way back to...
...last year.
Right, last year.
My point is this paper can't survive on just cafeteria stories alone.

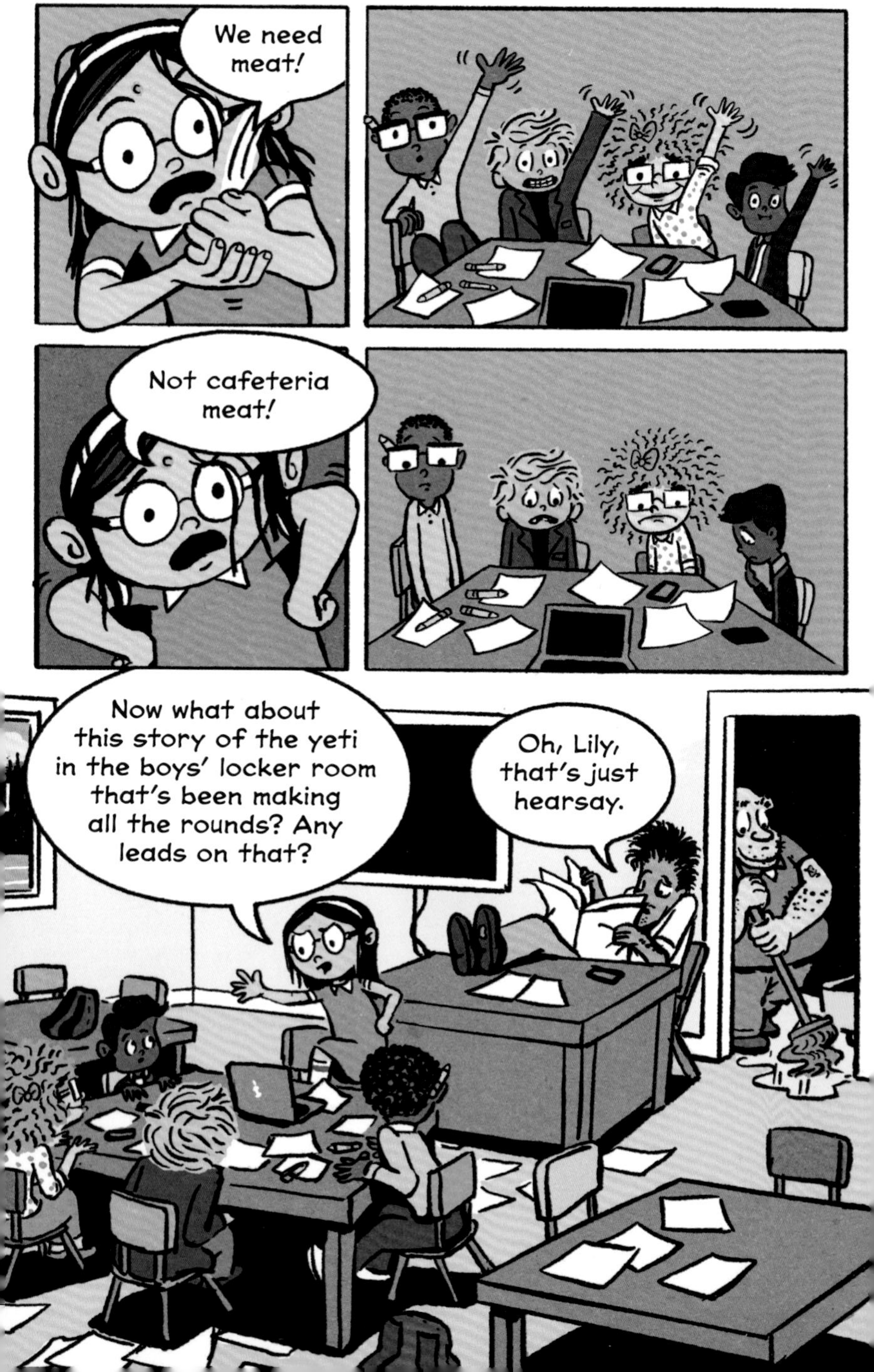
We need meat!
Not cafeteria meat!
Now what about this story of the yeti in the boys' locker room that's been making all the rounds? Any leads on that?
Oh, Lily, that's just hearsay.

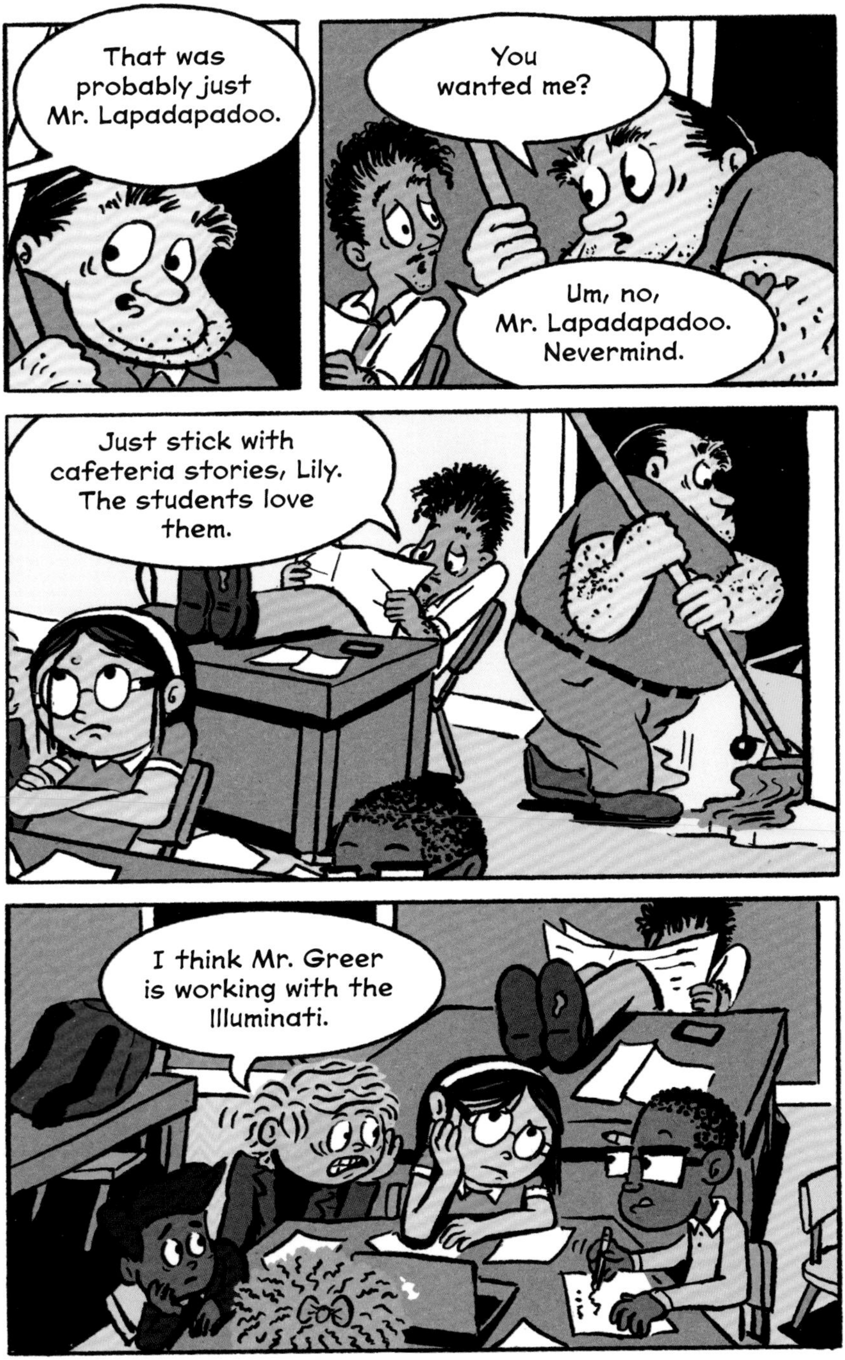
That was probably just Mr. Lapadapadoo.
You wanted me?
Um, no, Mr. Lapadapadoo. Nevermind.
Just stick with cafeteria stories, Lily. The students love them.
I think Mr. Greer is working with the Illuminati.

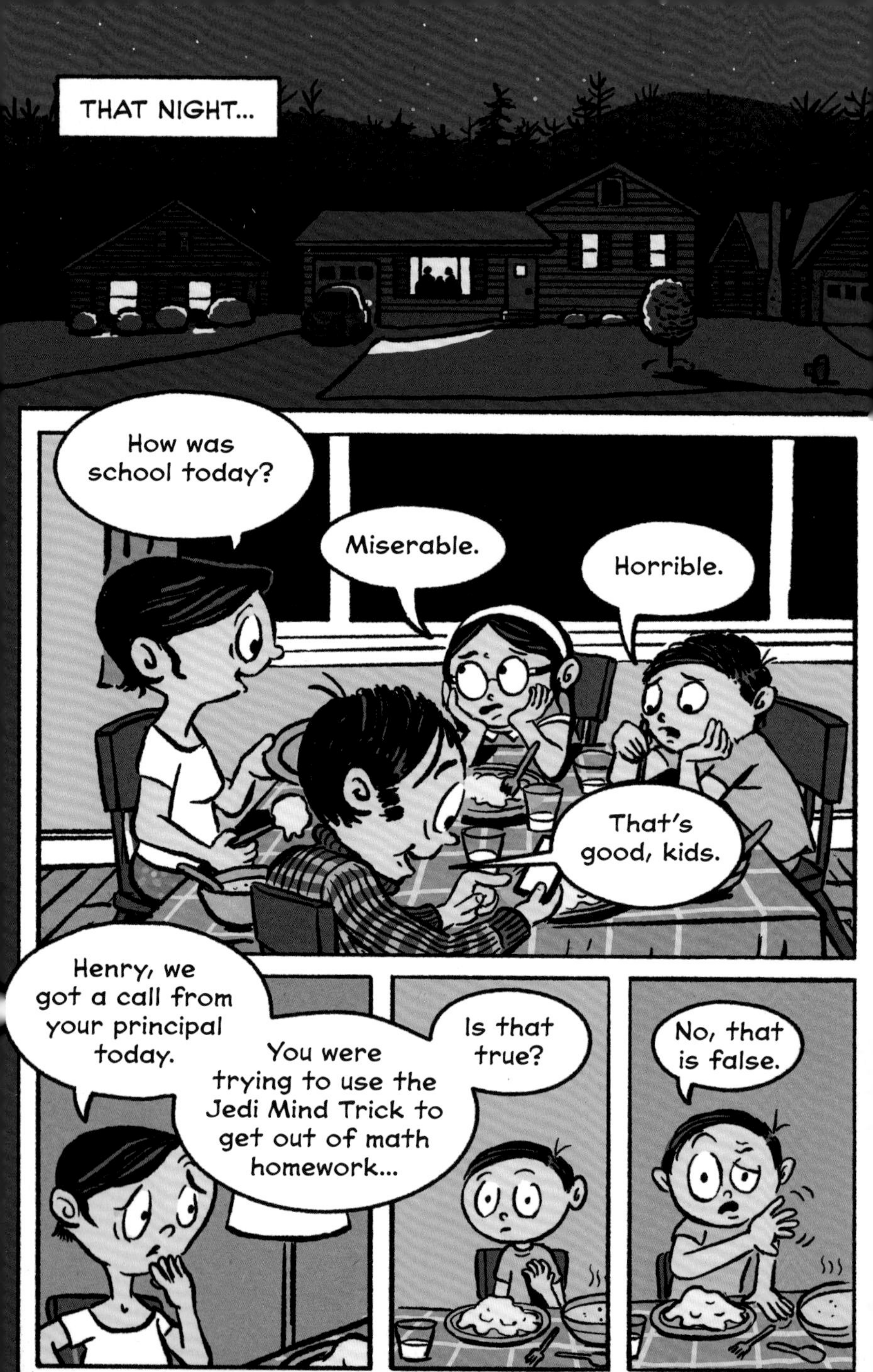
THAT NIGHT...
How was school today?
Miserable.
Horrible.
That's good, kids.
Henry, we got a call from your principal today.
You were trying to use the Jedi Mind Trick to get out of math homework...
Is that true?
No, that is false.

Mom, the neighbor kid is pressing his face against the window again.

I know.

He likes the funny faces it makes.

Just pull the shade down and he'll go away.

What about you, Lily? Anything interesting happen at school today?

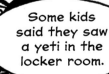

Some kids said they saw a yeti in the locker room.

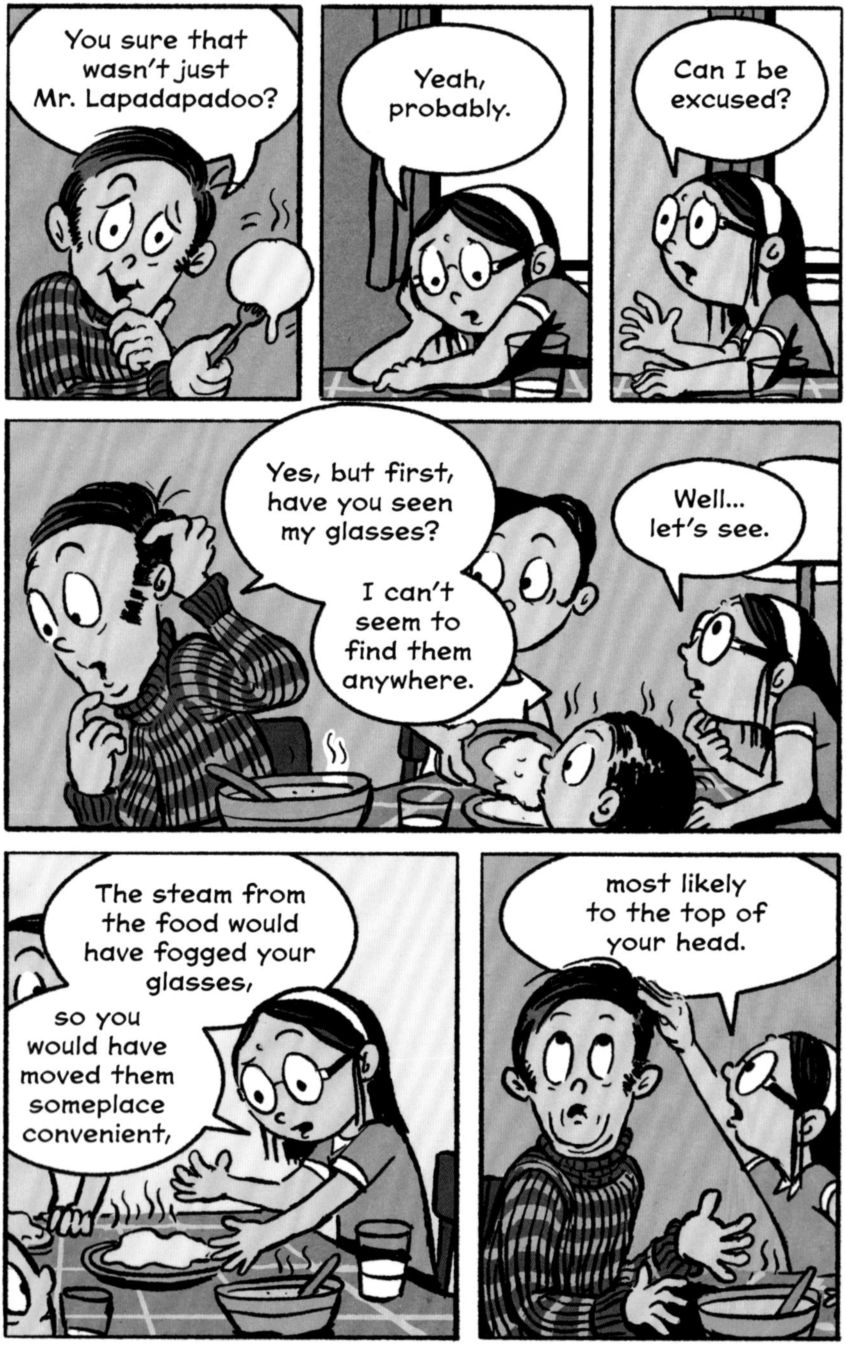
You sure that wasn't just Mr. Lapadapadoo?
Yeah, probably.
Can I be excused?
Yes, but first, have you seen my glasses?
I can't seem to find them anywhere.
Well... let's see.
The steam from the food would have fogged your glasses,
so you would have moved them someplace convenient,
most likely to the top of your head.

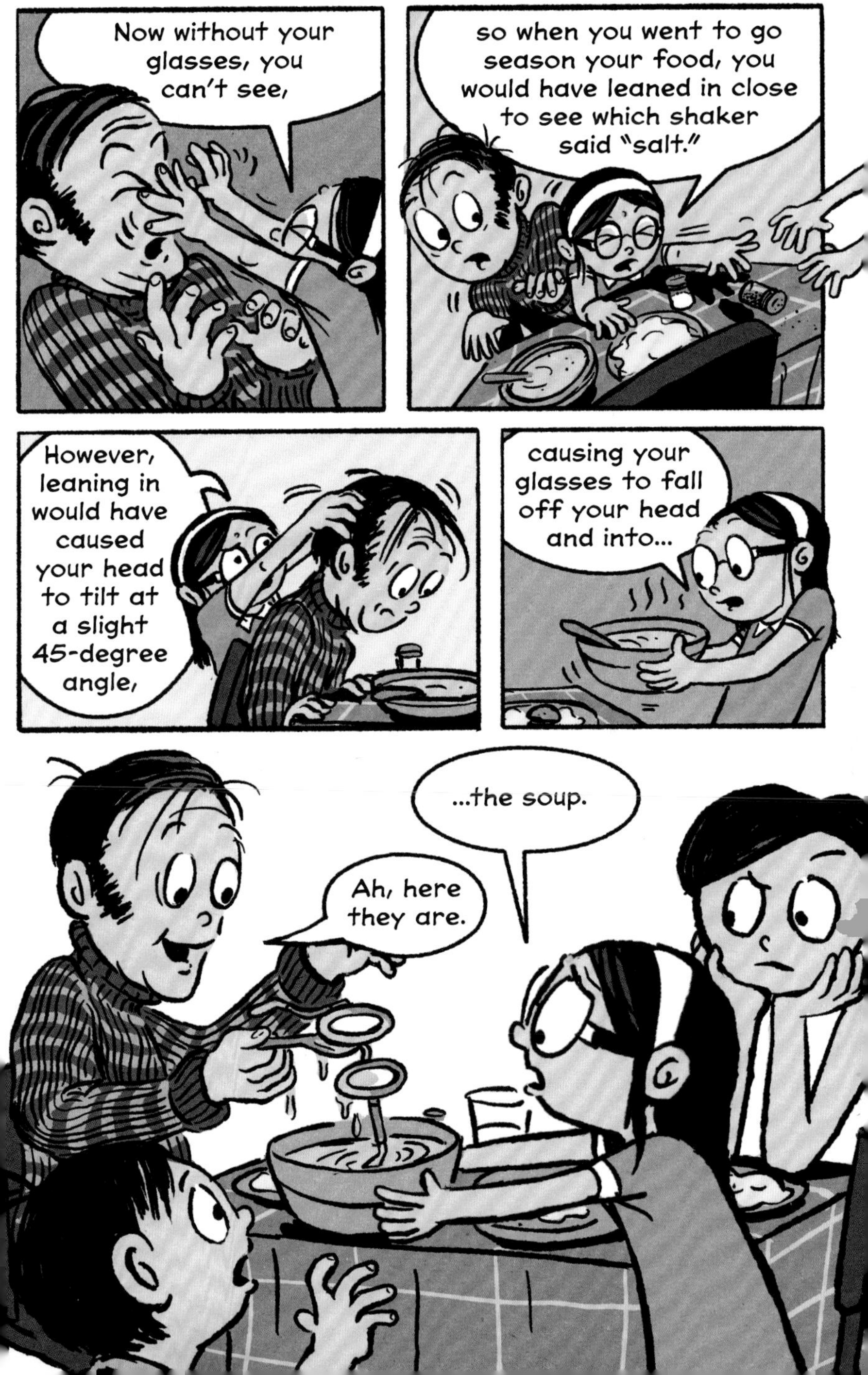
Now without your glasses, you can't see,
so when you went to go season your food, you would have leaned in close to see which shaker said "salt."
However, leaning in would have caused your head to tilt at a slight 45-degree angle,
causing your glasses to fall off your head and into...
...the soup.
Ah, here they are.

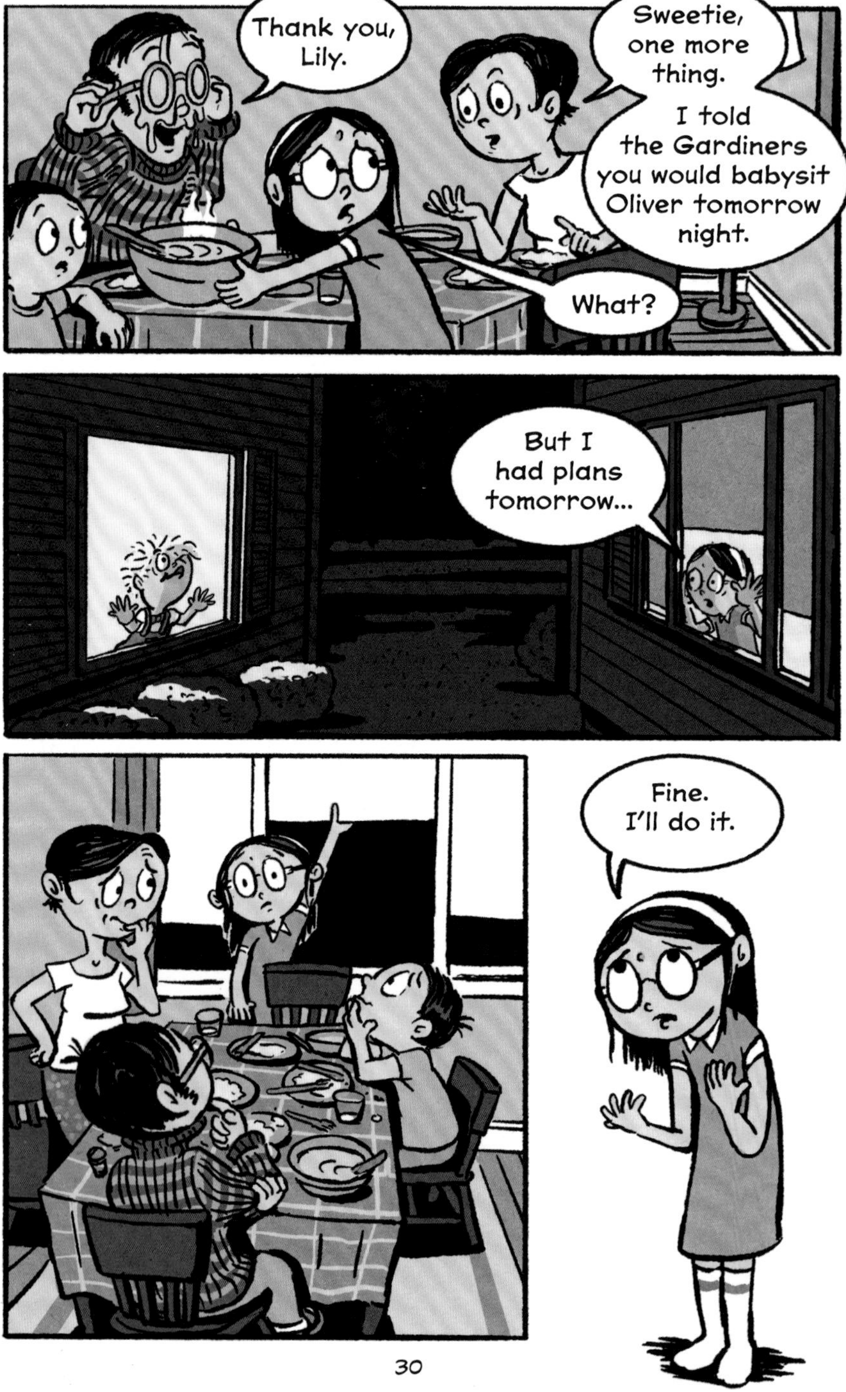
Thank you, Lily.
Sweetie, one more thing.
I told the Gardiners you would babysit Oliver tomorrow night.
What?
But I had plans tomorrow...
Fine. I'll do it.

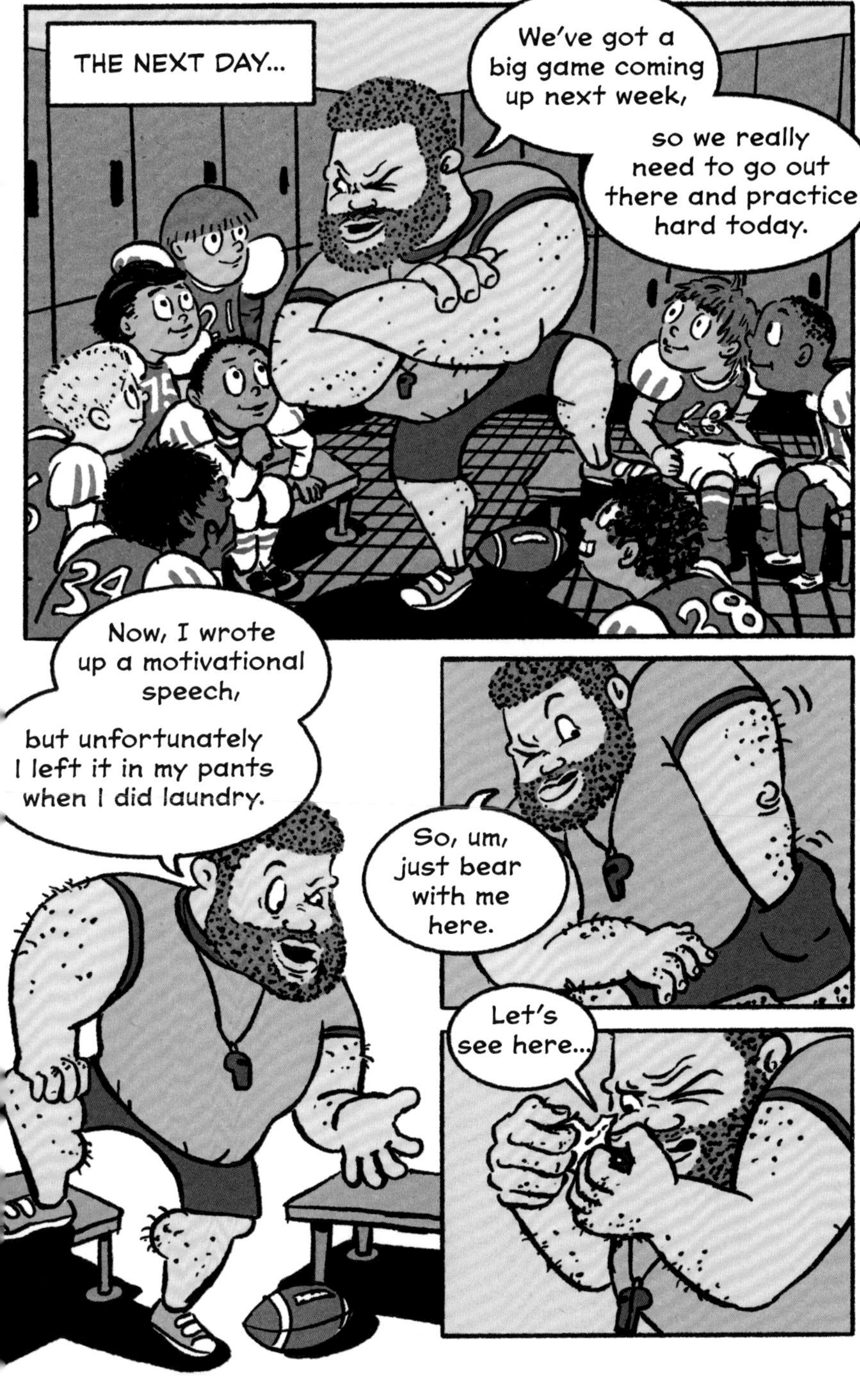
THE NEXT DAY...
We've got a big game coming up next week,
so we really need to go out there and practice hard today.
Now, I wrote up a motivational speech,
but unfortunately I left it in my pants when I did laundry.
So, um, just bear with me here.
Let's see here...

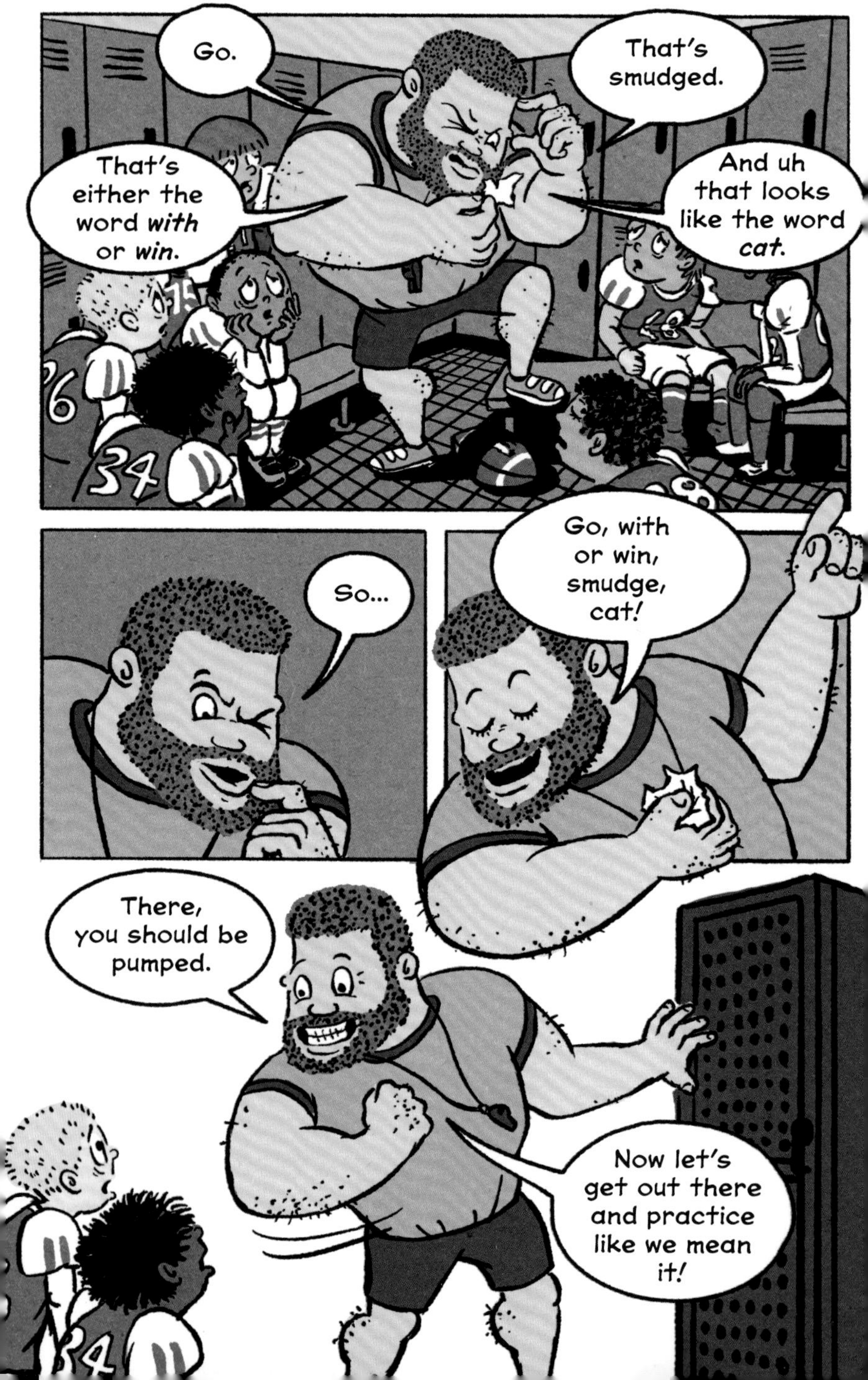
Go.
That's smudged.
That's either the word *with* or *win*.
And uh that looks like the word *cat*.
So...
Go, with or win, smudge, cat!
There, you should be pumped.
Now let's get out there and practice like we mean it!

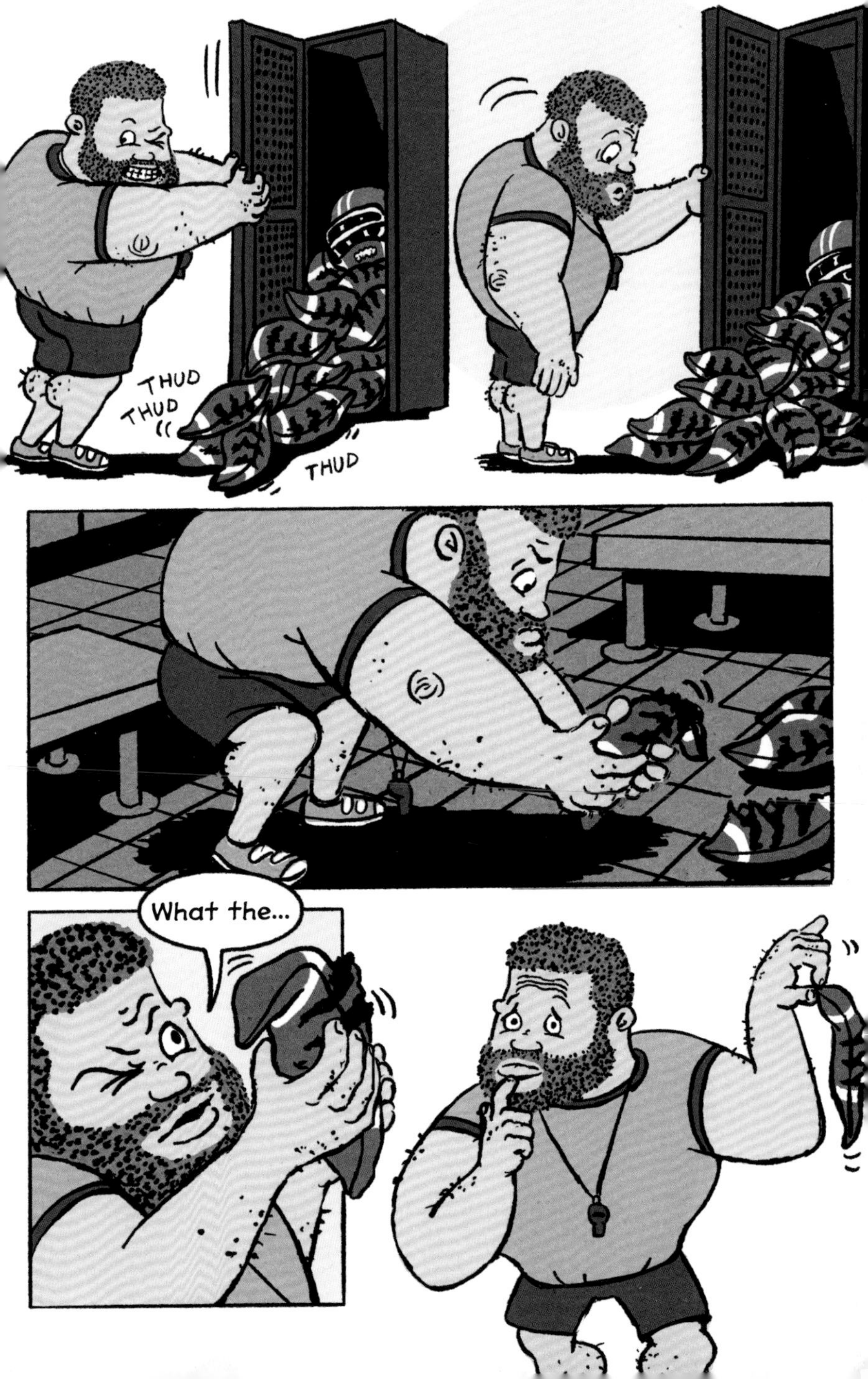
THUD
THUD
THUD
What the...

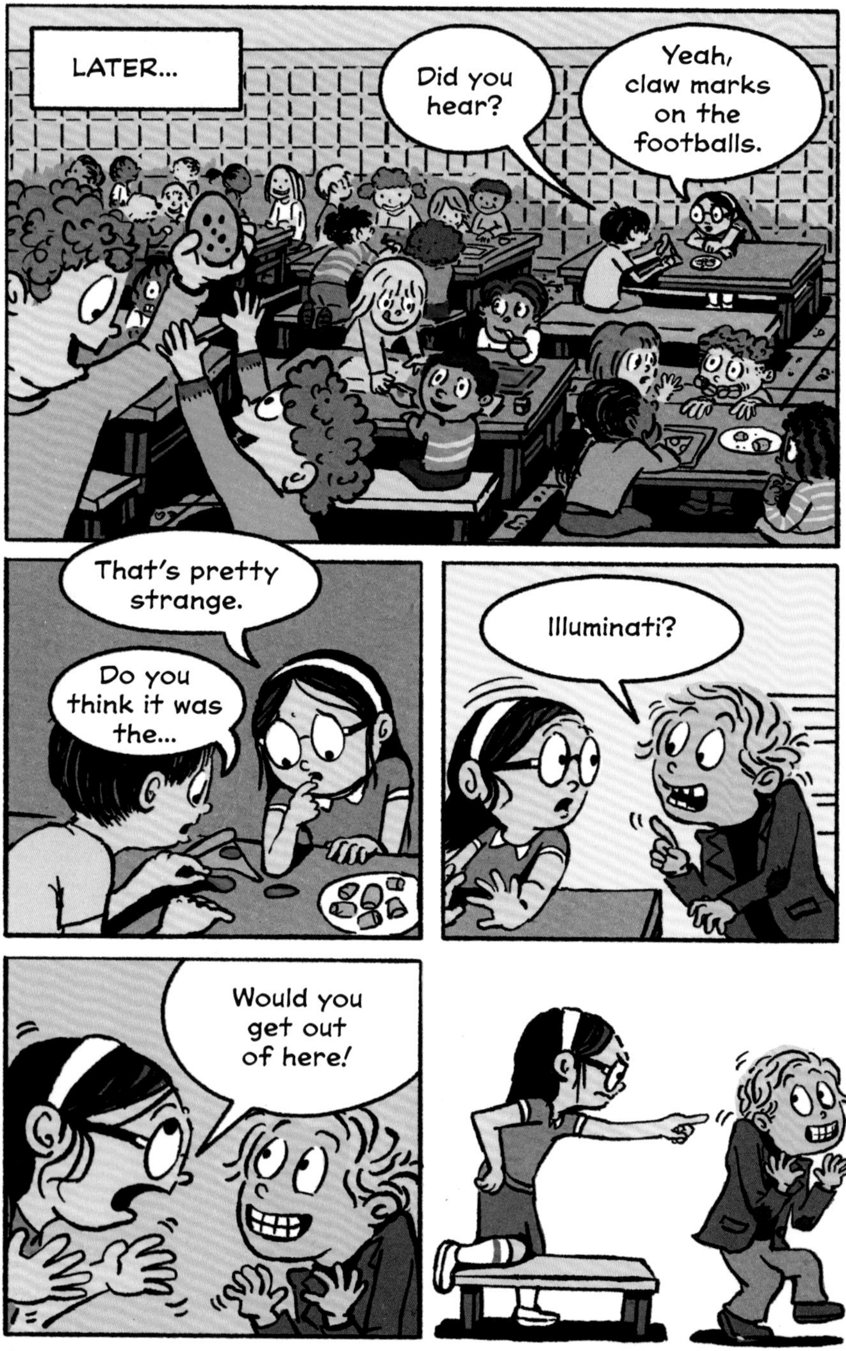
LATER...
Did you hear?
Yeah, claw marks on the footballs.
That's pretty strange.
Do you think it was the...
Illuminati?
Would you get out of here!

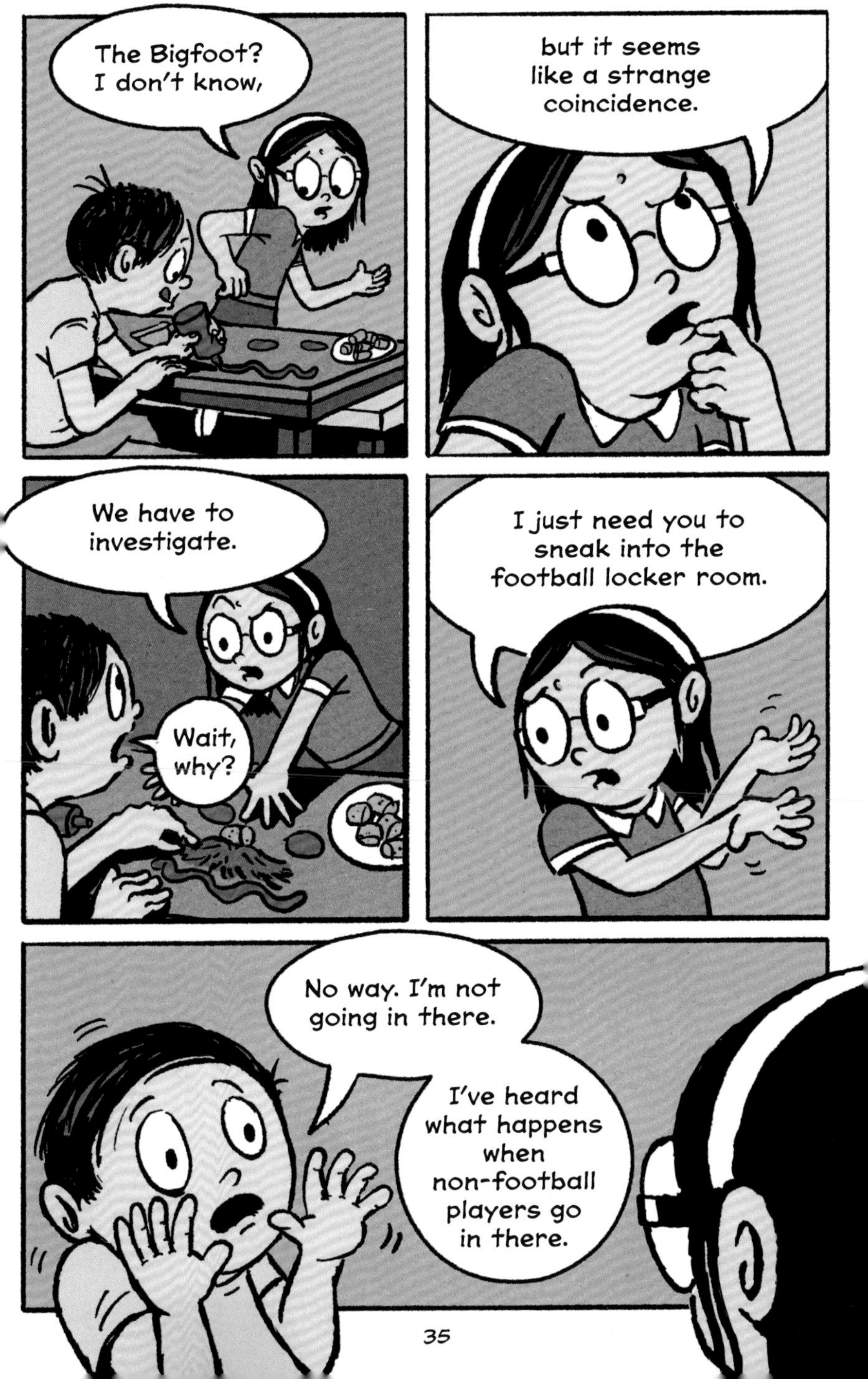
The Bigfoot? I don't know,
but it seems like a strange coincidence.
We have to investigate.
Wait, why?
I just need you to sneak into the football locker room.
No way. I'm not going in there.
I've heard what happens when non-football players go in there.

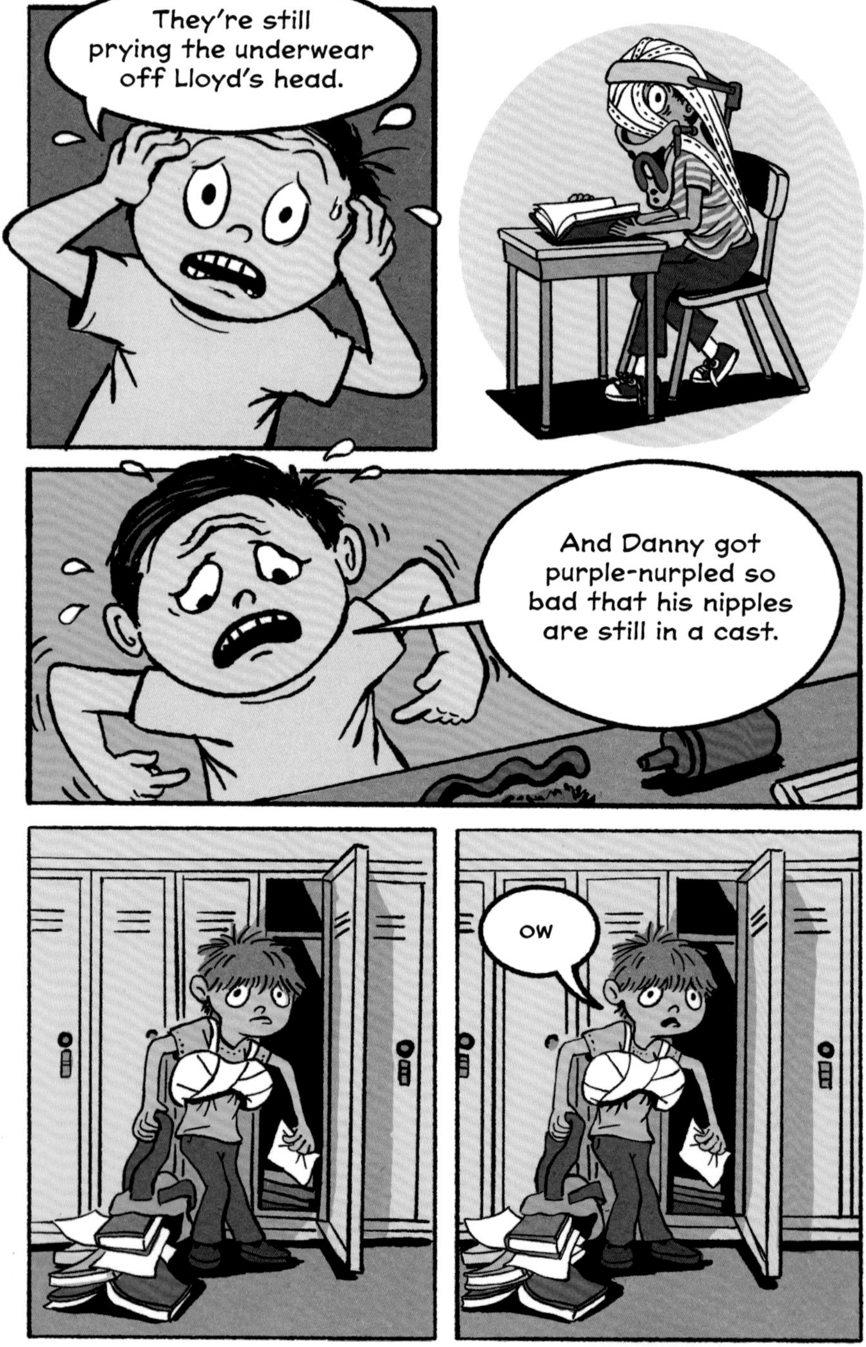
They're still prying the underwear off Lloyd's head.
And Danny got purple-nurpled so bad that his nipples are still in a cast.
OW

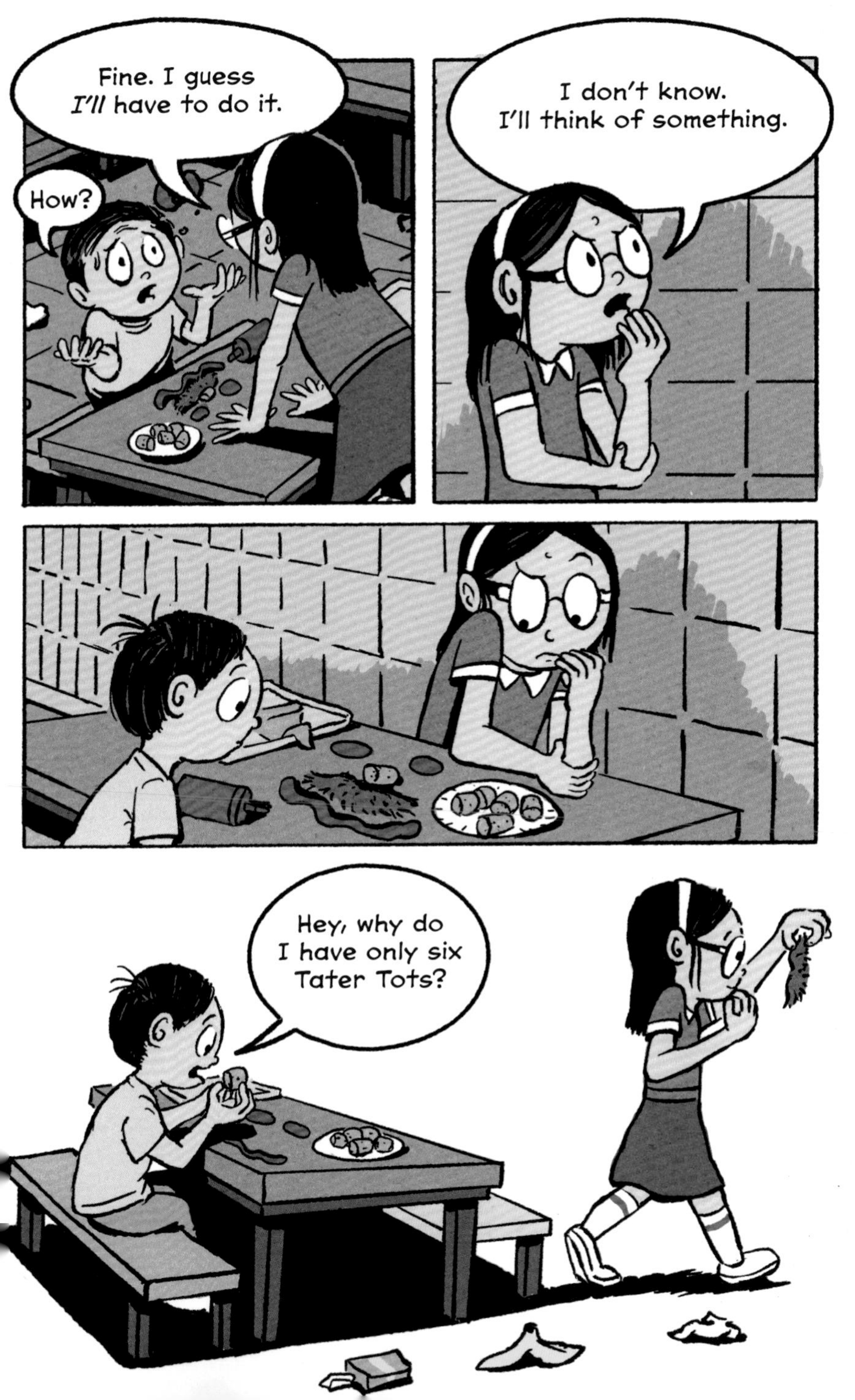
Fine. I guess *I'll* have to do it.
How?
I don't know. I'll think of something.
Hey, why do I have only six Tater Tots?

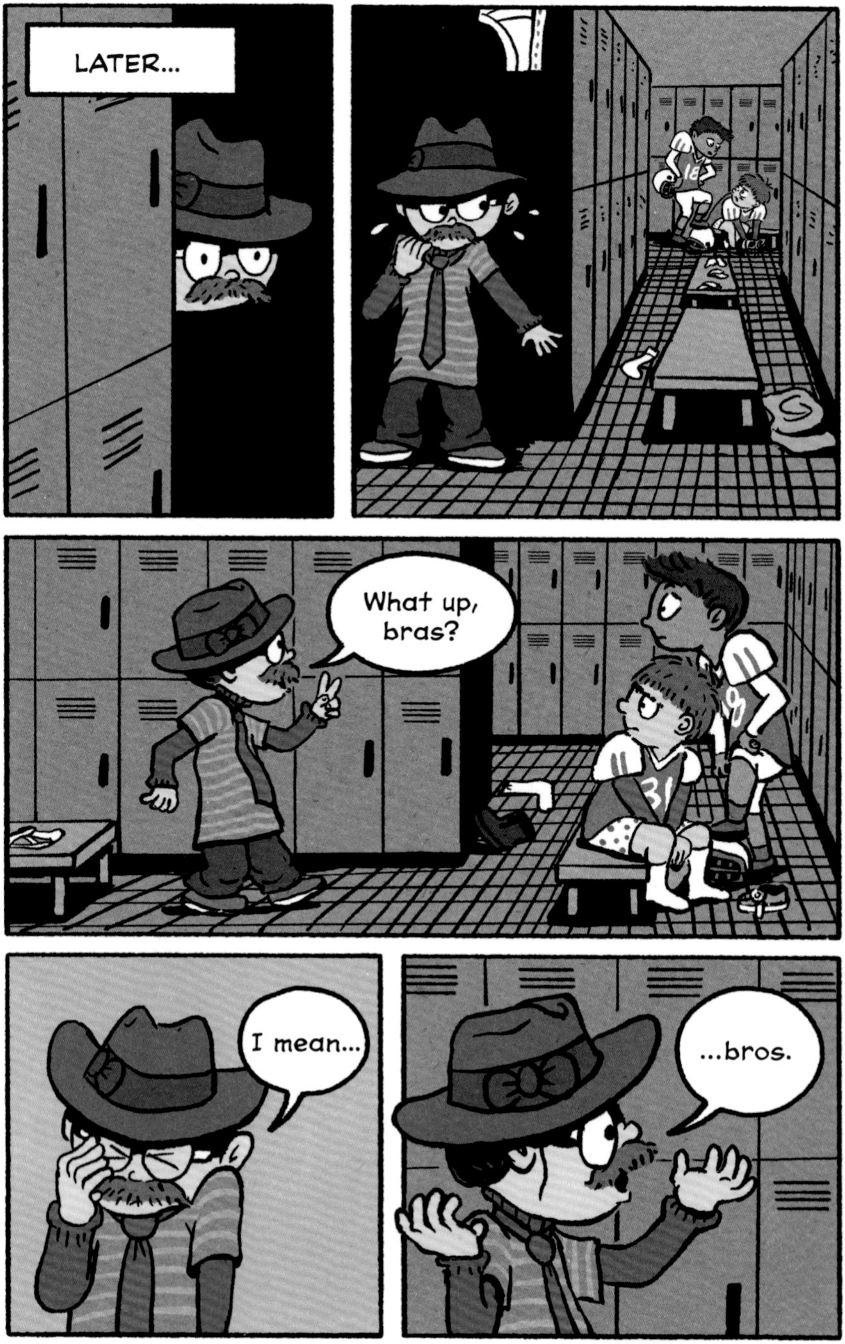
LATER...
What up, bras?
I mean...
...bros.

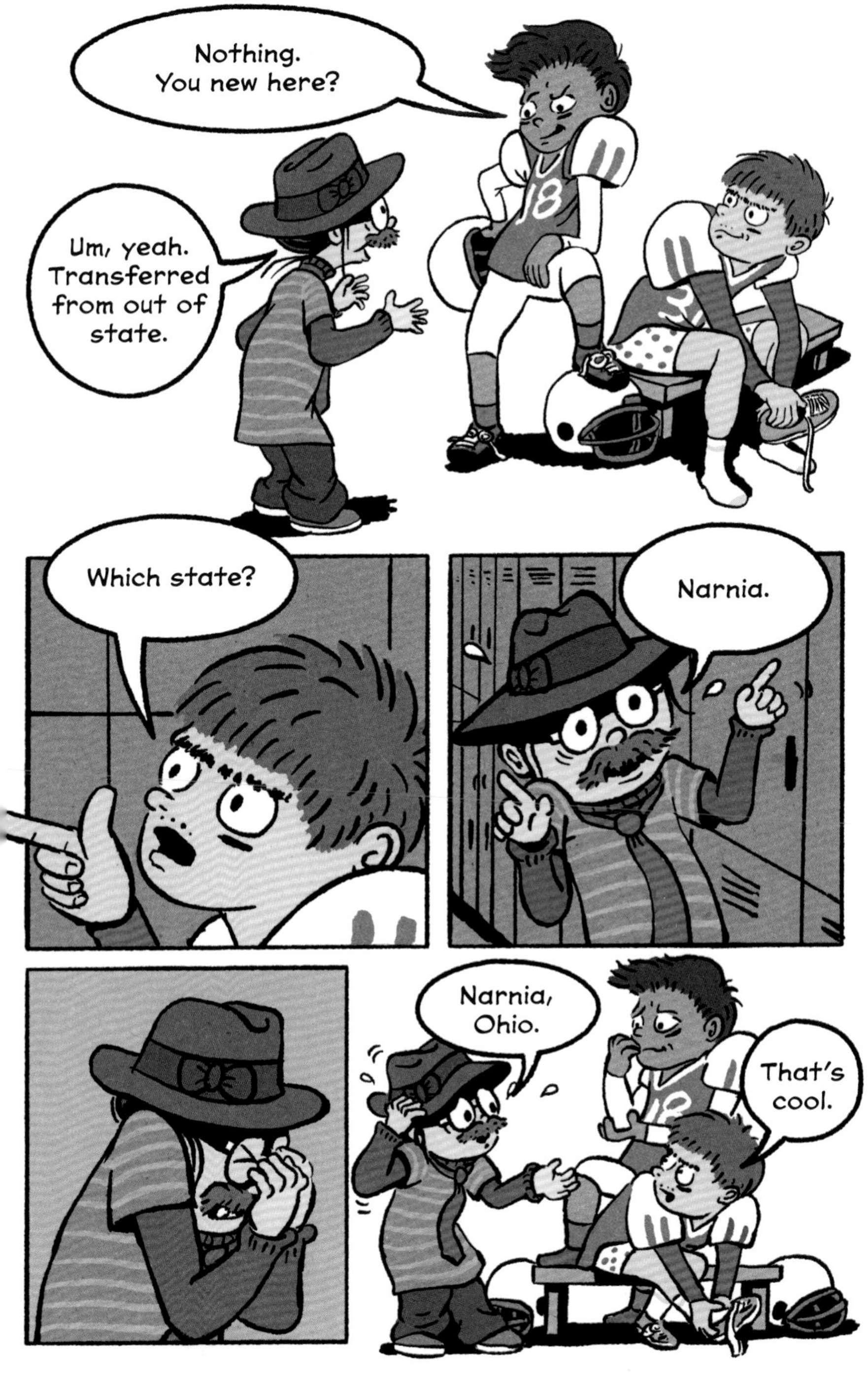
Nothing. You new here?
Um, yeah. Transferred from out of state.
Which state?
Narnia.
Narnia, Ohio.
That's cool.

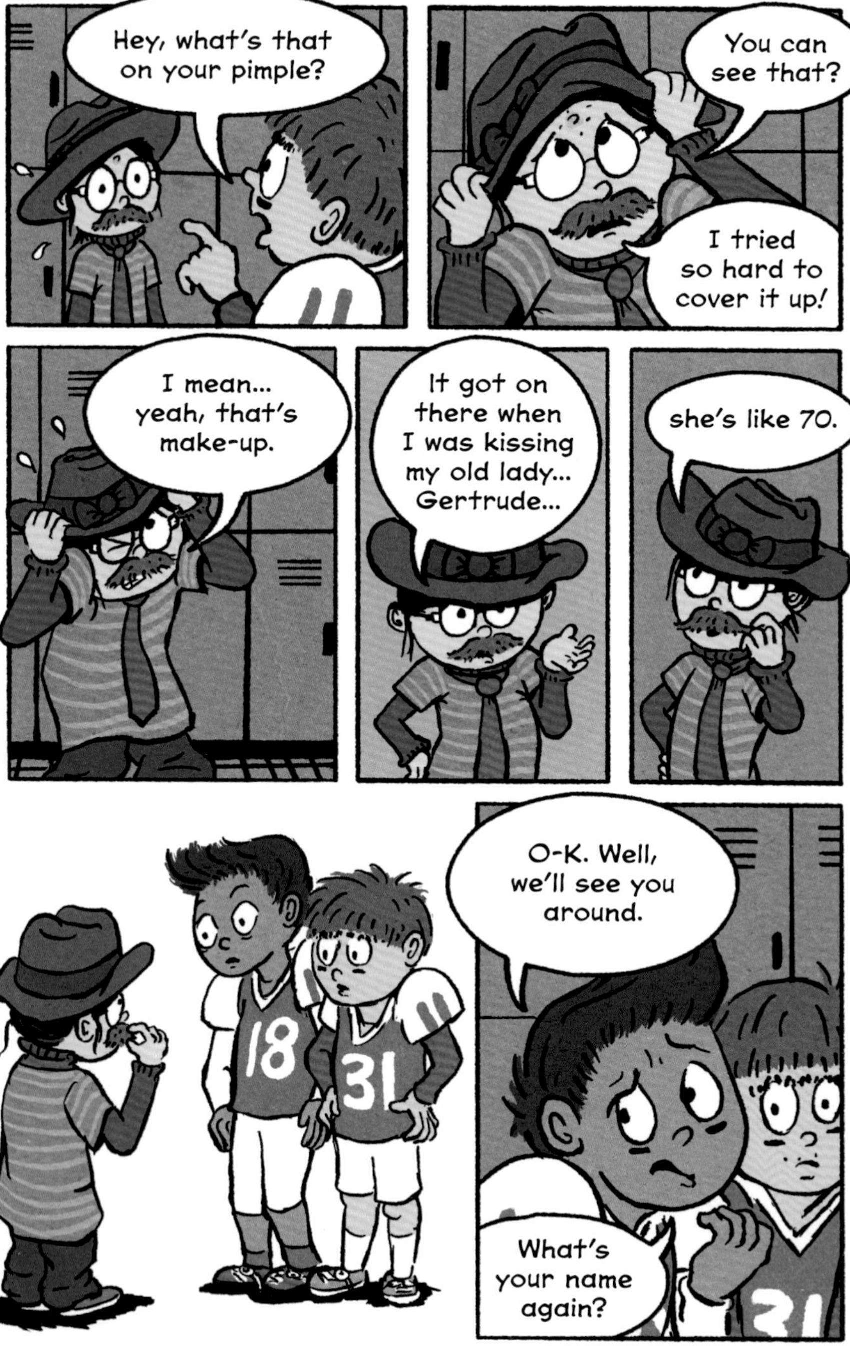
Hey, what's that on your pimple?
You can see that?
I tried so hard to cover it up!
I mean... yeah, that's make-up.
It got on there when I was kissing my old lady... Gertrude...
she's like 70.
O-K. Well, we'll see you around.
What's your name again?
18
31

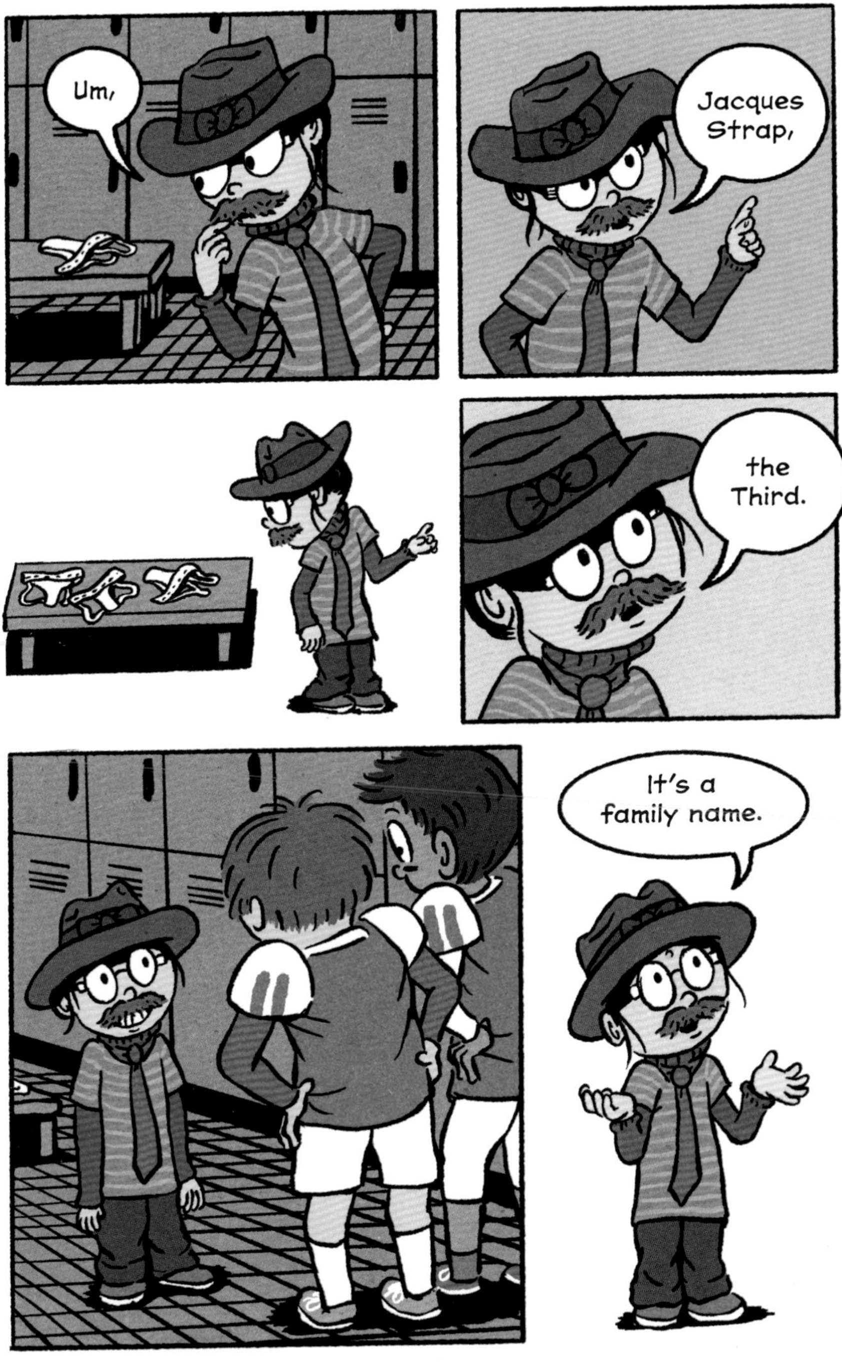
Um,
Jacques Strap,
the Third.
It's a family name.

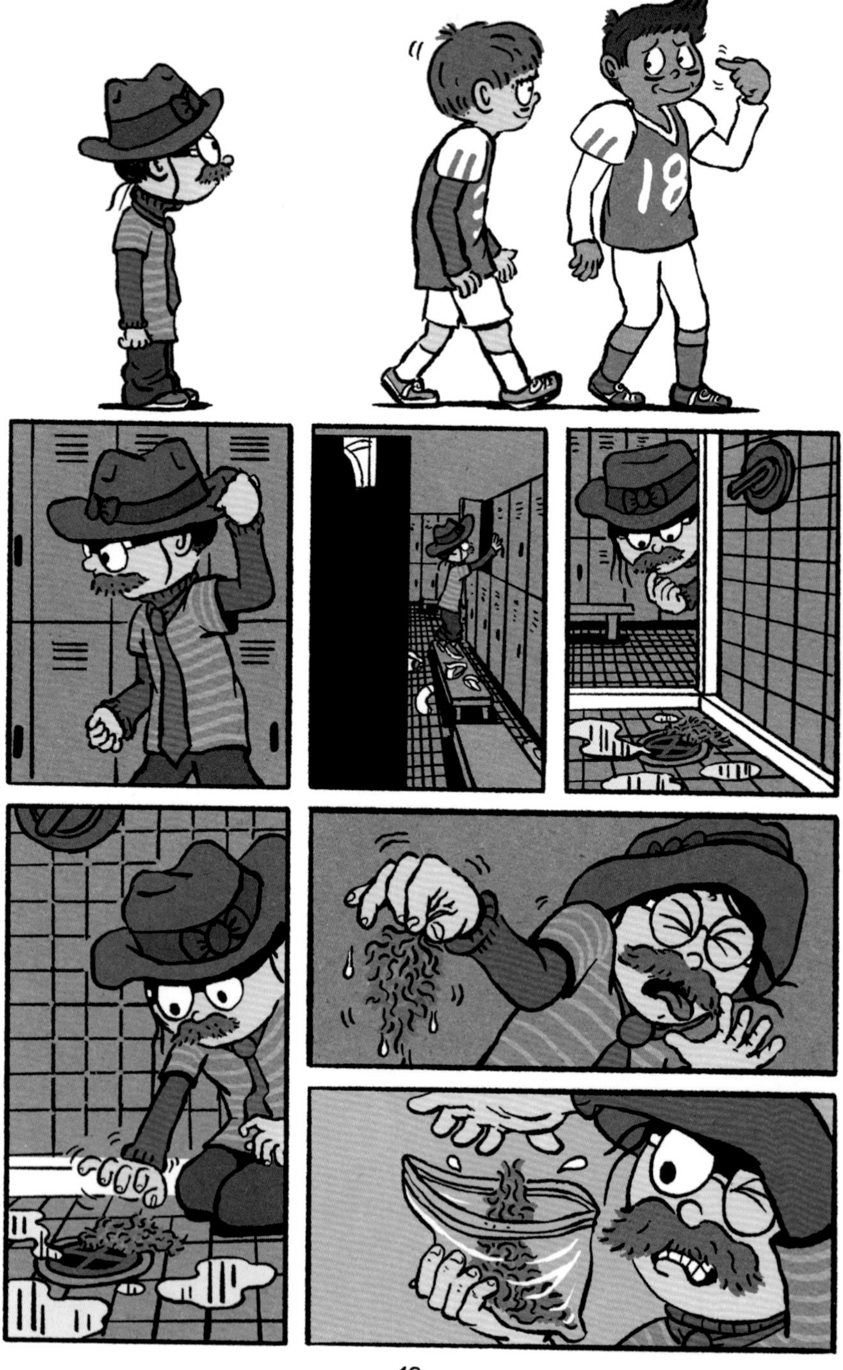
18

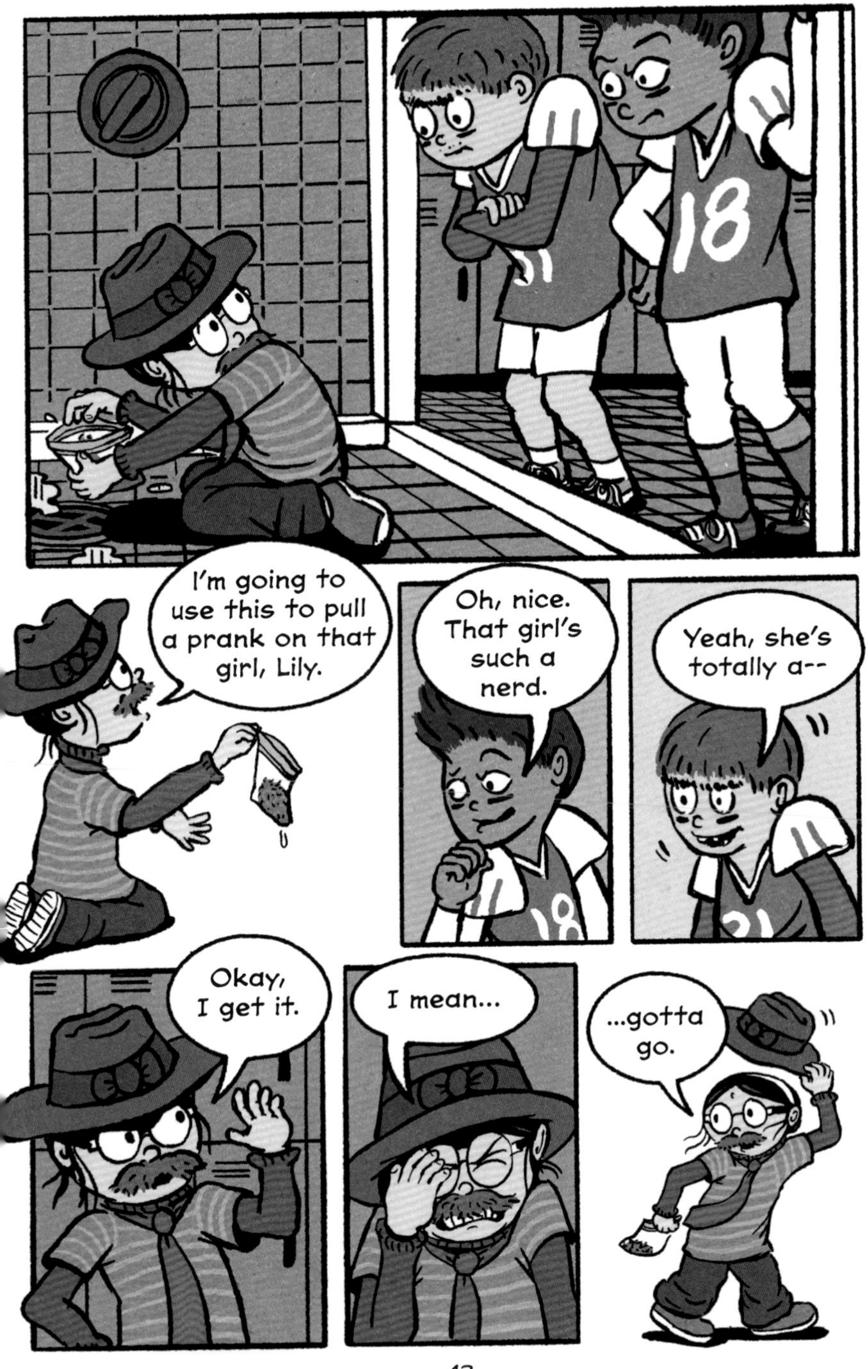
I'm going to use this to pull a prank on that girl, Lily.
Oh, nice. That girl's such a nerd.
Yeah, she's totally a--
Okay, I get it.
I mean...
...gotta go.

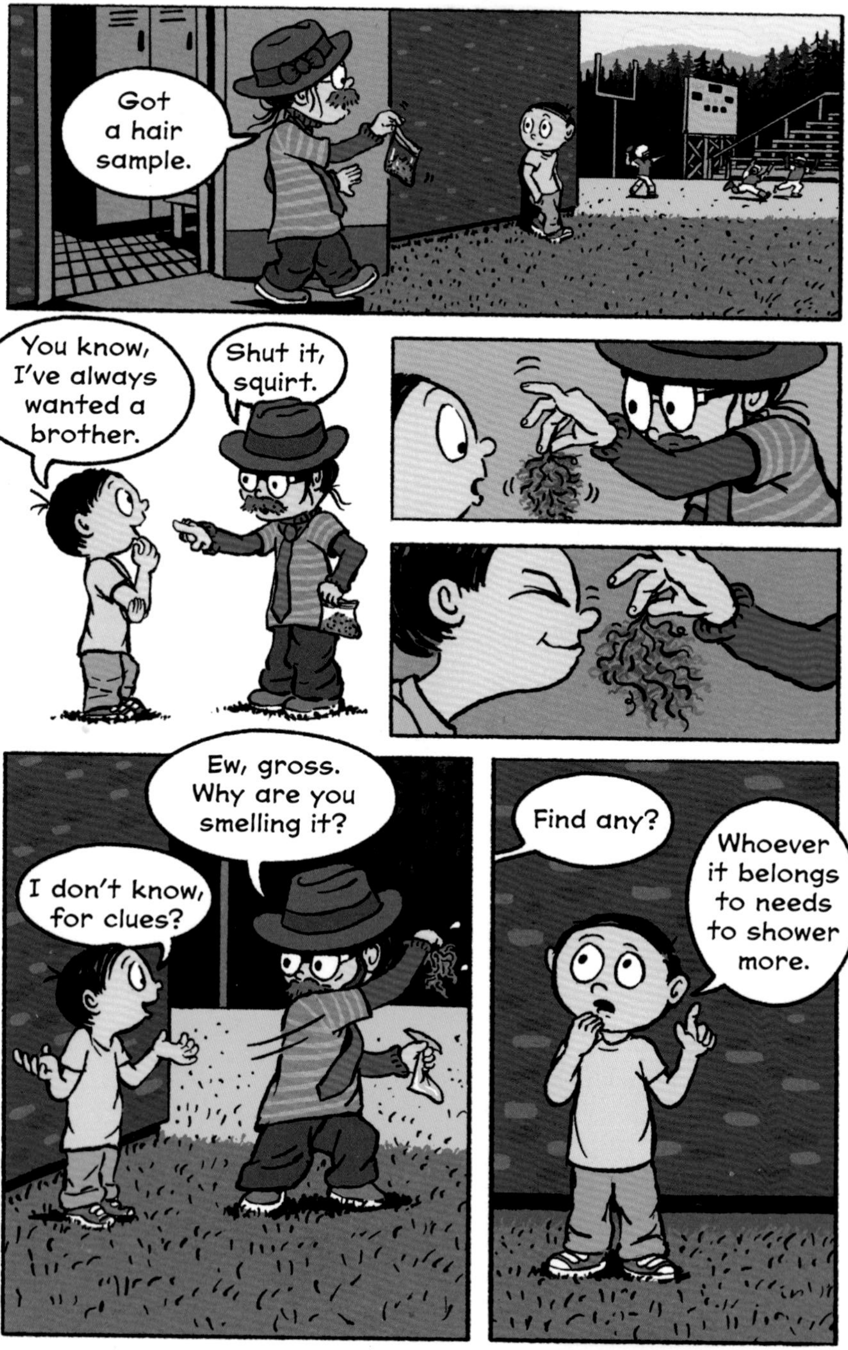
Got a hair sample.
You know, I've always wanted a brother.
Shut it, squirt.
Ew, gross. Why are you smelling it?
I don't know, for clues?
Find any?
Whoever it belongs to needs to shower more.

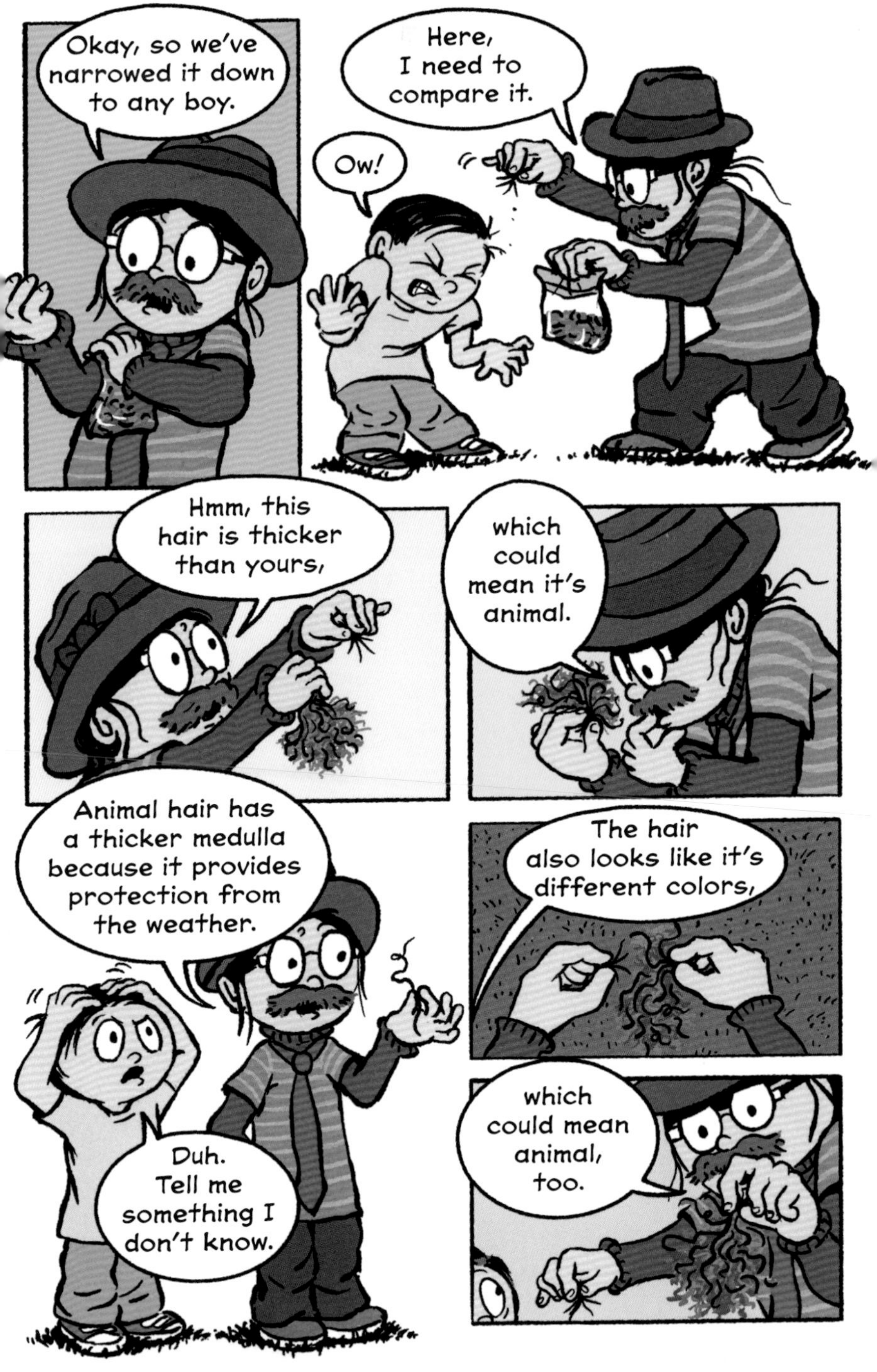
Okay, so we've narrowed it down to any boy.
Ow!
Here, I need to compare it.
Hmm, this hair is thicker than yours,
which could mean it's animal.
Animal hair has a thicker medulla because it provides protection from the weather.
Duh. Tell me something I don't know.
The hair also looks like it's different colors,
which could mean animal, too.

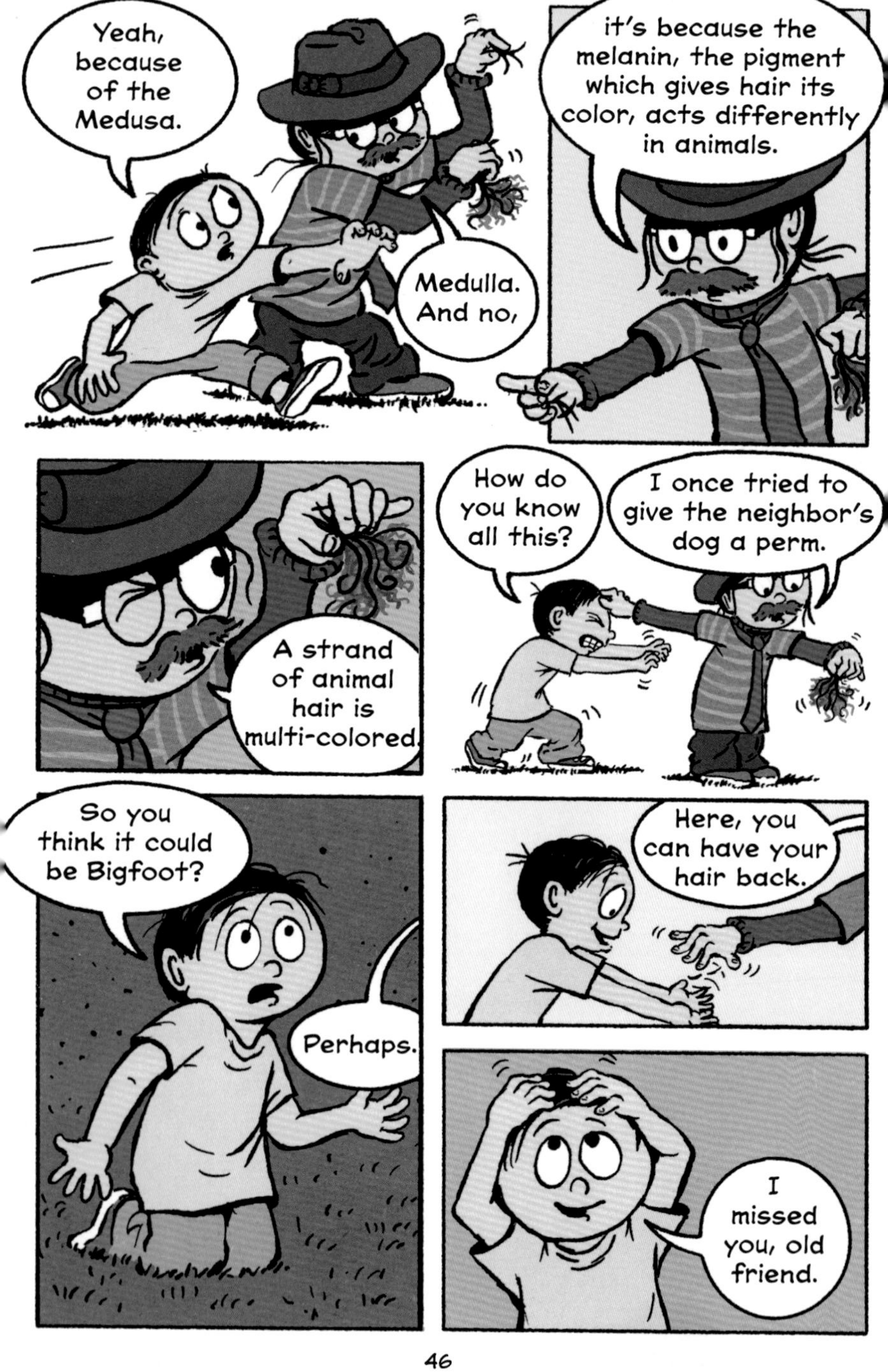
Yeah, because of the Medusa.
Medulla. And no,
it's because the melanin, the pigment which gives hair its color, acts differently in animals.
A strand of animal hair is multi-colored.
How do you know all this?
I once tried to give the neighbor's dog a perm.
So you think it could be Bigfoot?
Perhaps.
Here, you can have your hair back.
I missed you, old friend.

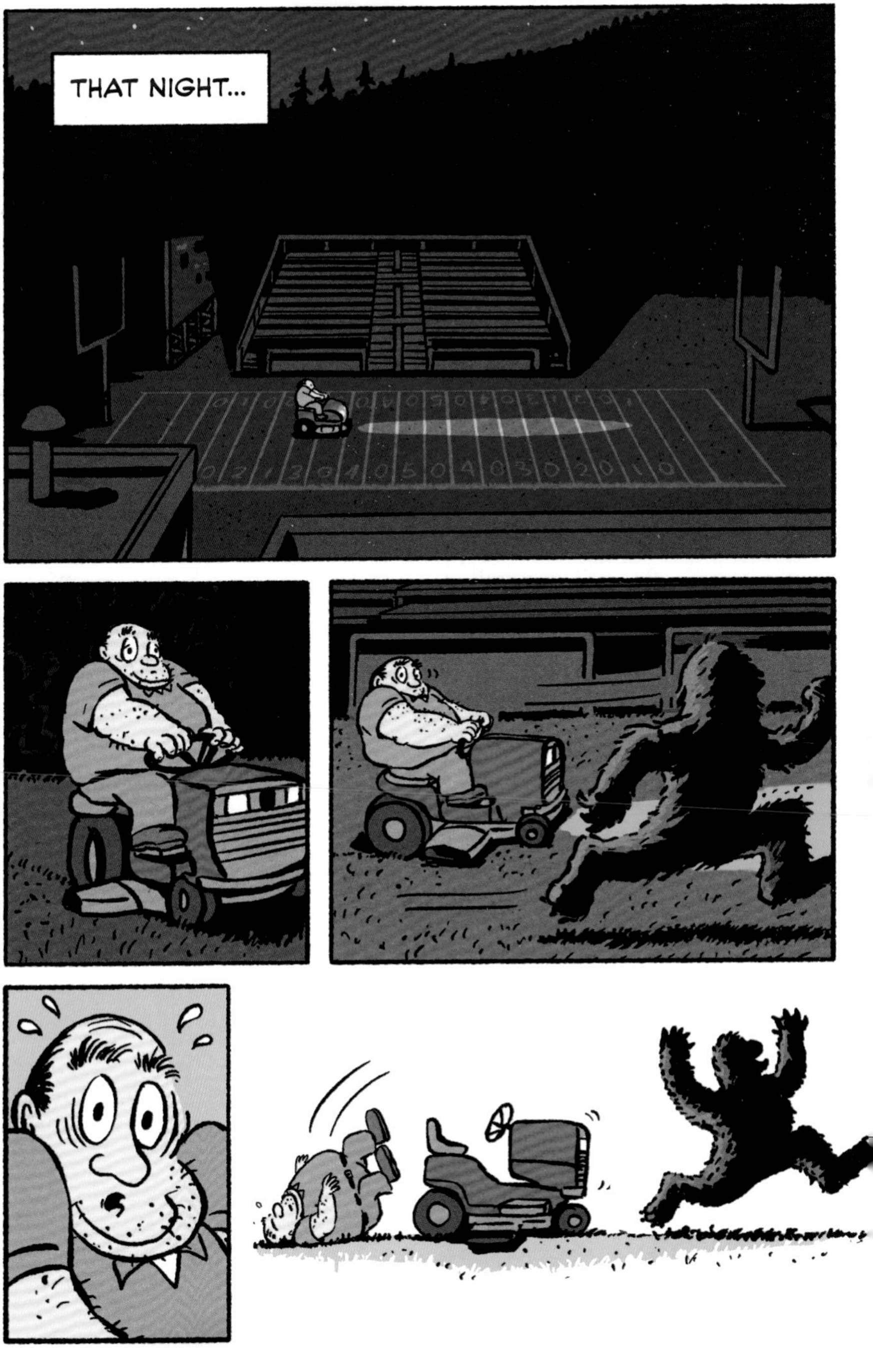
THAT NIGHT...

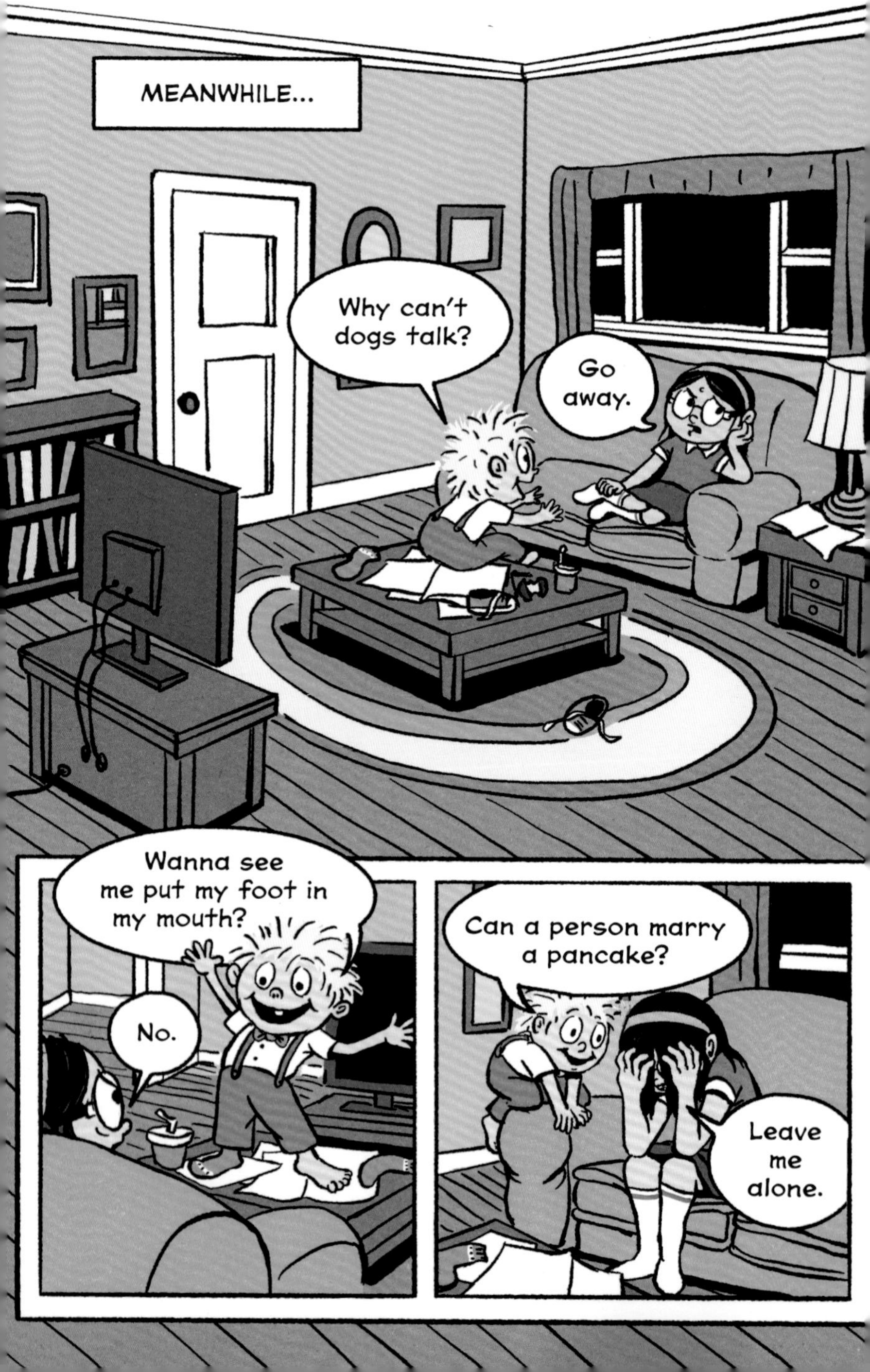
MEANWHILE...
Why can't dogs talk?
Go away.
Wanna see me put my foot in my mouth?
No.
Can a person marry a pancake?
Leave me alone.

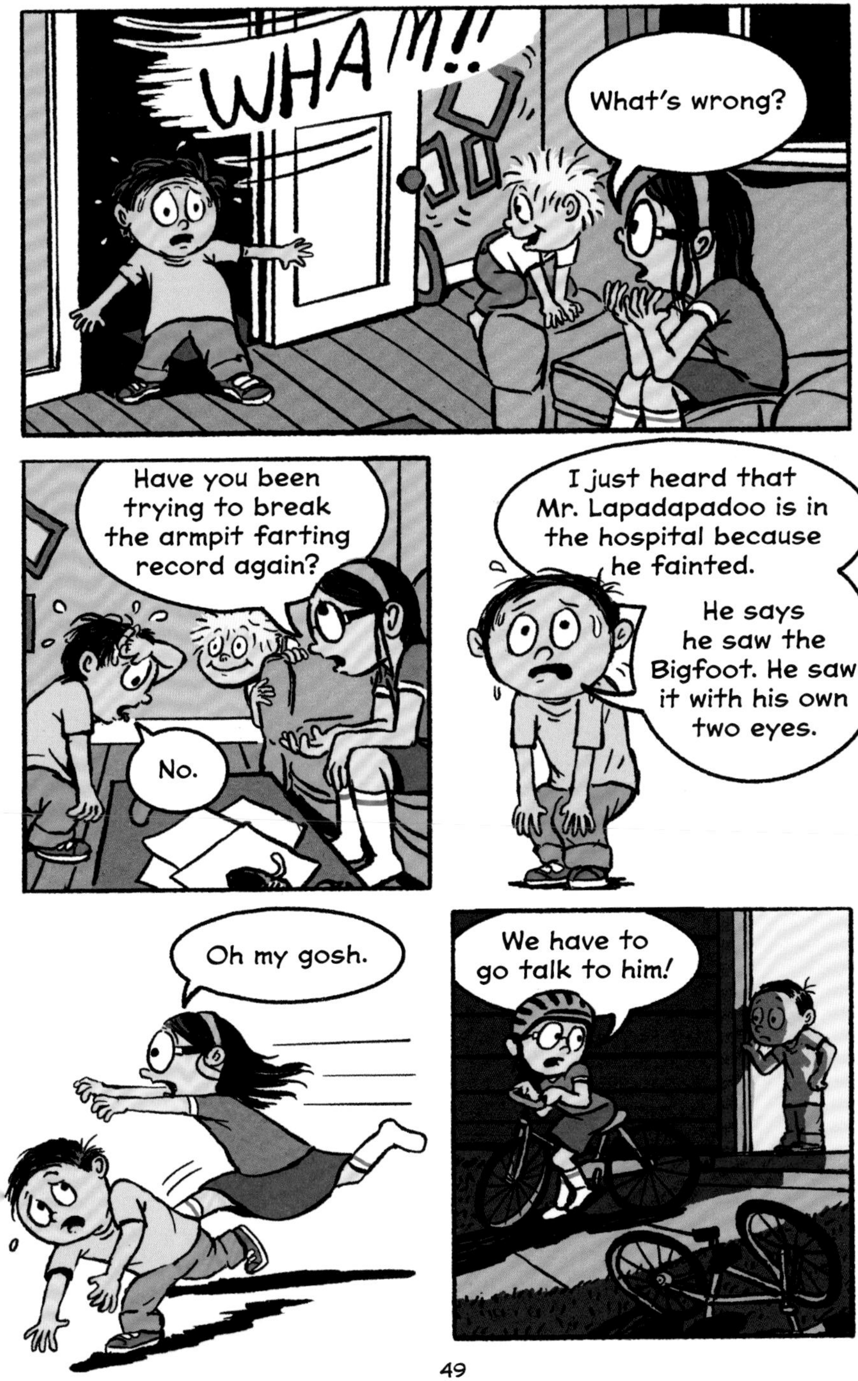
WHAM!!
What's wrong?
Have you been trying to break the armpit farting record again?
No.
I just heard that Mr. Lapadapadoo is in the hospital because he fainted.
He says he saw the Bigfoot. He saw it with his own two eyes.
Oh my gosh.
We have to go talk to him!

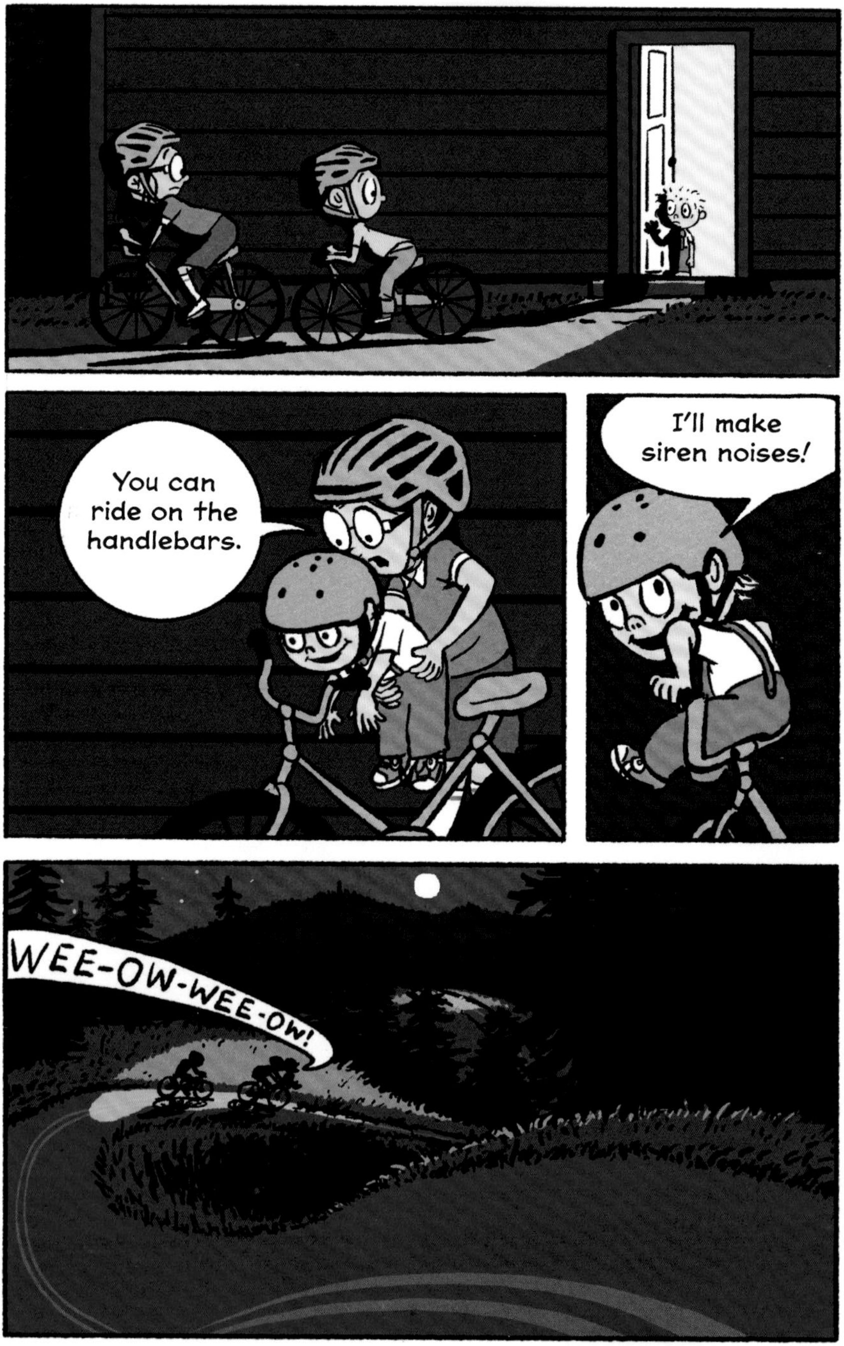
You can ride on the handlebars.
I'll make siren noises!
WEE-OW-WEE-OW!

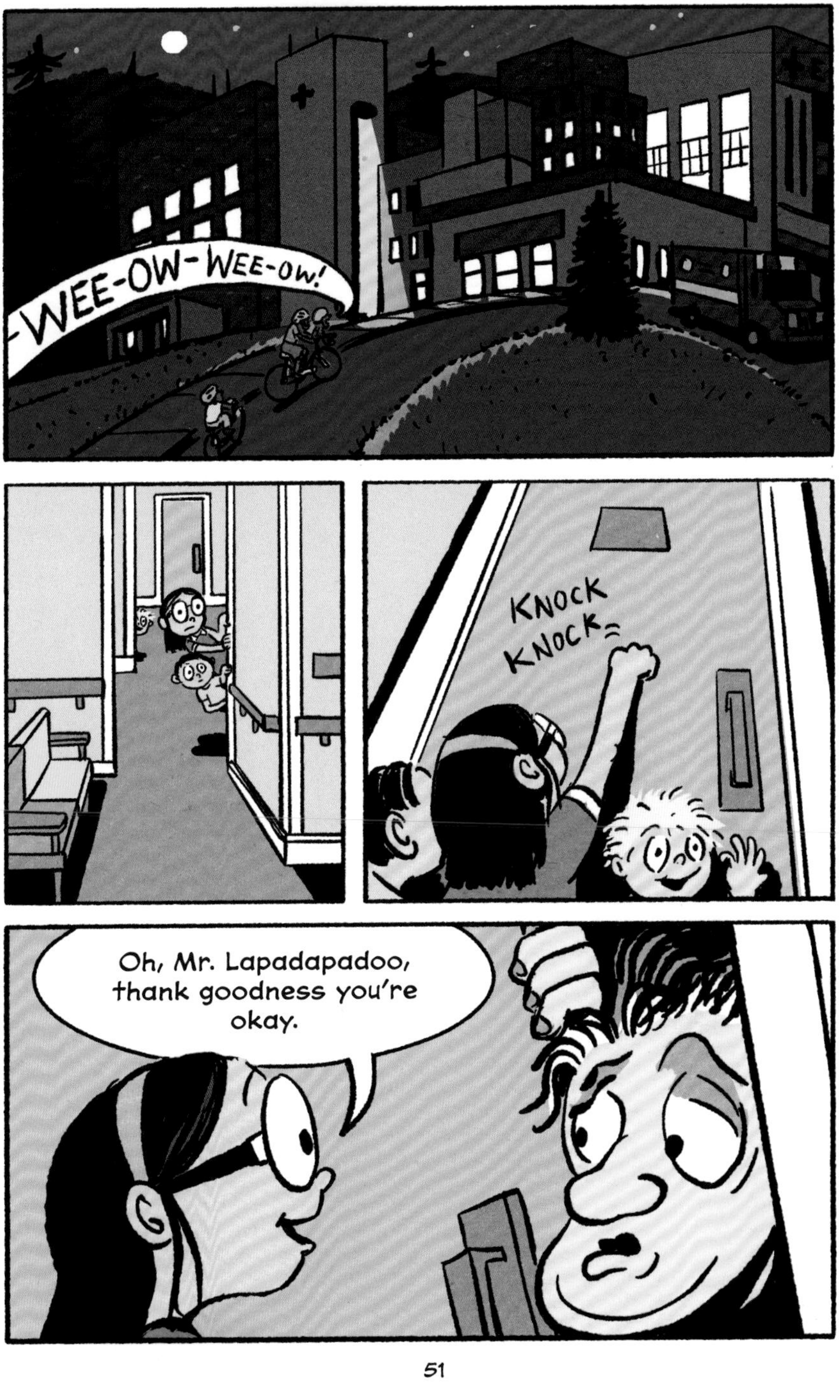
WEE-OW-WEE-OW!
KNOCK KNOCK
Oh, Mr. Lapadapadoo, thank goodness you're okay.

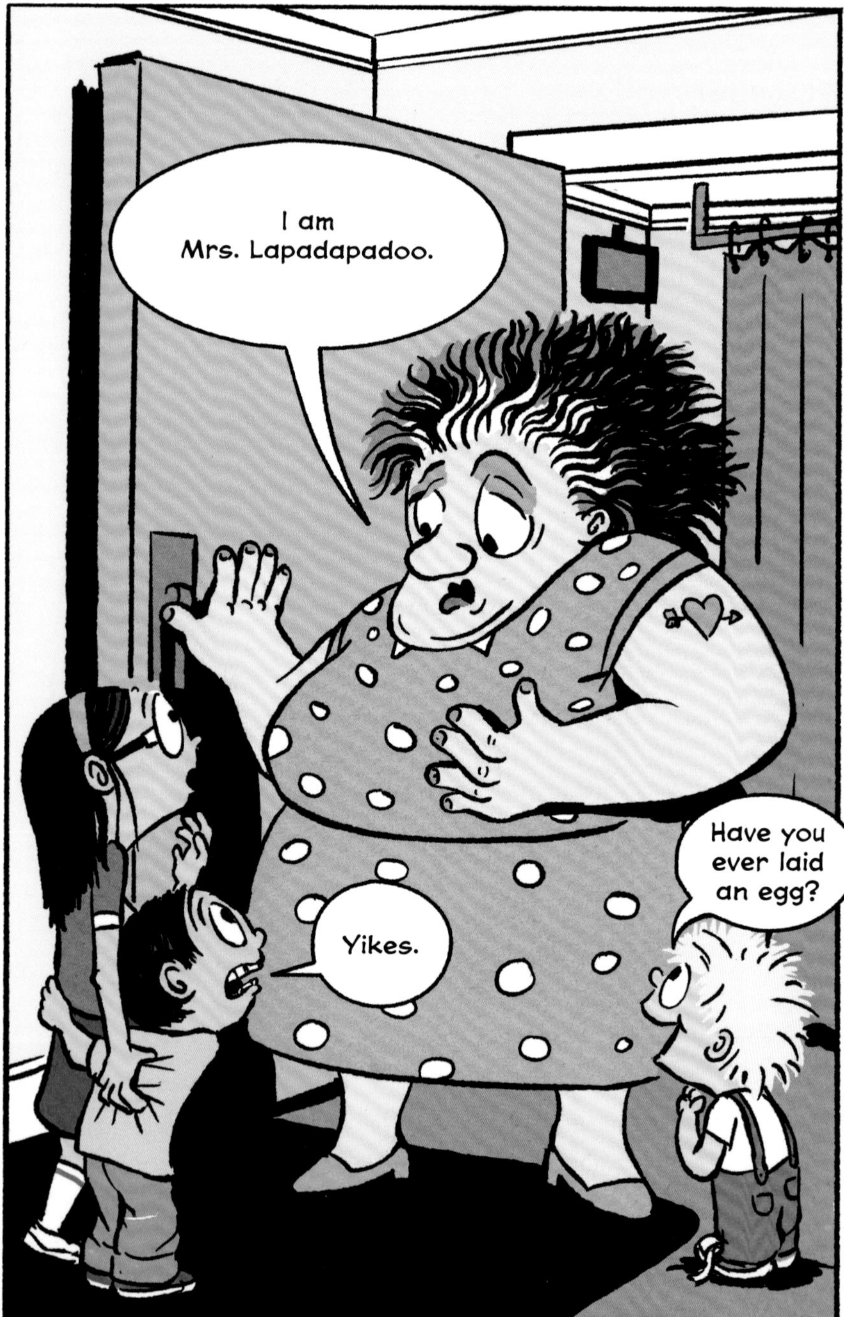
I am
Mrs. Lapadapadoo.
Yikes.
Have you ever laid an egg?

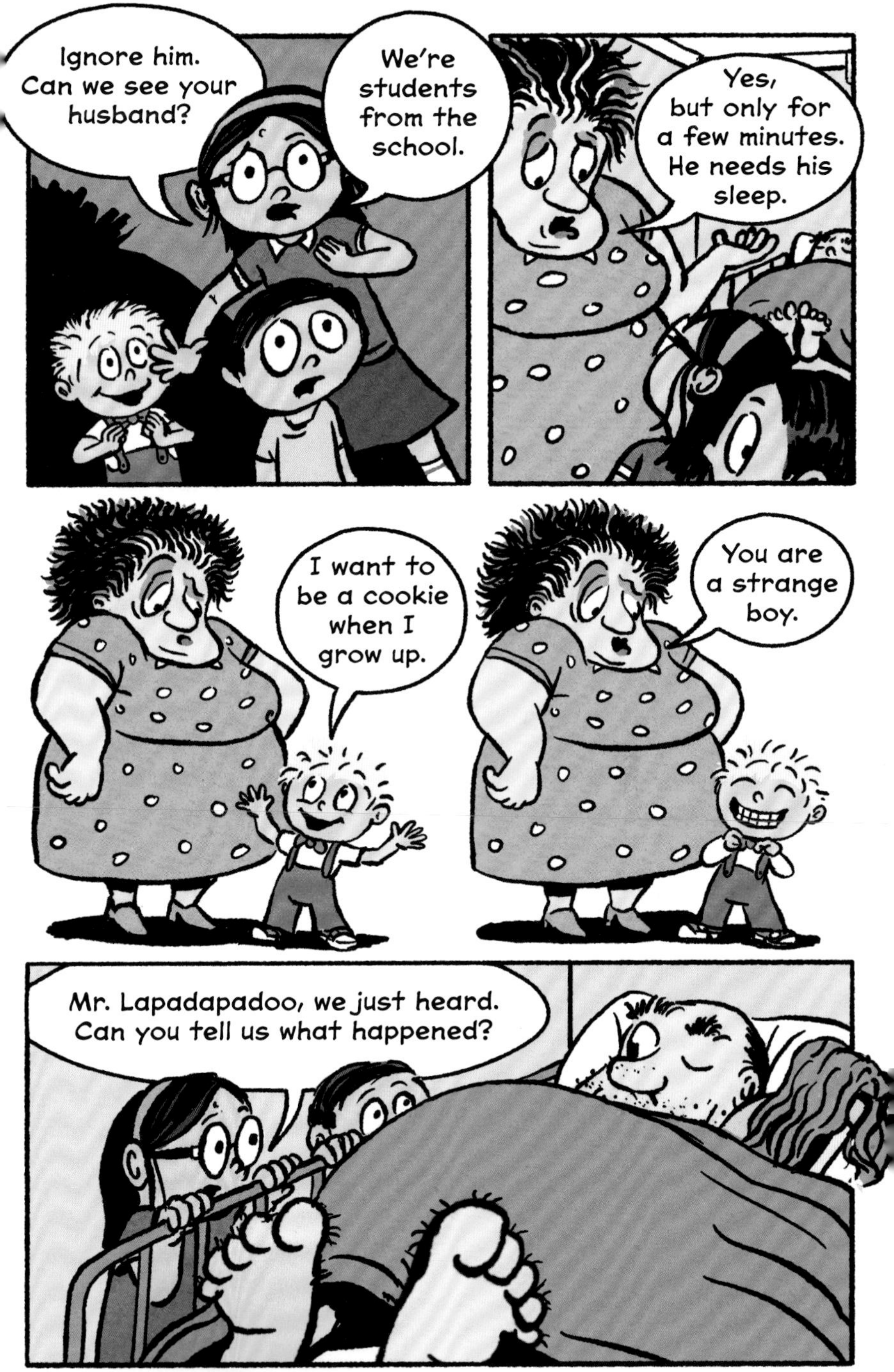
Ignore him. Can we see your husband?
We're students from the school.
Yes, but only for a few minutes. He needs his sleep.
I want to be a cookie when I grow up.
You are a strange boy.
Mr. Lapadapadoo, we just heard. Can you tell us what happened?

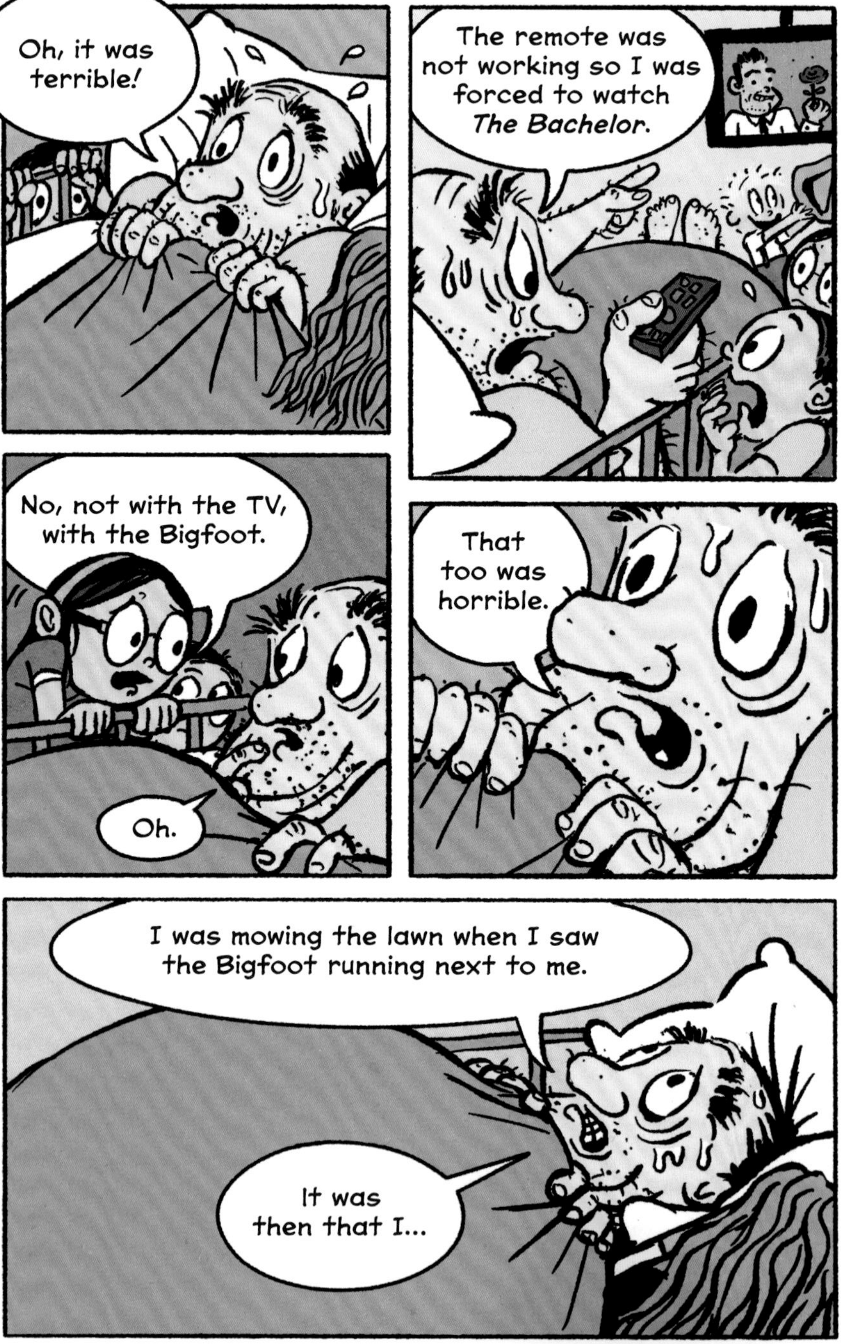
Oh, it was terrible!
The remote was not working so I was forced to watch *The Bachelor*.
No, not with the TV, with the Bigfoot.
Oh.
That too was horrible.
I was mowing the lawn when I saw the Bigfoot running next to me.
It was then that I...

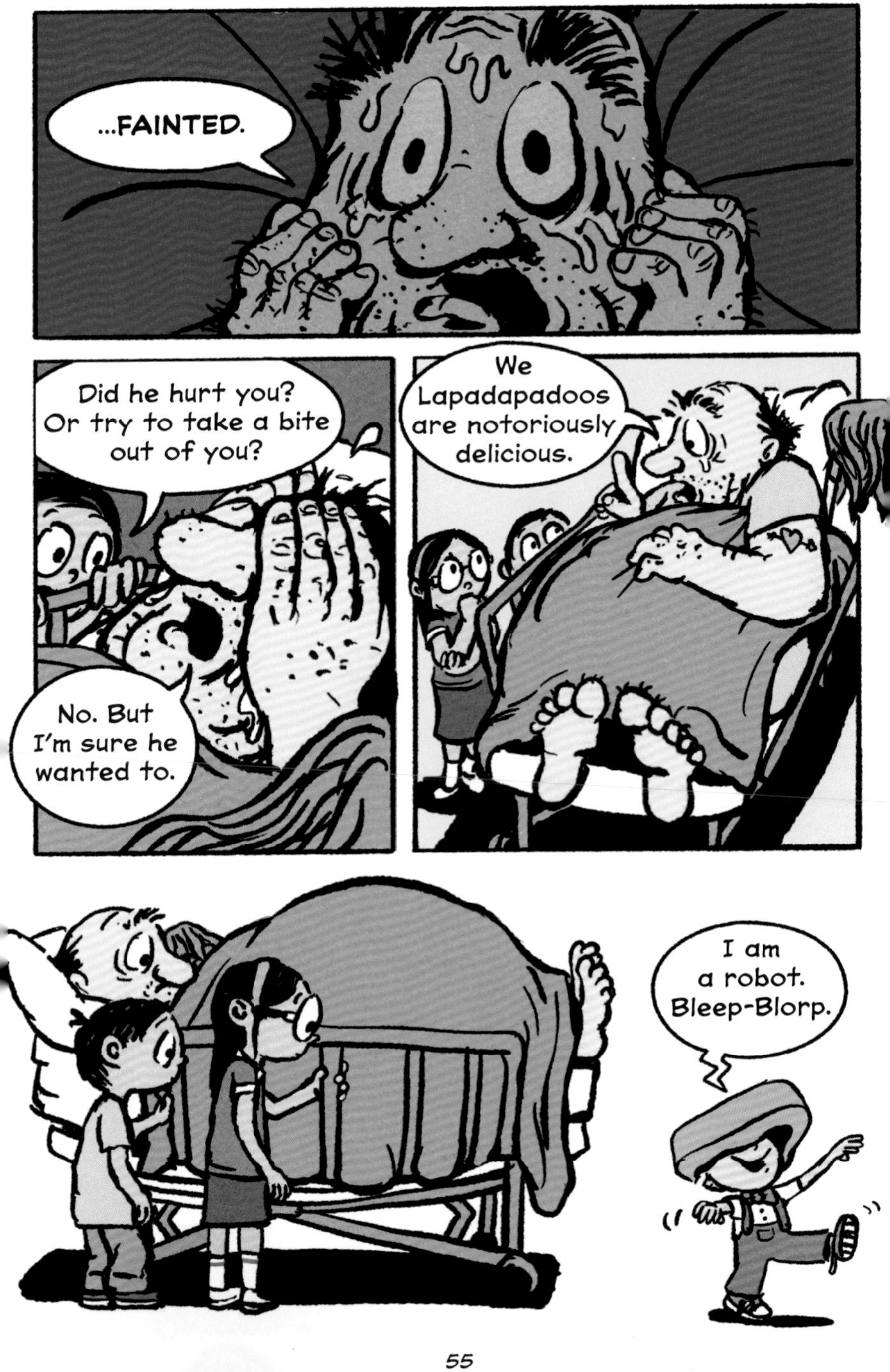
...FAINTED.
Did he hurt you? Or try to take a bite out of you?
No. But I'm sure he wanted to.
We Lapadapadoos are notoriously delicious.
I am a robot. Bleep-Blorp.

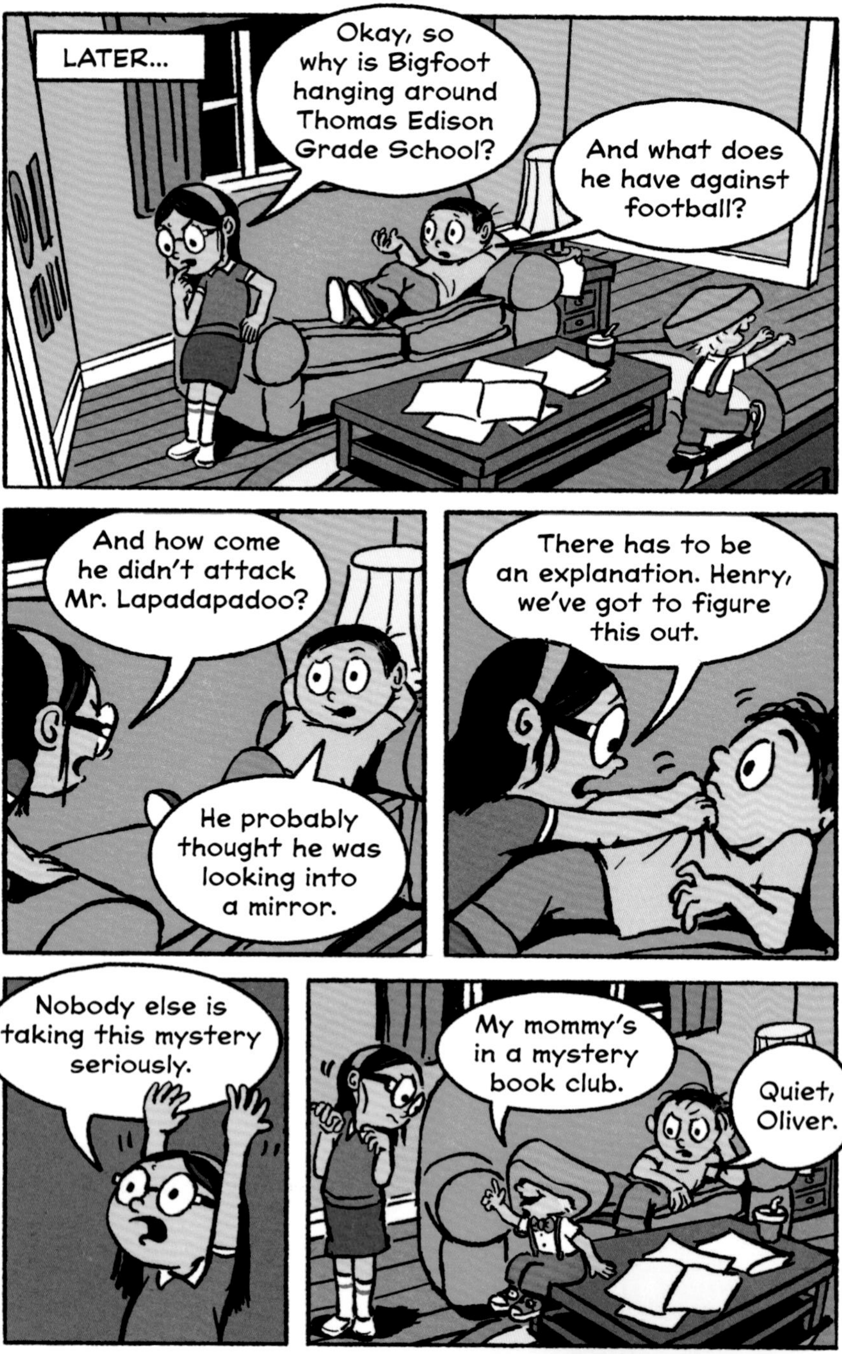
LATER...
Okay, so why is Bigfoot hanging around Thomas Edison Grade School?
And what does he have against football?
And how come he didn't attack Mr. Lapadapadoo?
He probably thought he was looking into a mirror.
There has to be an explanation. Henry, we've got to figure this out.
Nobody else is taking this mystery seriously.
My mommy's in a mystery book club.
Quiet, Oliver.

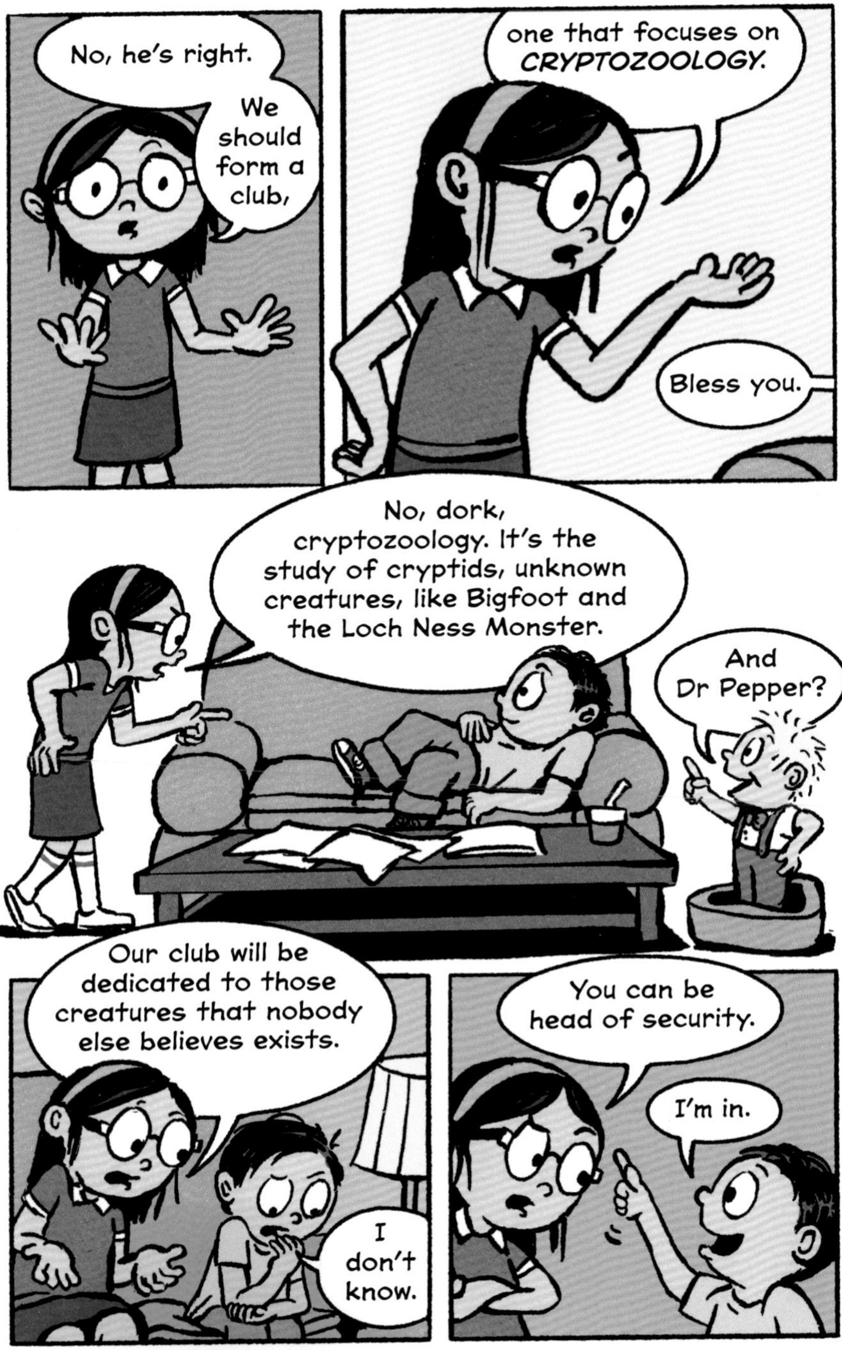
No, he's right.
We should form a club,
one that focuses on *CRYPTOZOOLOGY.*
Bless you.
No, dork, cryptozoology. It's the study of cryptids, unknown creatures, like Bigfoot and the Loch Ness Monster.
And Dr Pepper?
Our club will be dedicated to those creatures that nobody else believes exists.
I don't know.
You can be head of security.
I'm in.

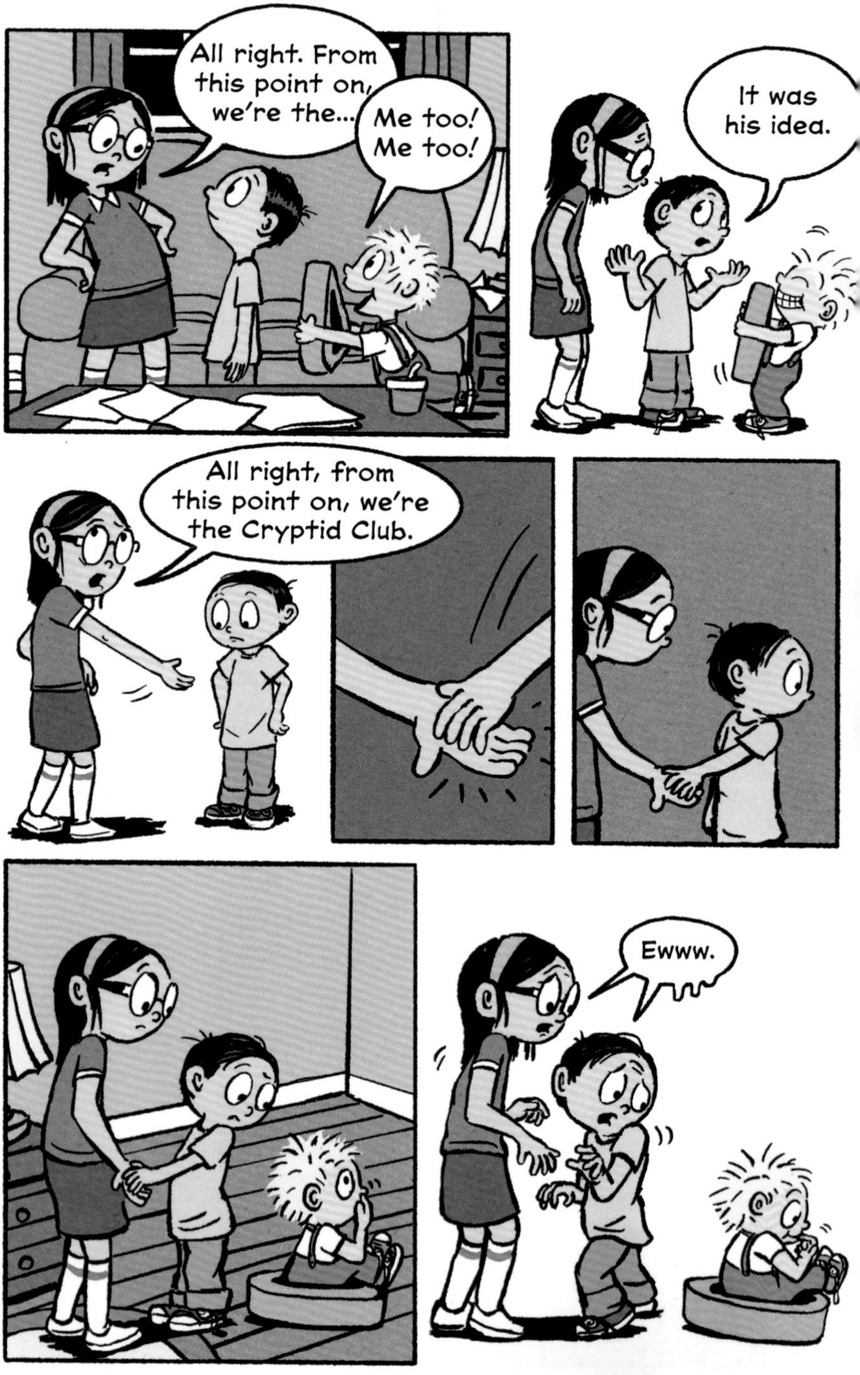
All right. From this point on, we're the...
Me too! Me too!
It was his idea.
All right, from this point on, we're the Cryptid Club.
Ewww.

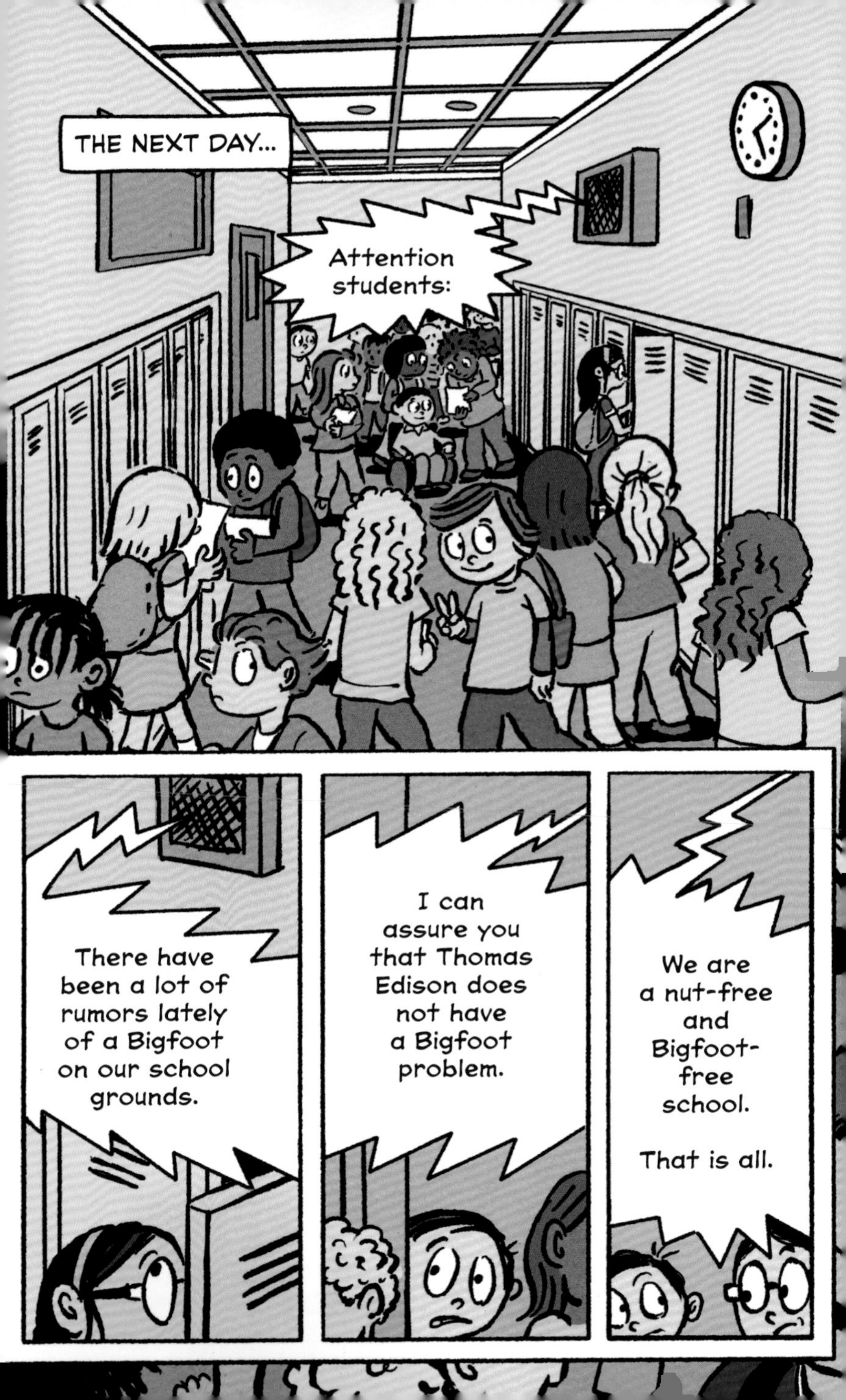
THE NEXT DAY...
Attention students:
There have been a lot of rumors lately of a Bigfoot on our school grounds.
I can assure you that Thomas Edison does not have a Bigfoot problem.
We are a nut-free and Bigfoot-free school.
That is all.

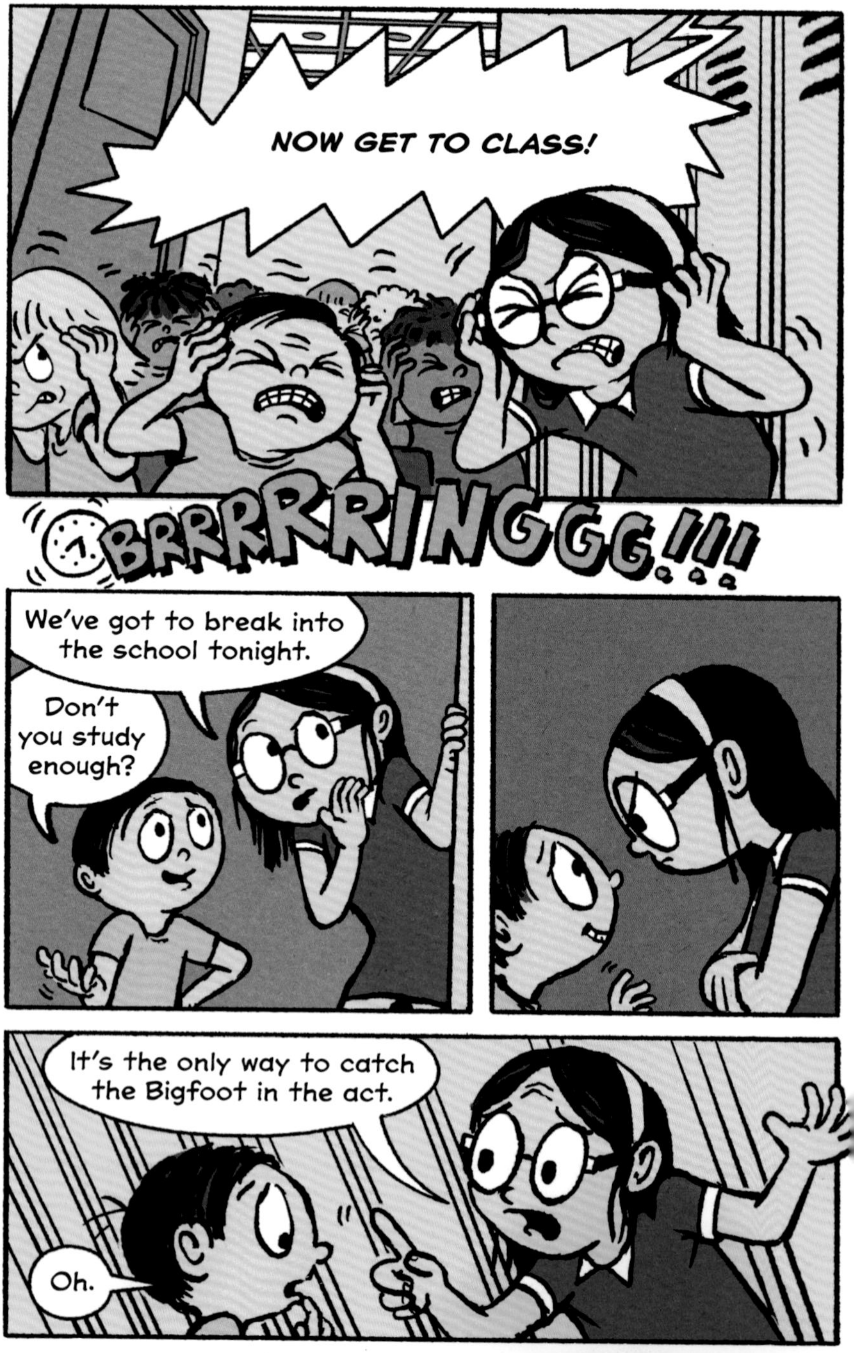
NOW GET TO CLASS!
BRRRRRINGGG!!!
We've got to break into the school tonight.
Don't you study enough?
It's the only way to catch the Bigfoot in the act.
Oh.

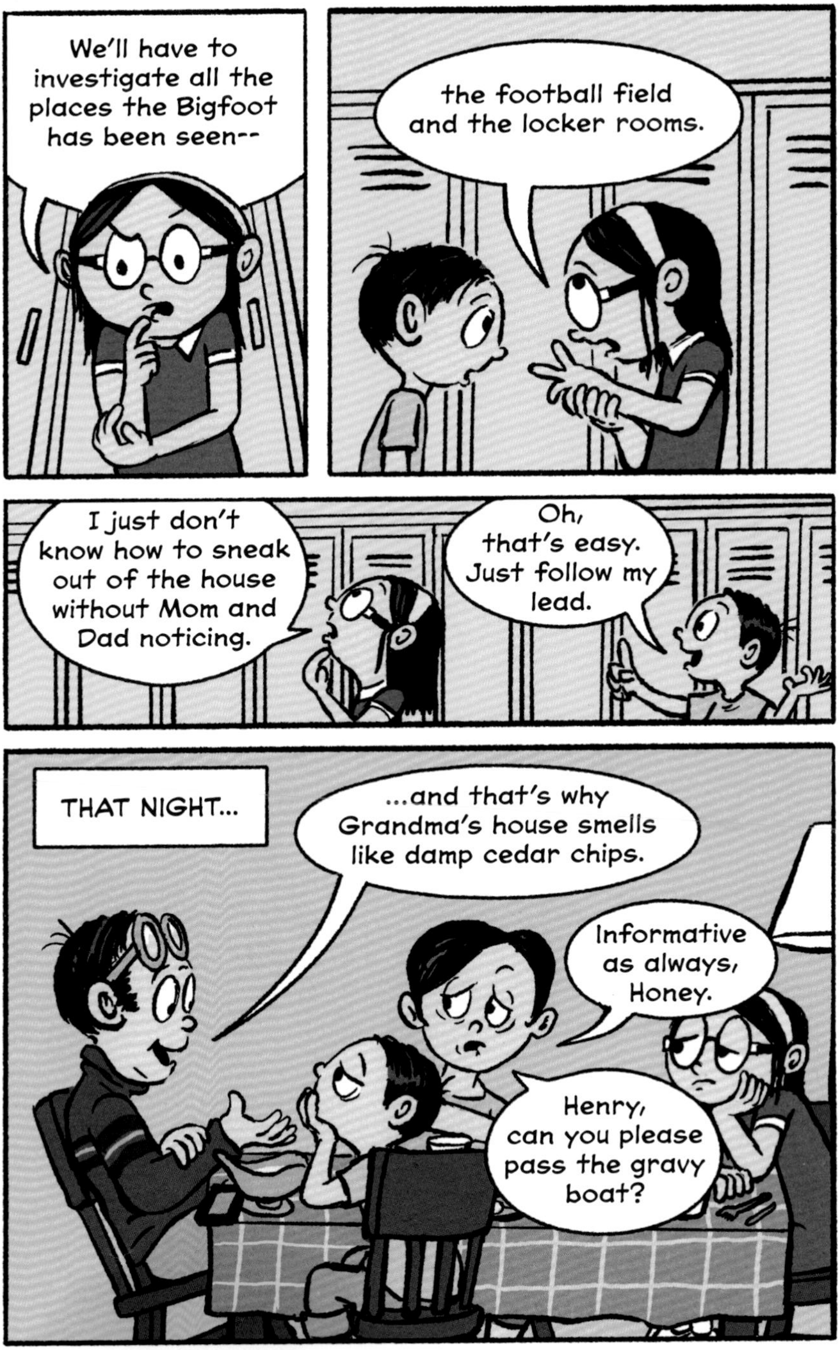

We'll have to investigate all the places the Bigfoot has been seen--
the football field and the locker rooms.
I just don't know how to sneak out of the house without Mom and Dad noticing.
Oh, that's easy. Just follow my lead.
THAT NIGHT...
...and that's why Grandma's house smells like damp cedar chips.
Informative as always, Honey.
Henry, can you please pass the gravy boat?

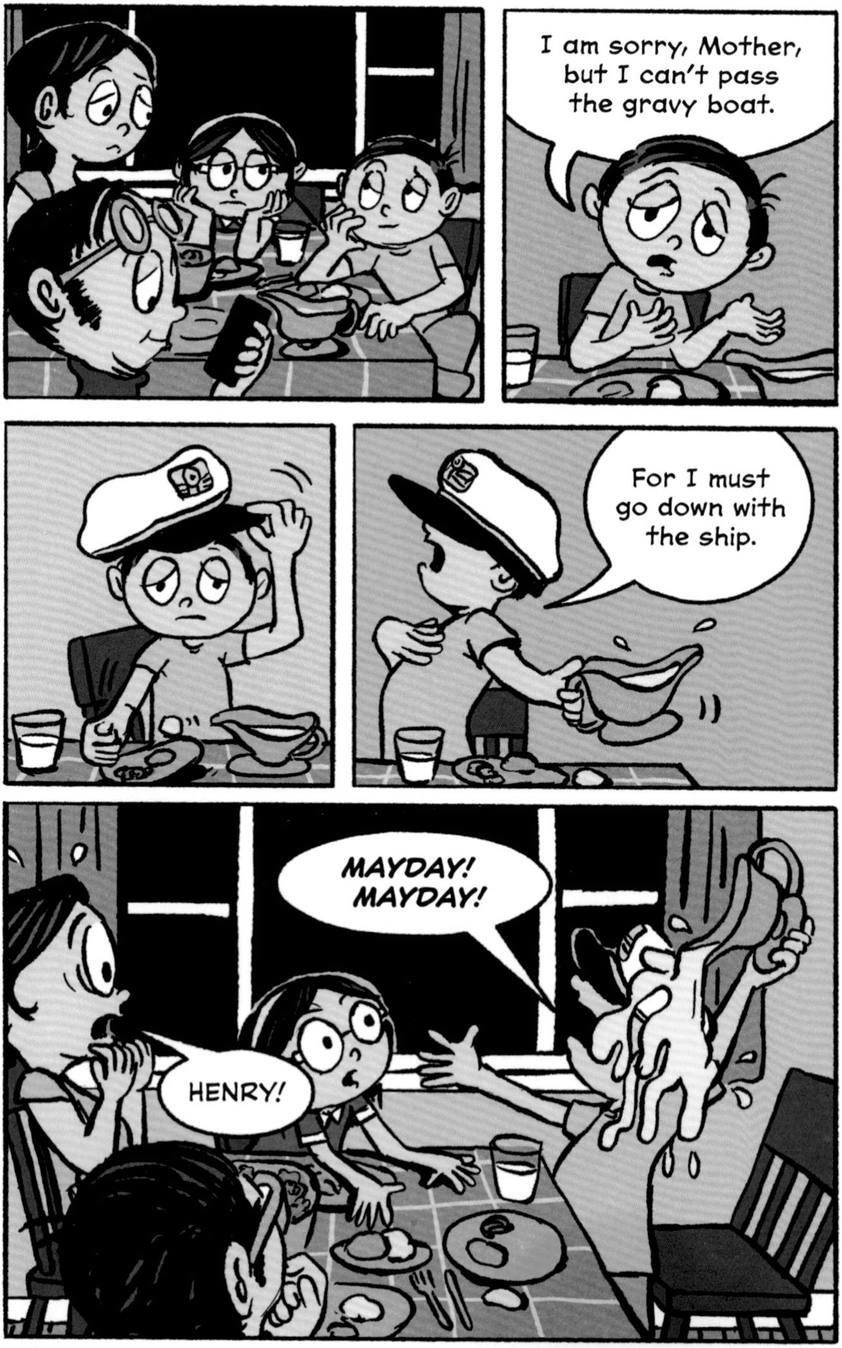
I am sorry, Mother, but I can't pass the gravy boat.
For I must go down with the ship.
MAYDAY! MAYDAY!
HENRY!

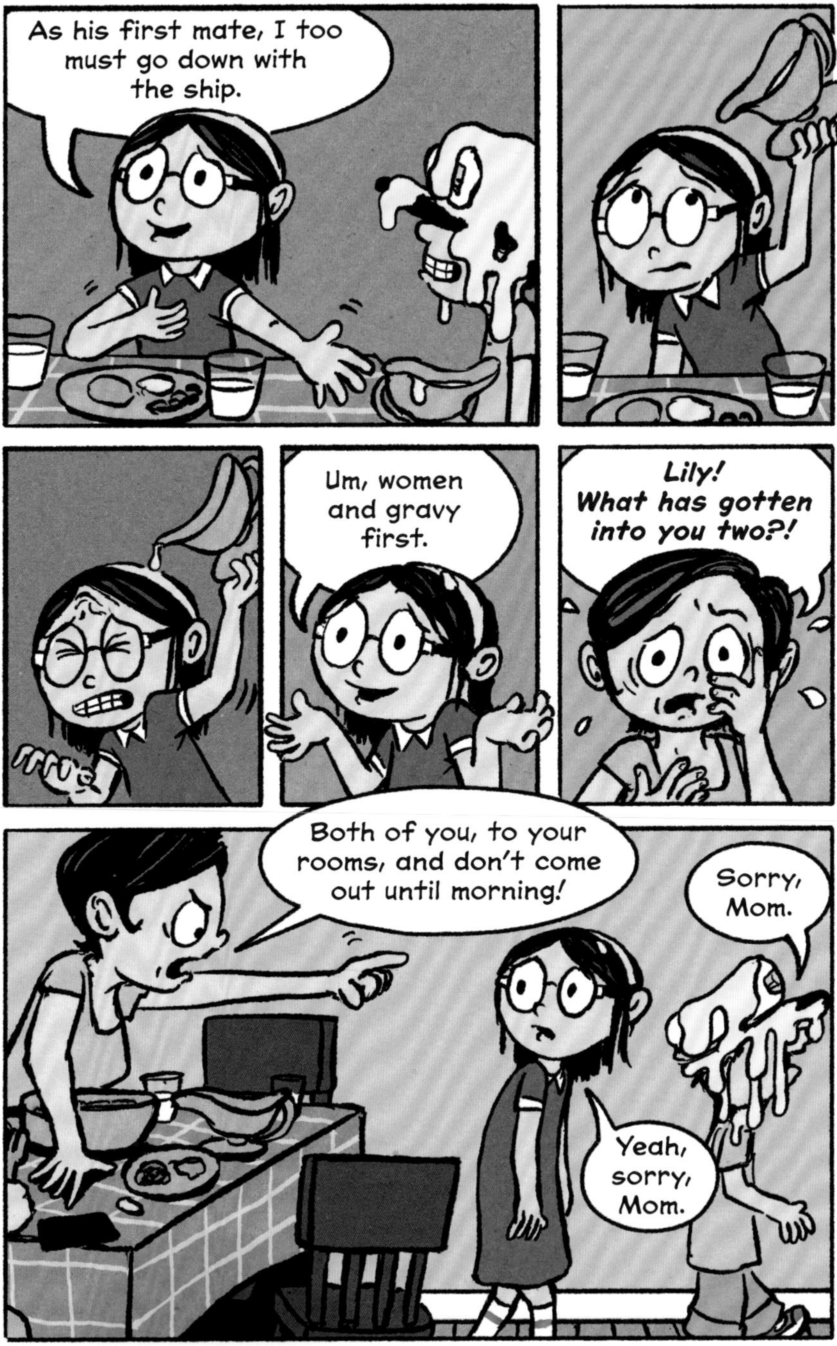
As his first mate, I too must go down with the ship.
Um, women and gravy first.
Lily! What has gotten into you two?!
Both of you, to your rooms, and don't come out until morning!
Sorry, Mom.
Yeah, sorry, Mom.

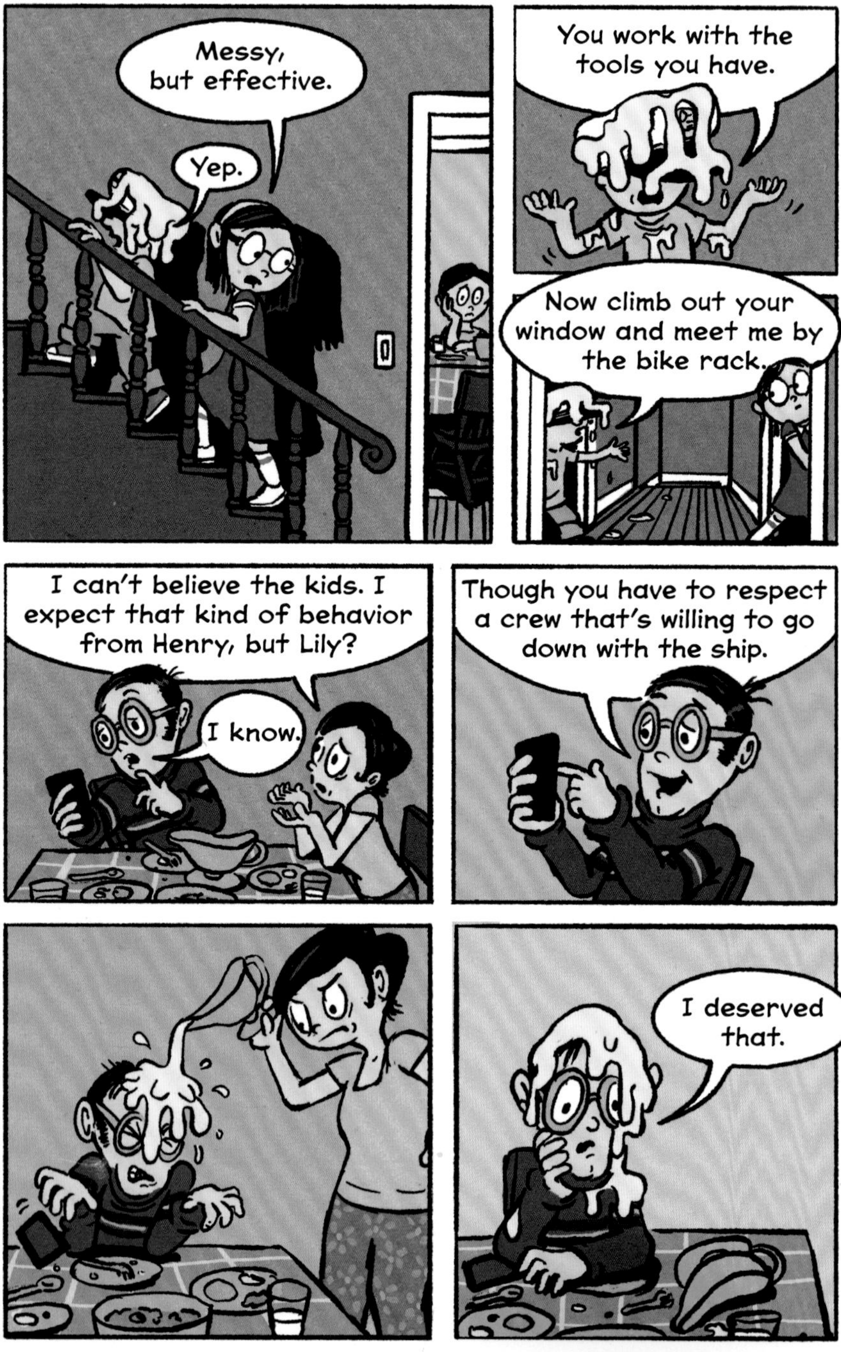
Messy, but effective.
Yep.
You work with the tools you have.
Now climb out your window and meet me by the bike rack.
I can't believe the kids. I expect that kind of behavior from Henry, but Lily?
I know.
Though you have to respect a crew that's willing to go down with the ship.
I deserved that.

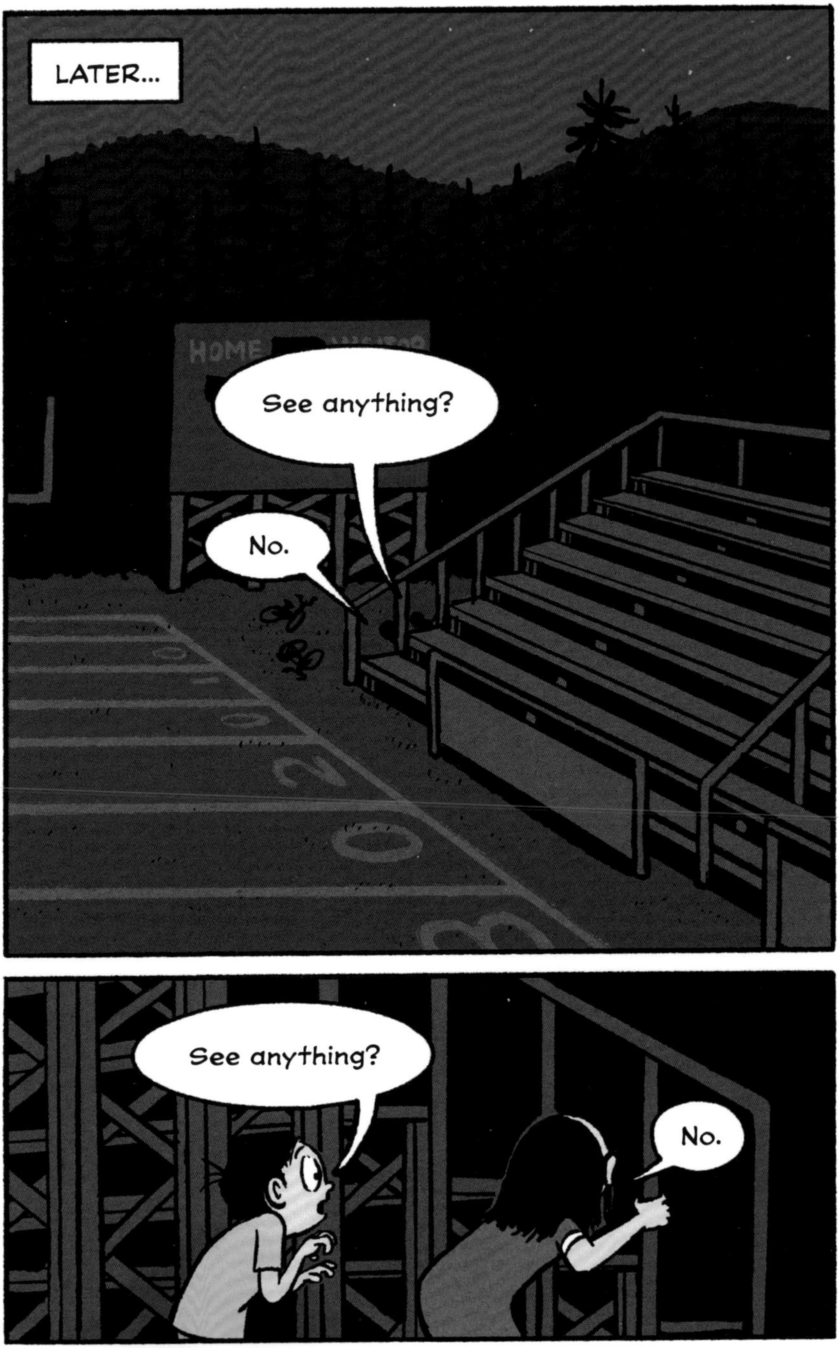
LATER...
HOME
See anything?
No.
See anything?
No.

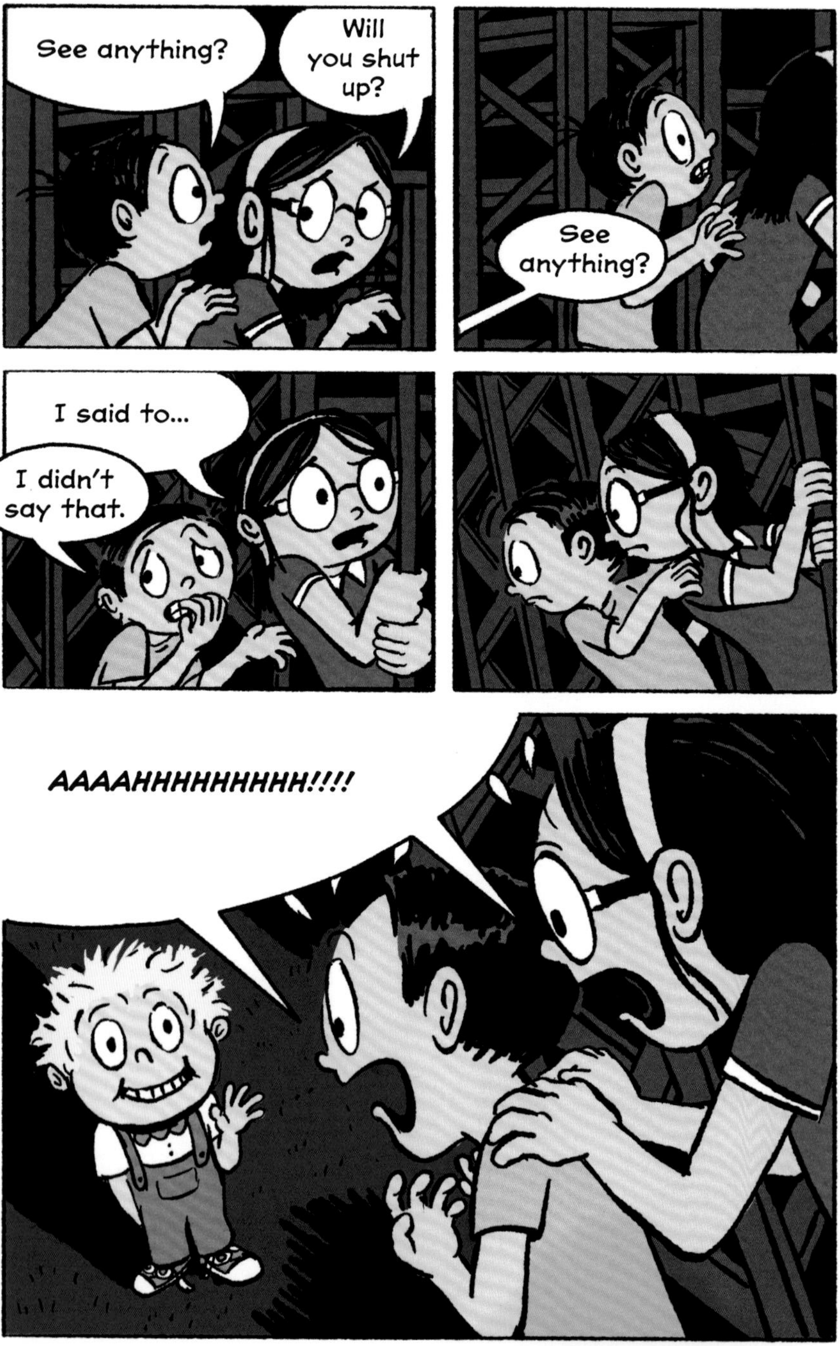
See anything?
Will you shut up?
See anything?
I said to...
I didn't say that.
AAAAHHHHHHHHH!!!!

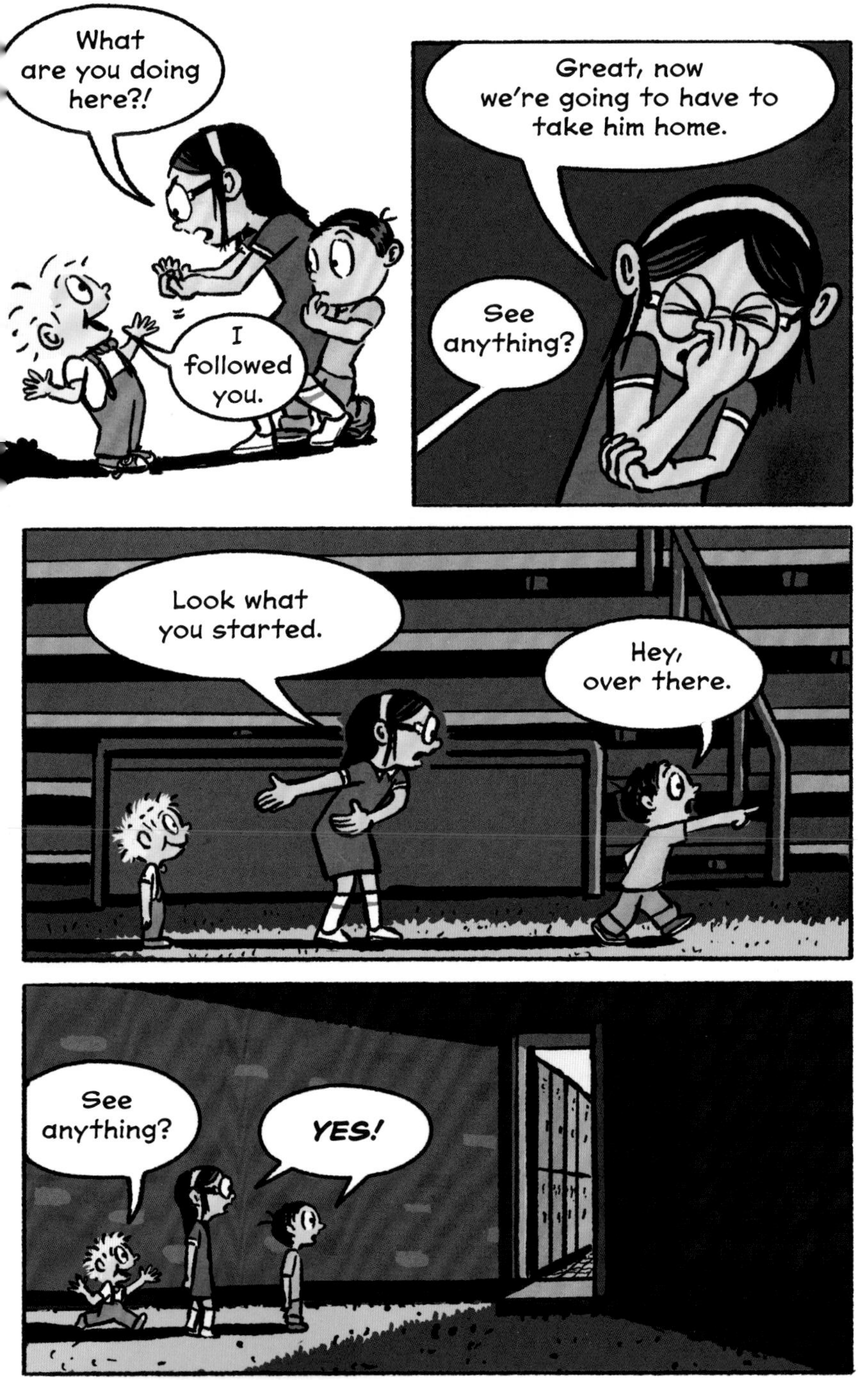
What are you doing here?!
I followed you.
Great, now we're going to have to take him home.
See anything?
Look what you started.
Hey, over there.
See anything?
YES!

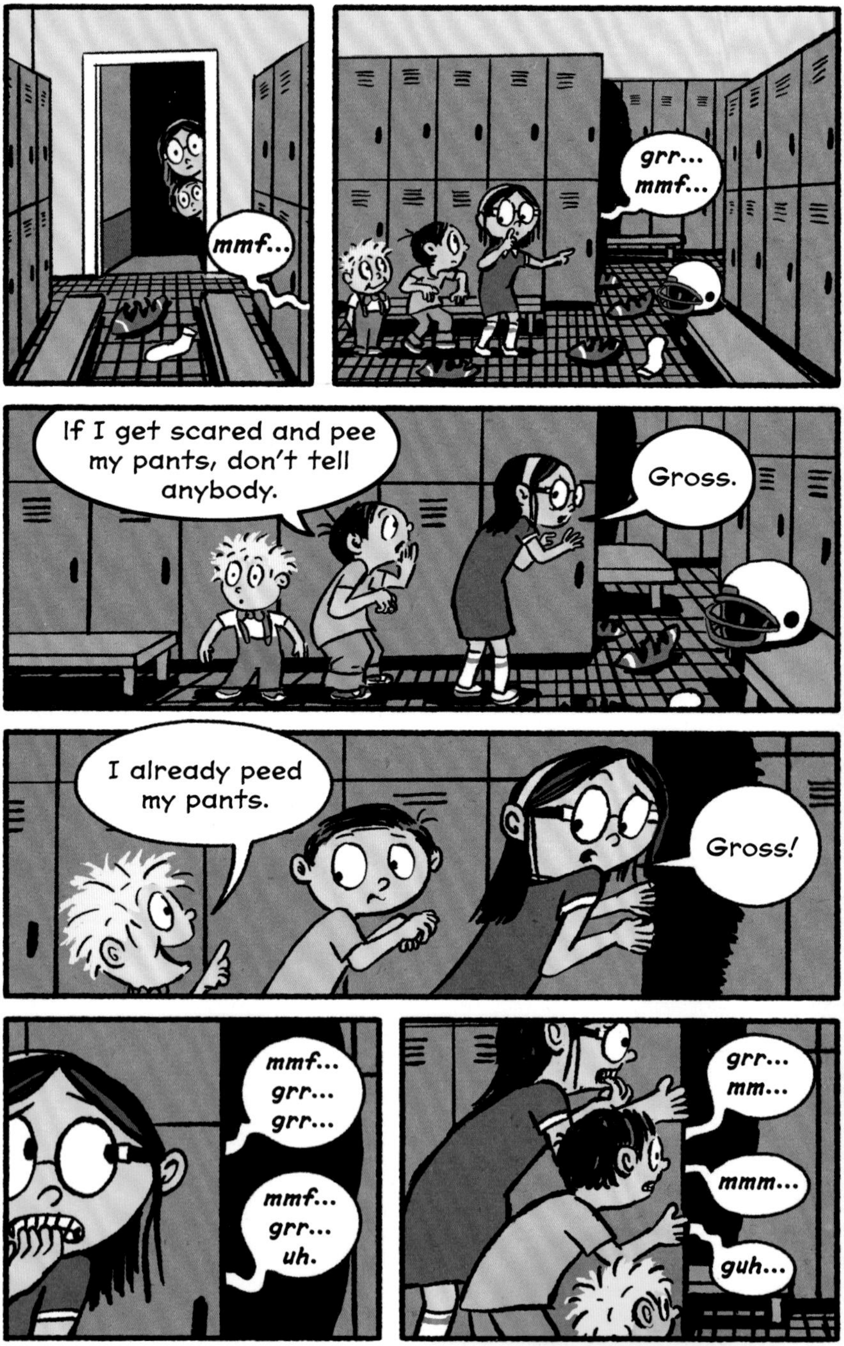
mmf...
grr...
mmf...
If I get scared and pee my pants, don't tell anybody.
Gross.
I already peed my pants.
Gross!
mmf...
grr...
grr...
mmf...
grr...
uh.
grr...
mm...
mmm...
guh...

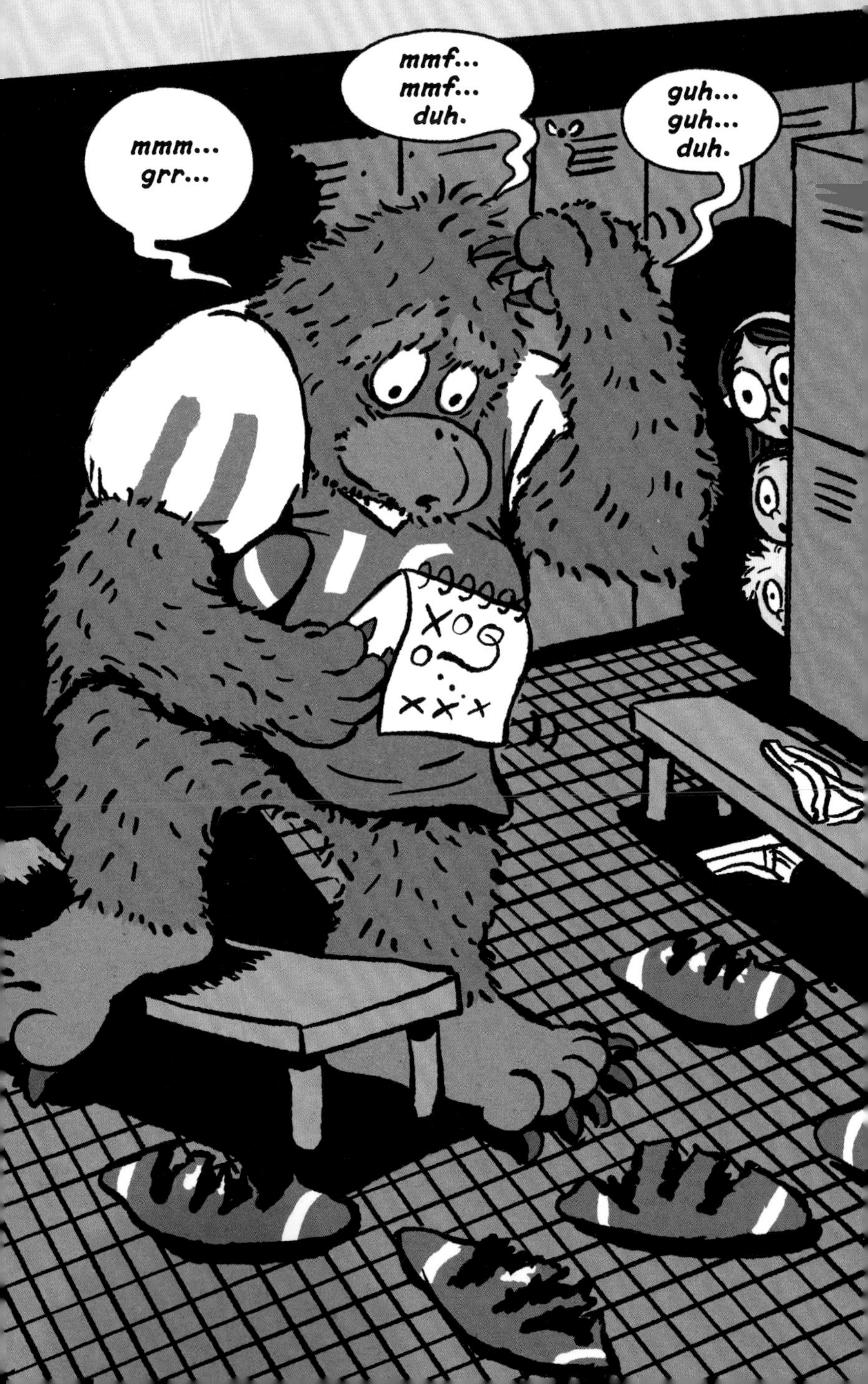
mmm...
grr...
mmf...
mmf...
duh.
guh...
guh...
duh.

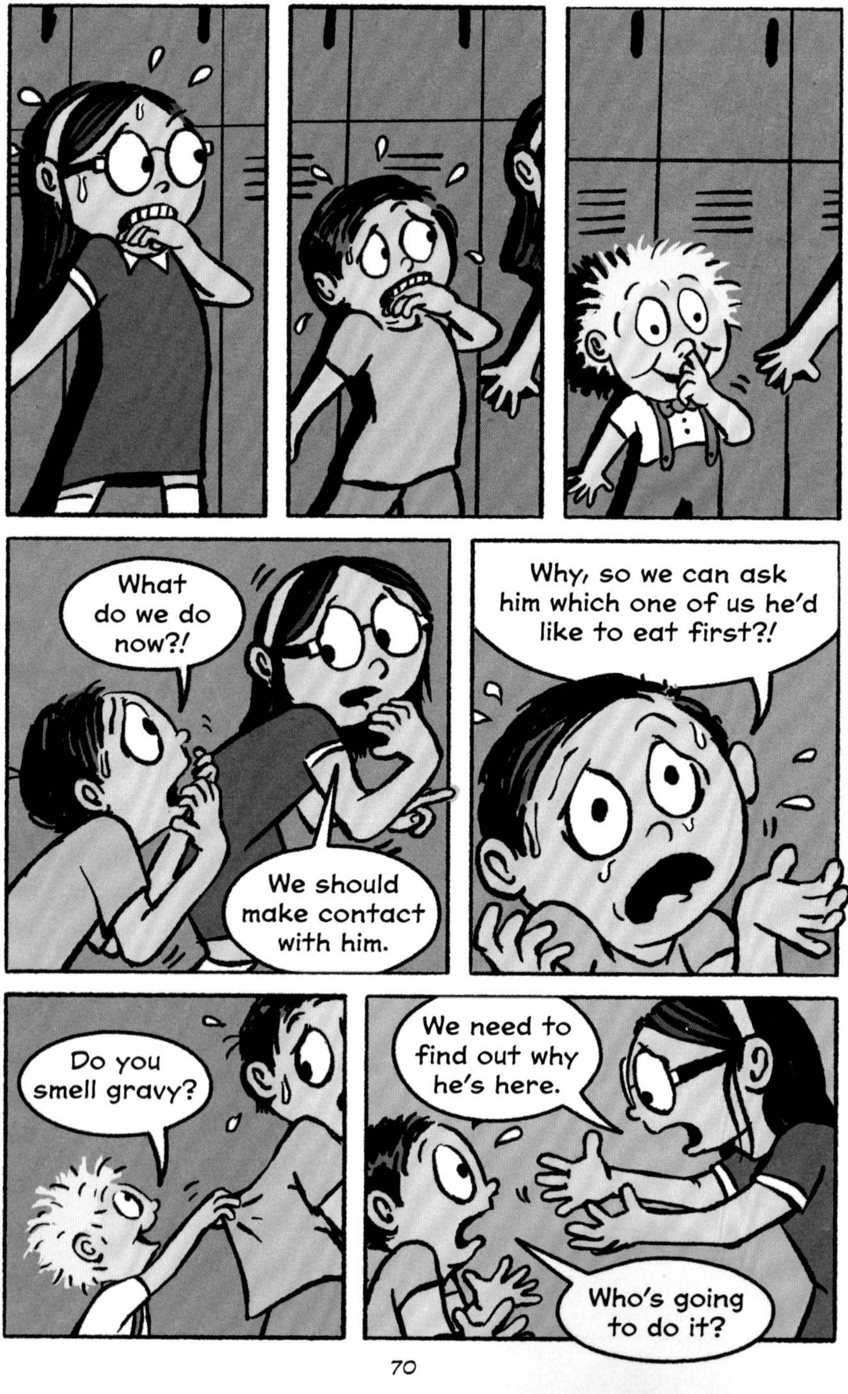
What do we do now?!
We should make contact with him.
Why, so we can ask him which one of us he'd like to eat first?!
Do you smell gravy?
We need to find out why he's here.
Who's going to do it?

Let's rock, paper, scissors for it.

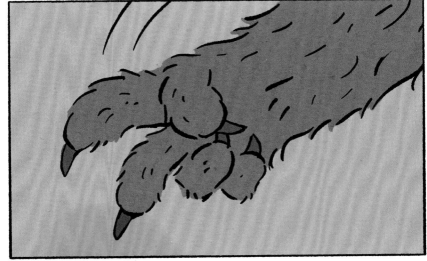

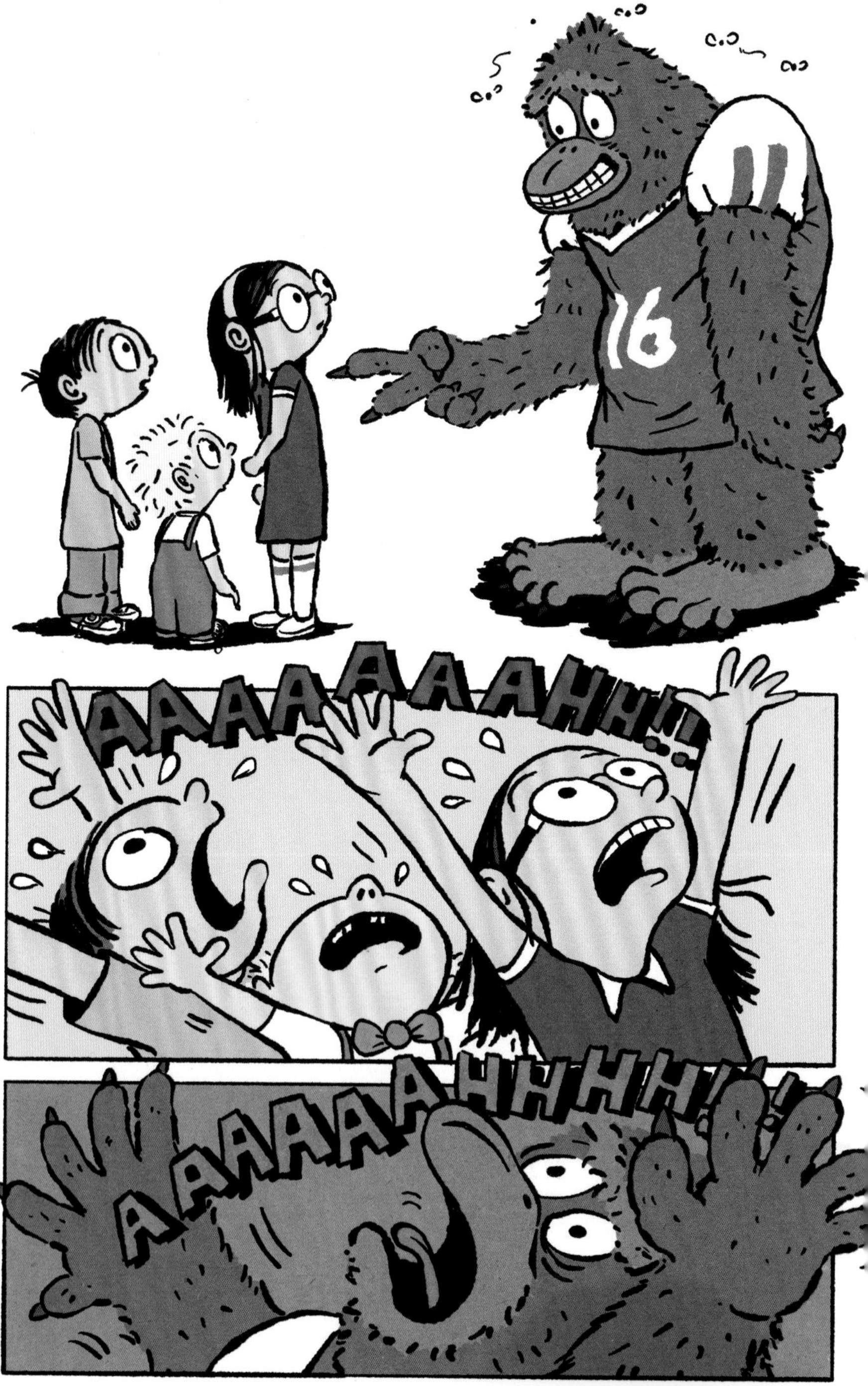
AAAAAAAHH!!!
AAAAAAAHHHHH!!

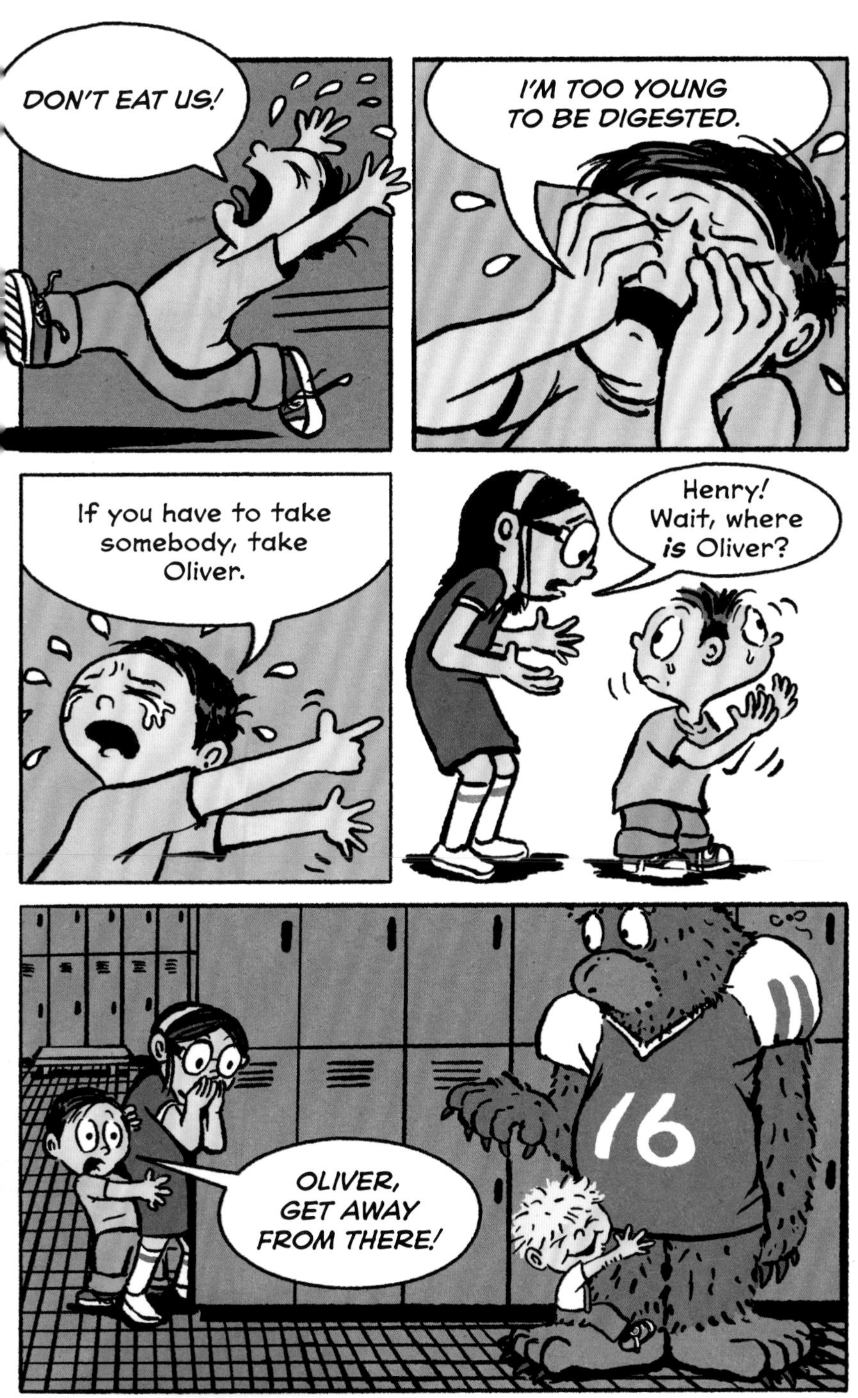
DON'T EAT US!
I'M TOO YOUNG TO BE DIGESTED.
If you have to take somebody, take Oliver.
Henry! Wait, where *is* Oliver?
OLIVER, GET AWAY FROM THERE!

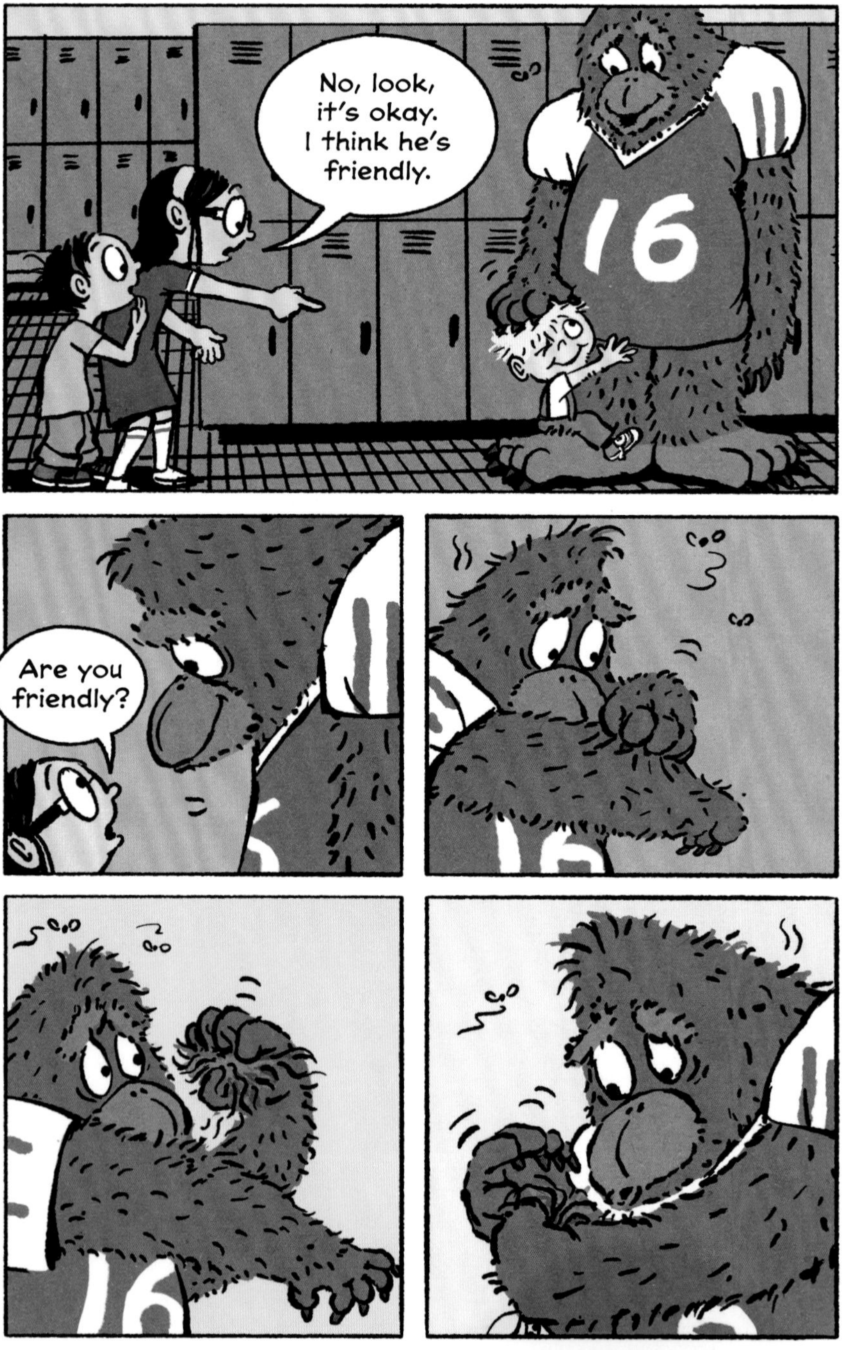
No, look, it's okay. I think he's friendly.
Are you friendly?

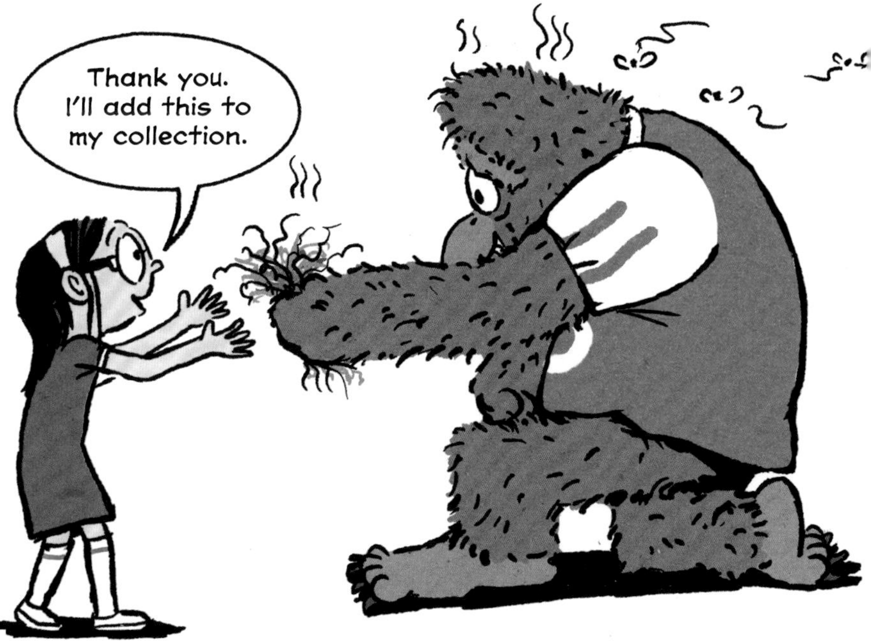
Thank you. I'll add this to my collection.

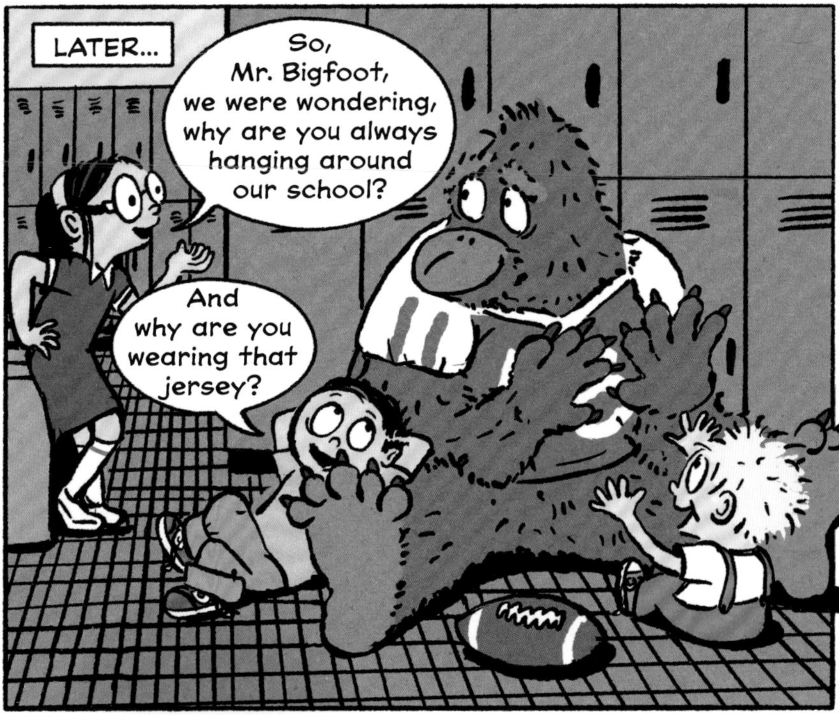
LATER...
So, Mr. Bigfoot, we were wondering, why are you always hanging around our school?
And why are you wearing that jersey?

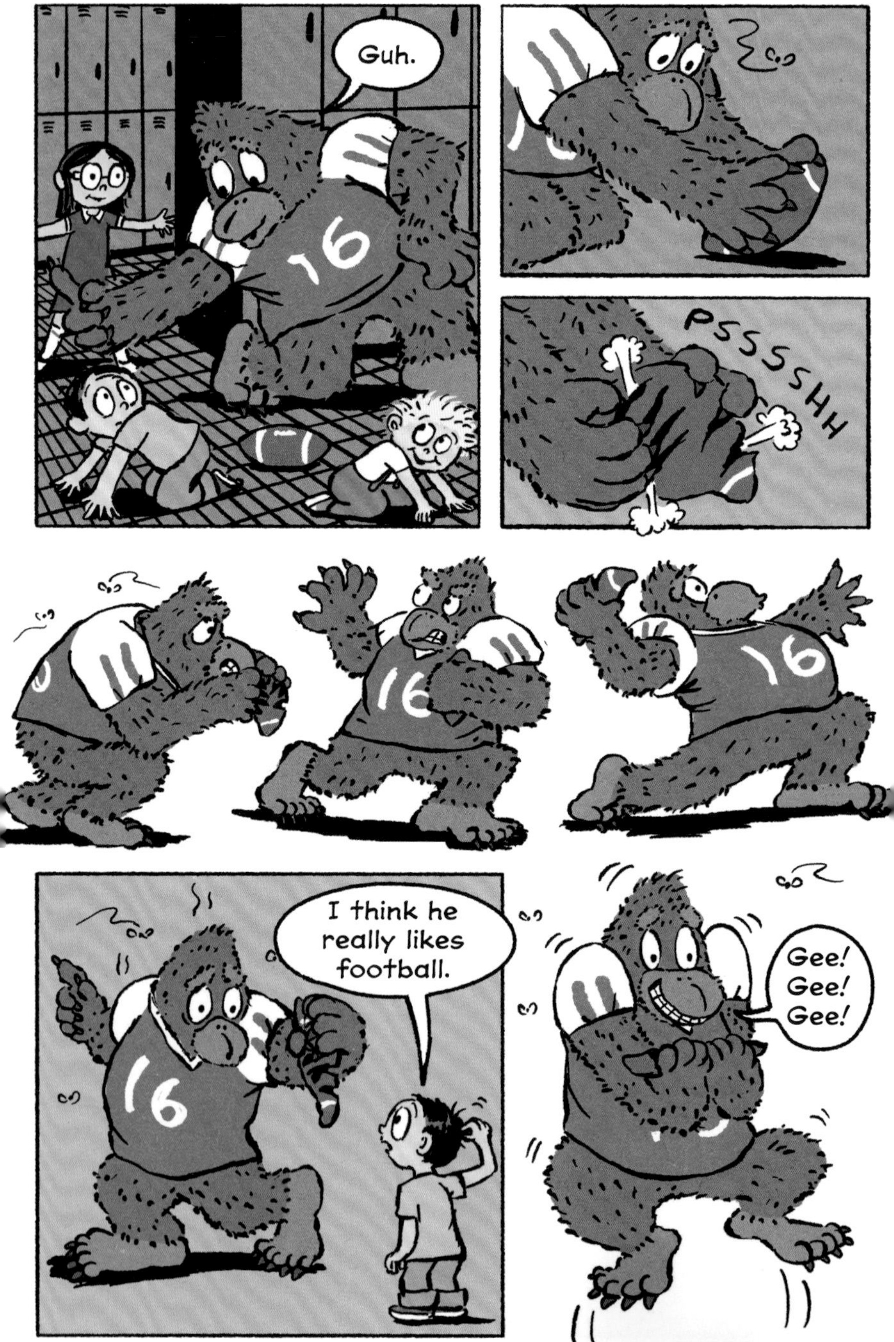
Guh.
PSSSSHH
I think he really likes football.
Gee! Gee! Gee!

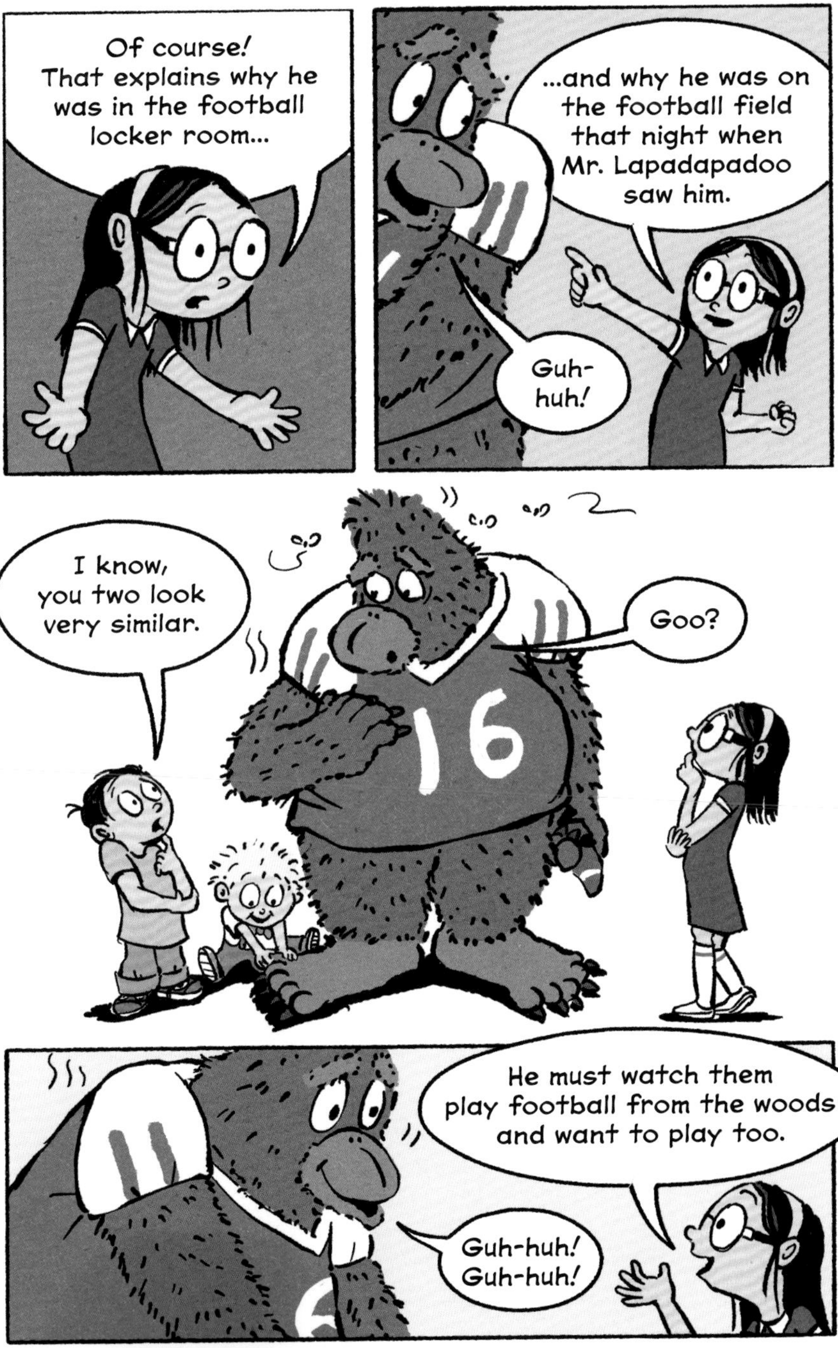
Of course! That explains why he was in the football locker room...
...and why he was on the football field that night when Mr. Lapadapadoo saw him.
Guh-huh!
I know, you two look very similar.
Goo?
He must watch them play football from the woods and want to play too.
Guh-huh! Guh-huh!

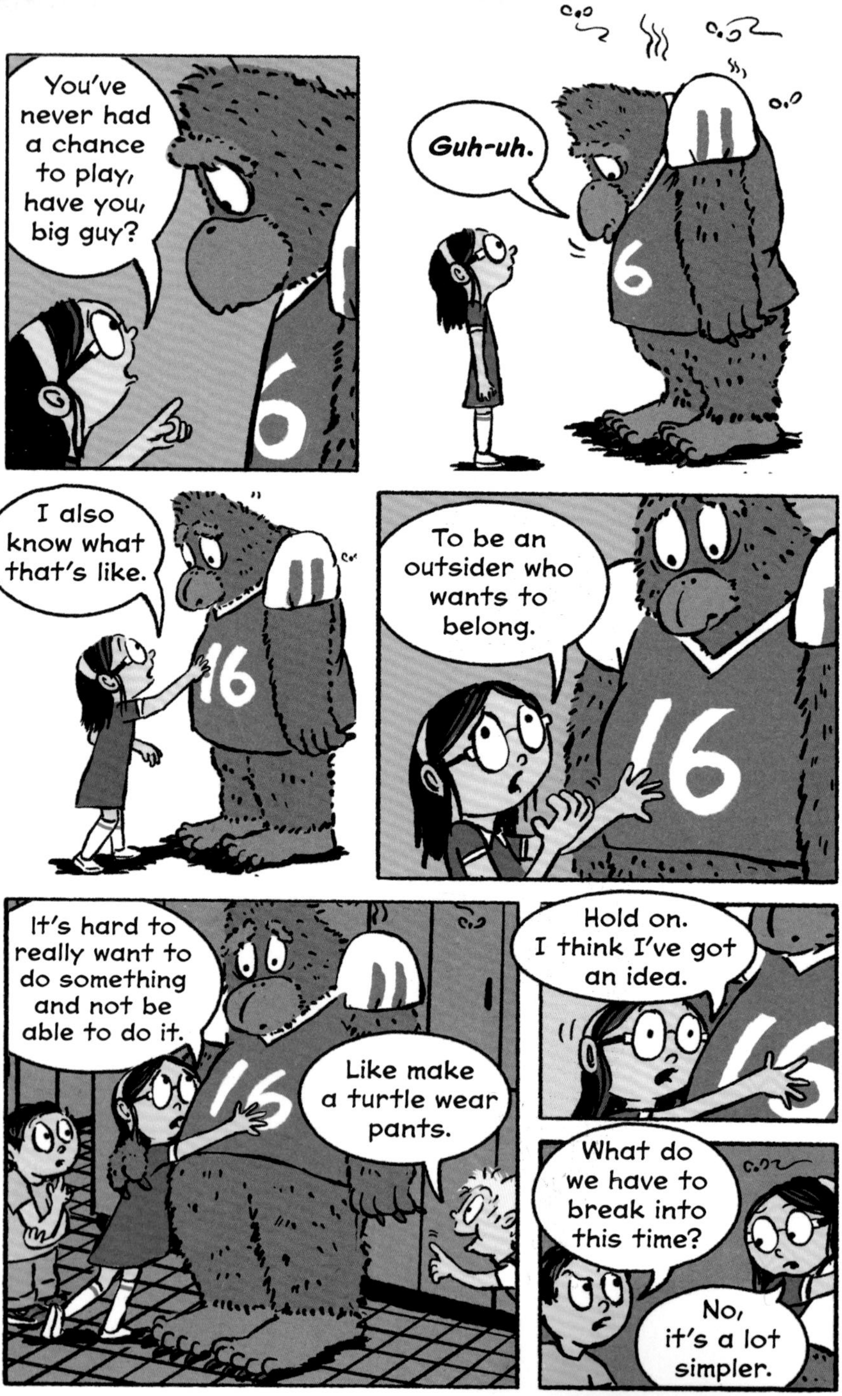
You've never had a chance to play, have you, big guy?
Guh-uh.
I also know what that's like.
To be an outsider who wants to belong.
It's hard to really want to do something and not be able to do it.
Like make a turtle wear pants.
Hold on. I think I've got an idea.
What do we have to break into this time?
No, it's a lot simpler.

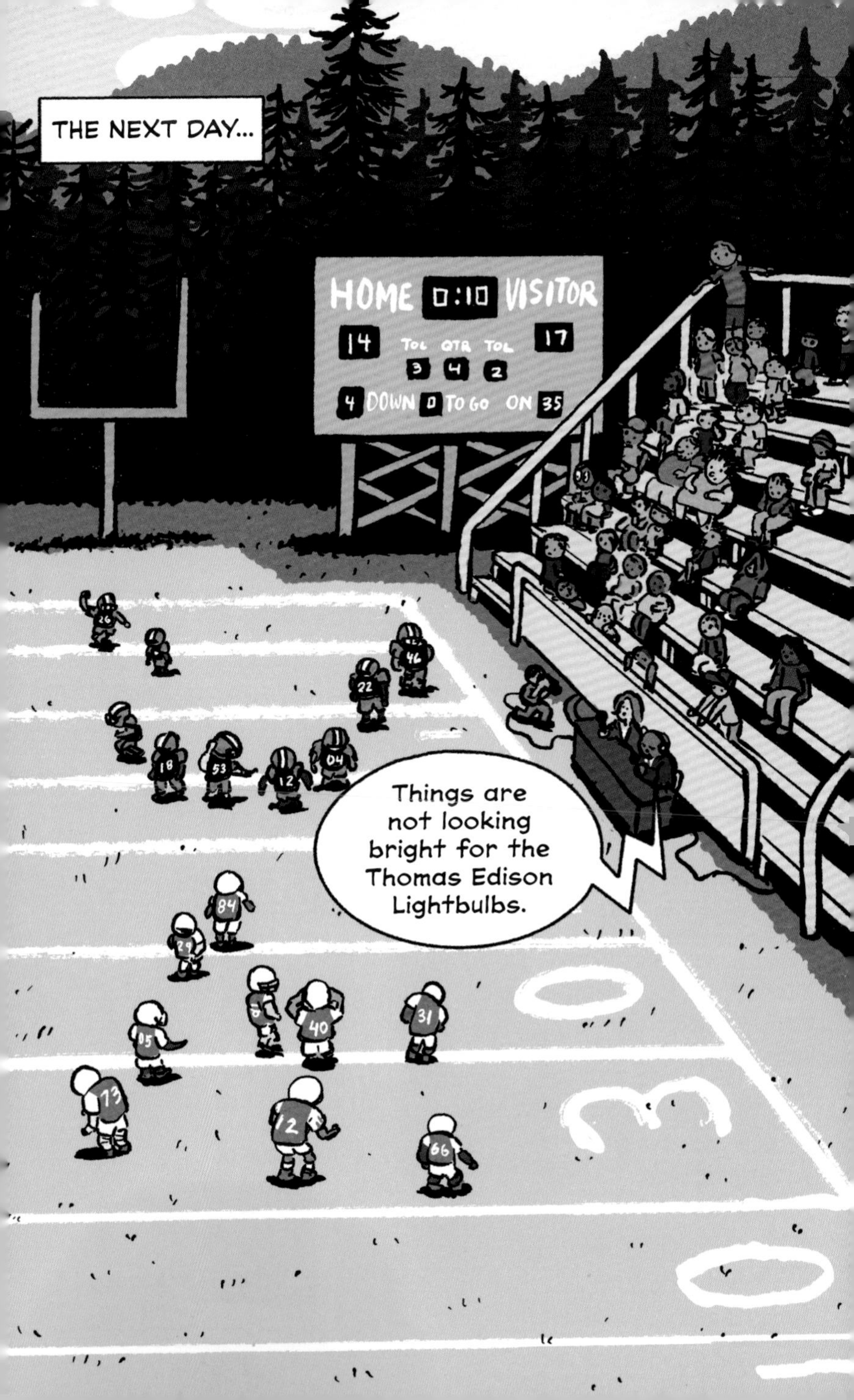
THE NEXT DAY...
HOME 0:10 VISITOR
14 17
TOL QTR TOL
3 4 2
4 DOWN 0 TO GO ON 35
Things are not looking bright for the Thomas Edison Lightbulbs.

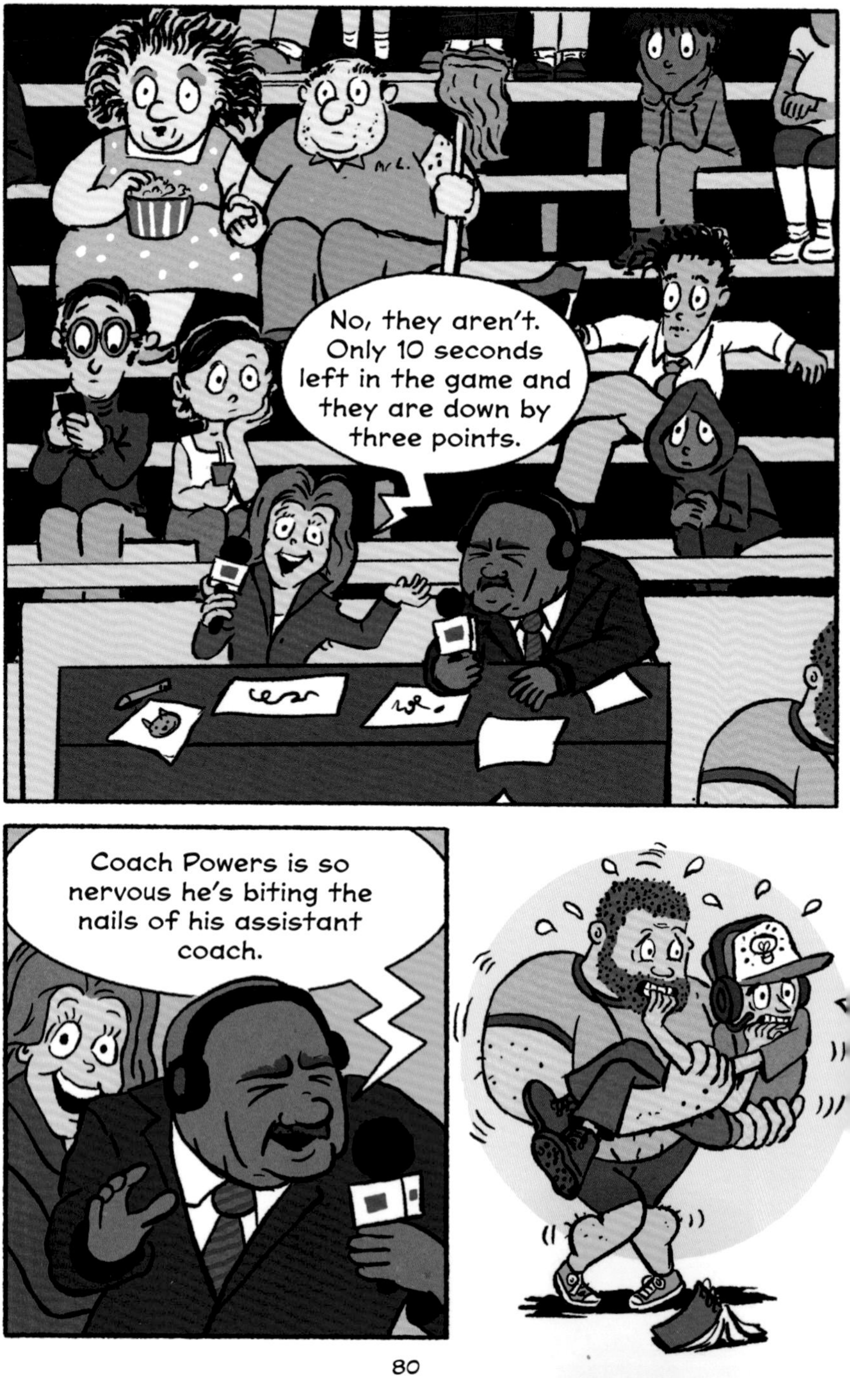
No, they aren't. Only 10 seconds left in the game and they are down by three points.
Coach Powers is so nervous he's biting the nails of his assistant coach.

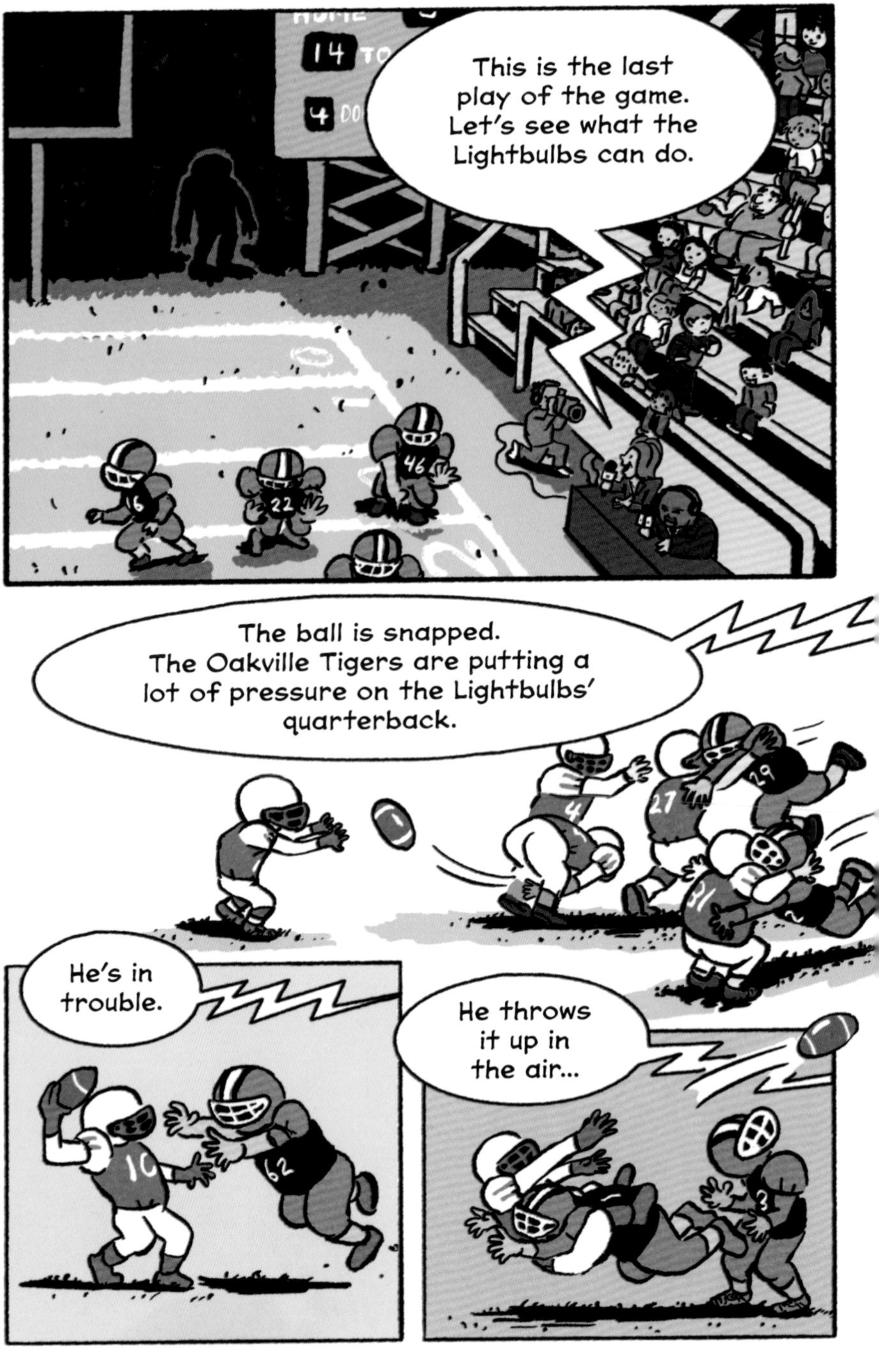
This is the last play of the game. Let's see what the Lightbulbs can do.
The ball is snapped. The Oakville Tigers are putting a lot of pressure on the Lightbulbs' quarterback.
He's in trouble.
He throws it up in the air...

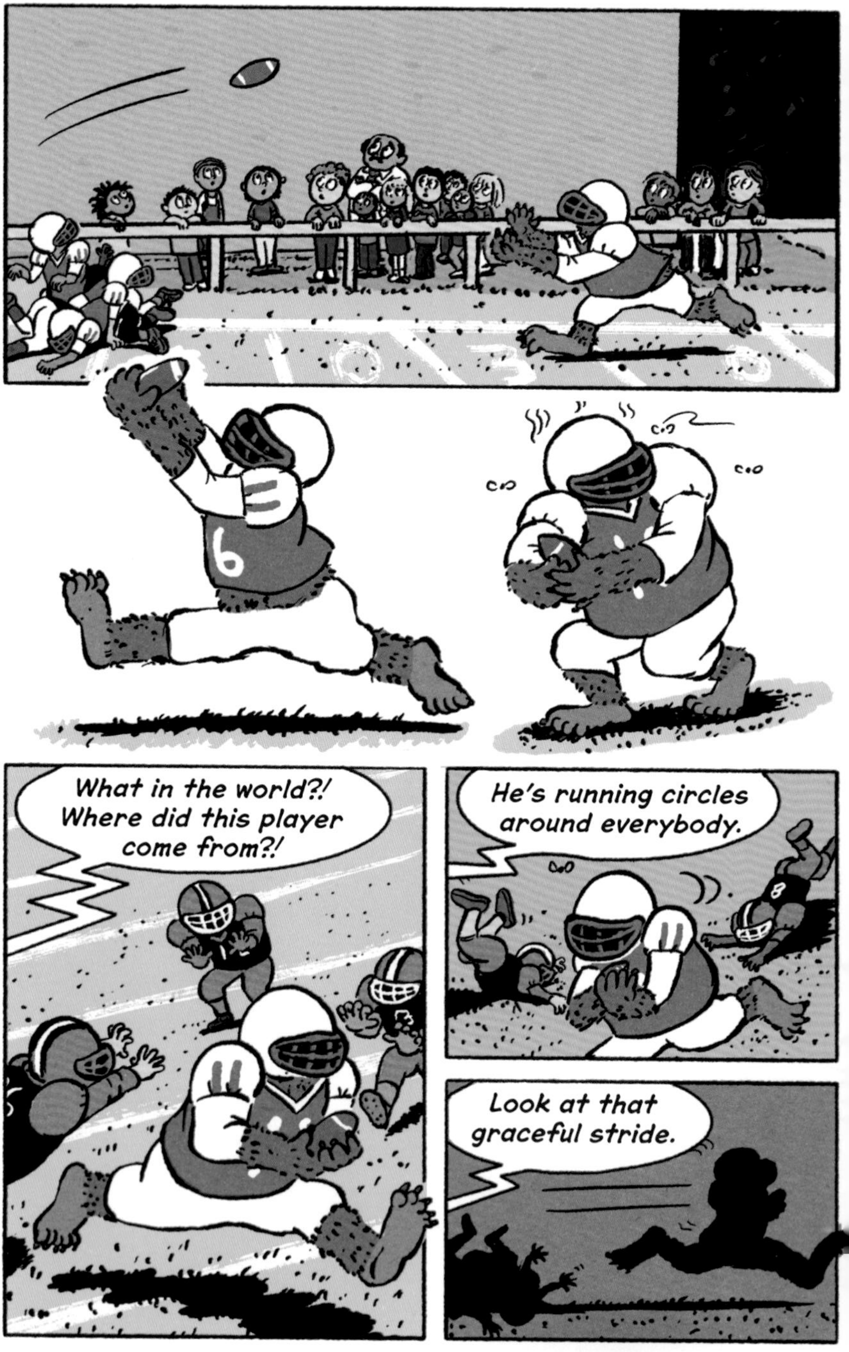
What in the world?! Where did this player come from?!
He's running circles around everybody.
Look at that graceful stride.

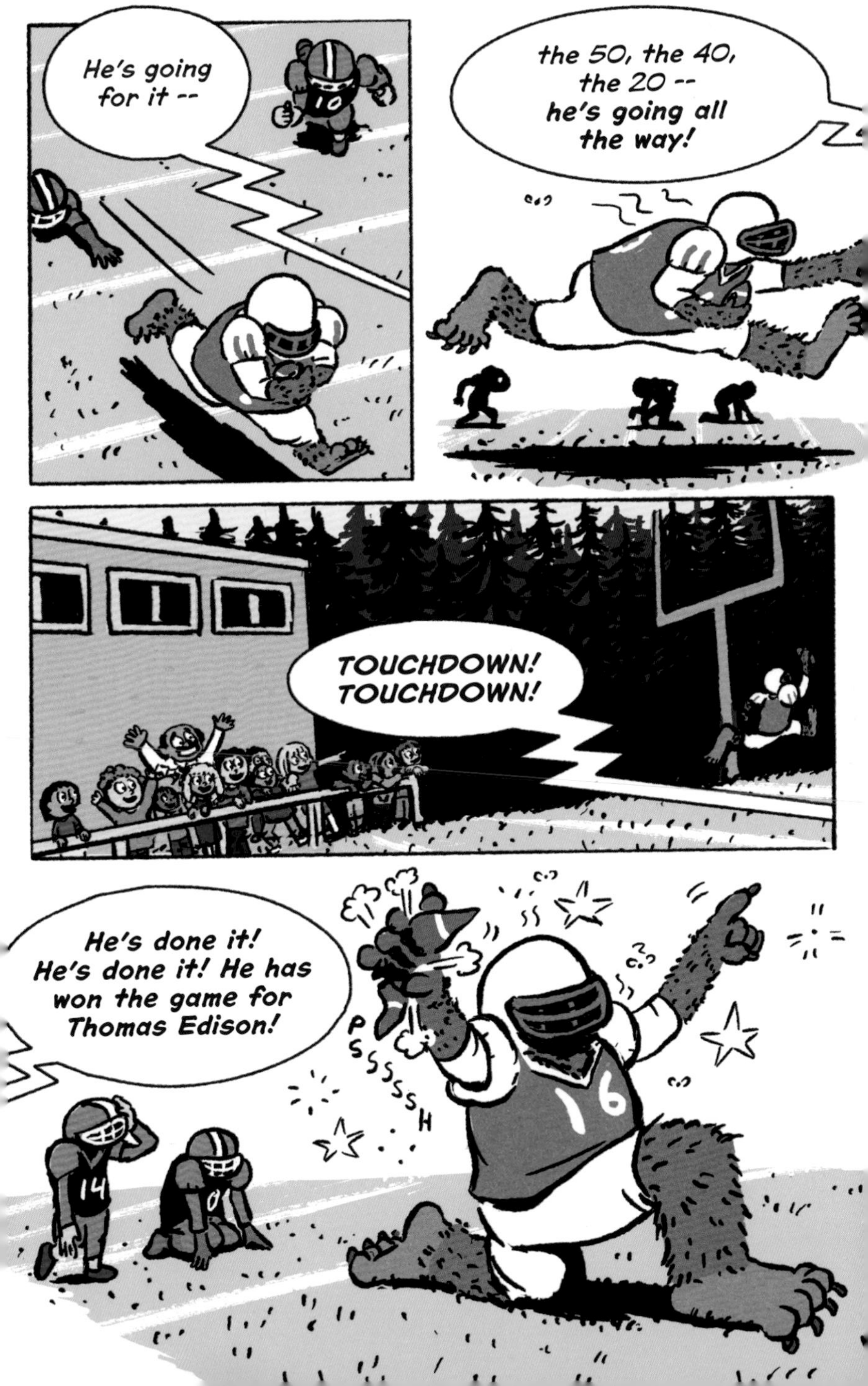
He's going for it --
the 50, the 40, the 20 -- he's going all the way!
TOUCHDOWN! TOUCHDOWN!
He's done it! He's done it! He has won the game for Thomas Edison!
PSSSSSSH

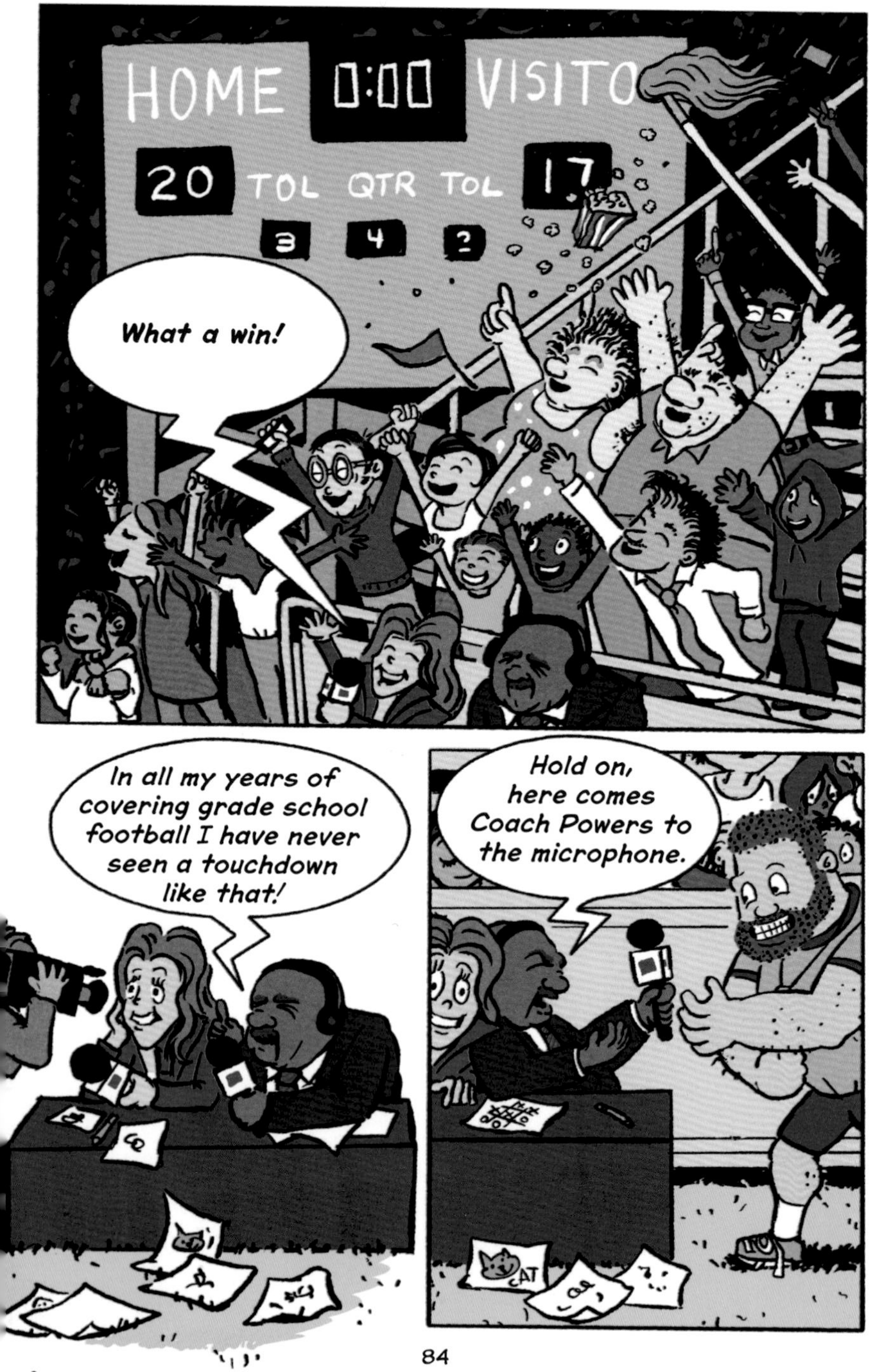
HOME 0:00 VISITO
20 TOL QTR TOL 17
3 4 2
What a win!
In all my years of covering grade school football I have never seen a touchdown like that!
Hold on, here comes Coach Powers to the microphone.
CAT

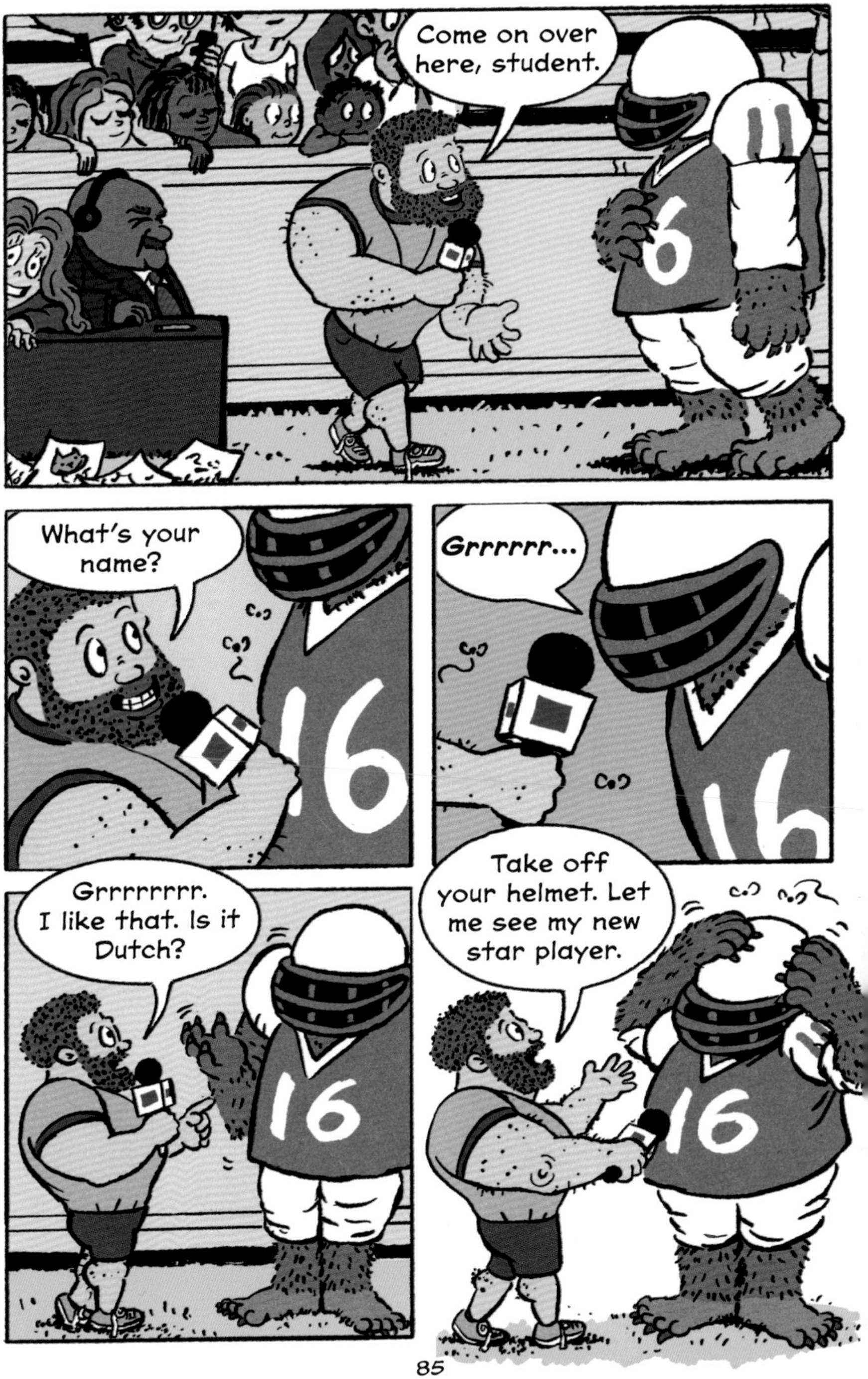
Come on over here, student.
What's your name?
Grrrrrr...
Grrrrrrr. I like that. Is it Dutch?
Take off your helmet. Let me see my new star player.

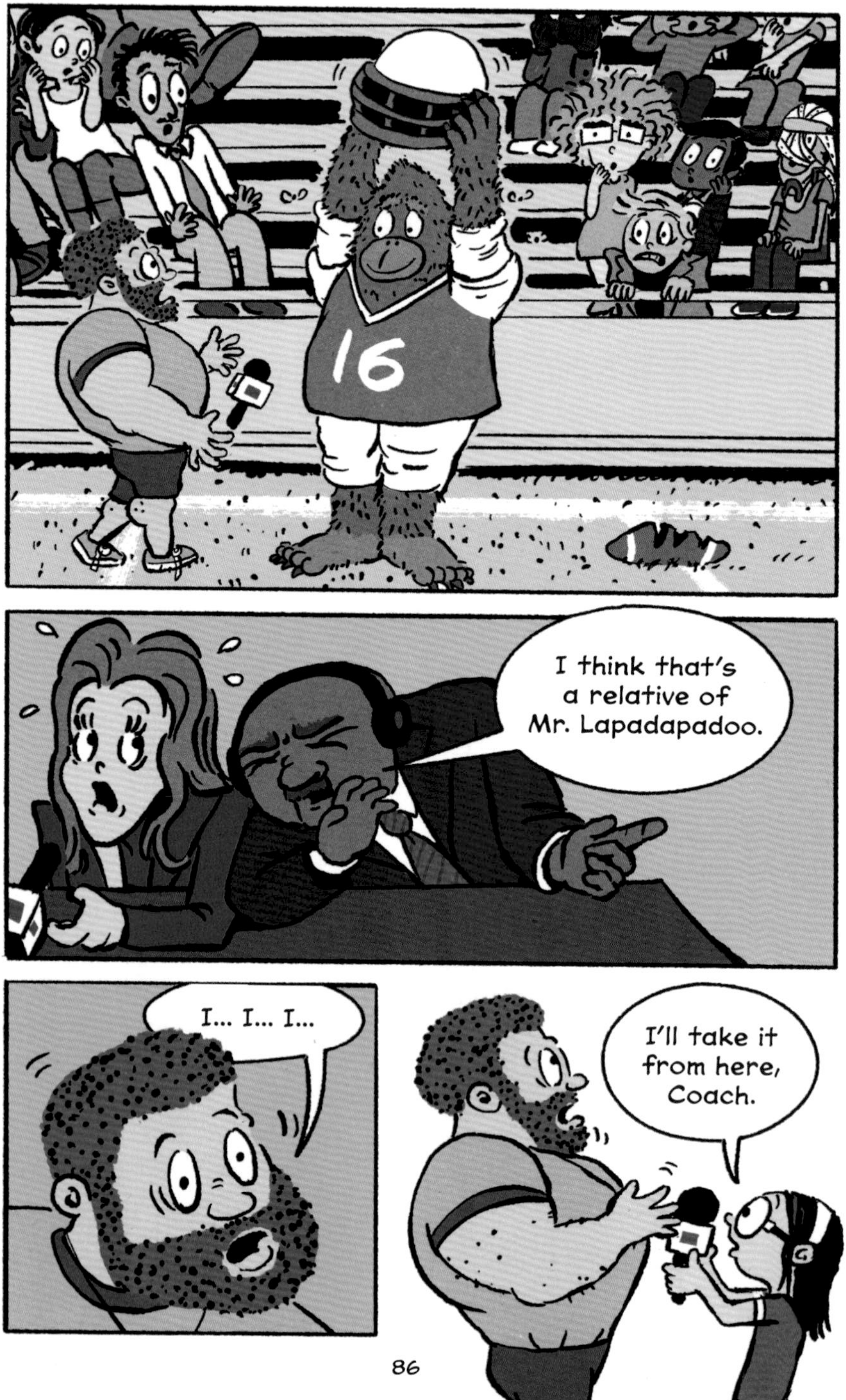
16
I think that's a relative of Mr. Lapadapadoo.
I... I... I...
I'll take it from here, Coach.

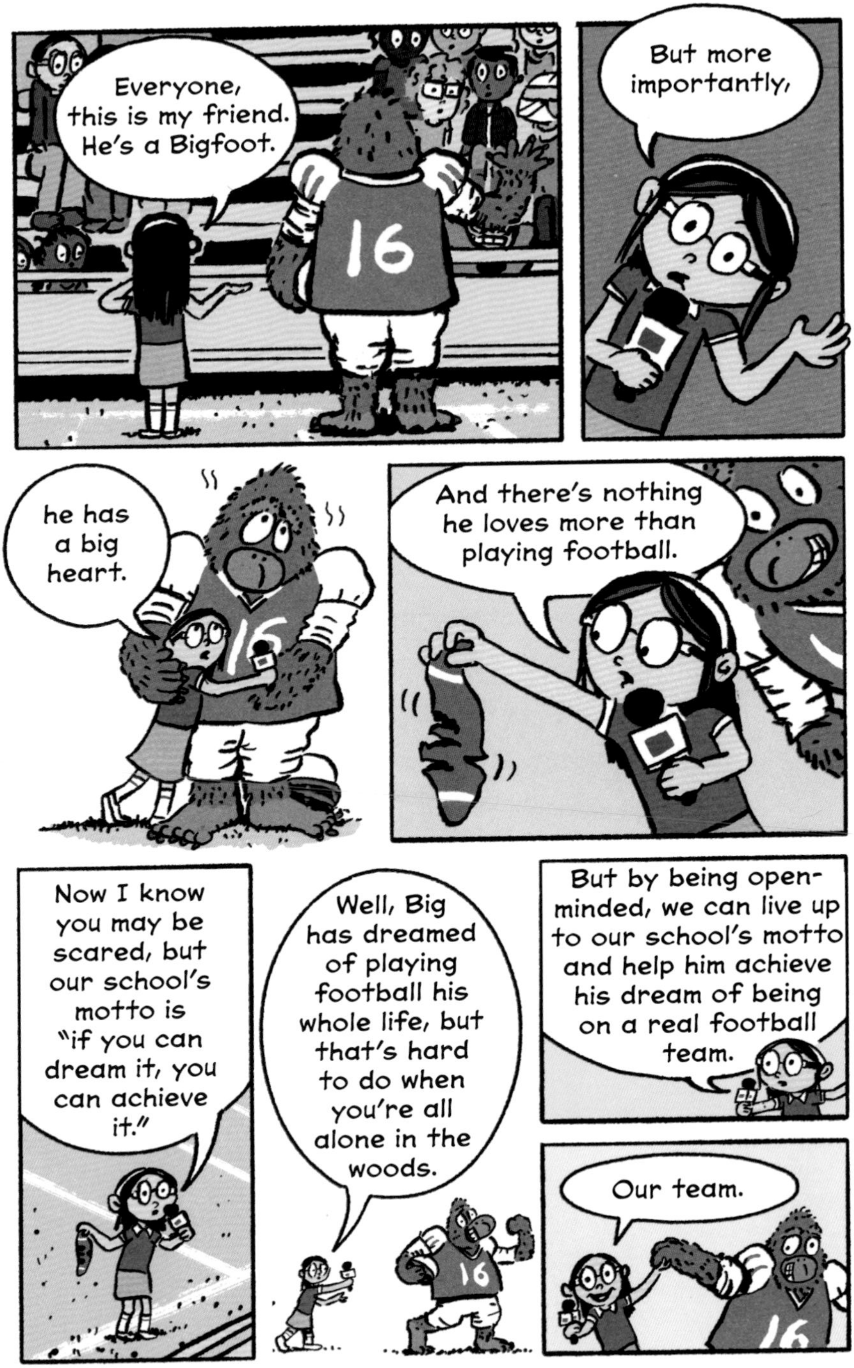
Everyone, this is my friend. He's a Bigfoot.
But more importantly,
he has a big heart.
And there's nothing he loves more than playing football.
Now I know you may be scared, but our school's motto is "if you can dream it, you can achieve it."
Well, Big has dreamed of playing football his whole life, but that's hard to do when you're all alone in the woods.
But by being open-minded, we can live up to our school's motto and help him achieve his dream of being on a real football team.
Our team.

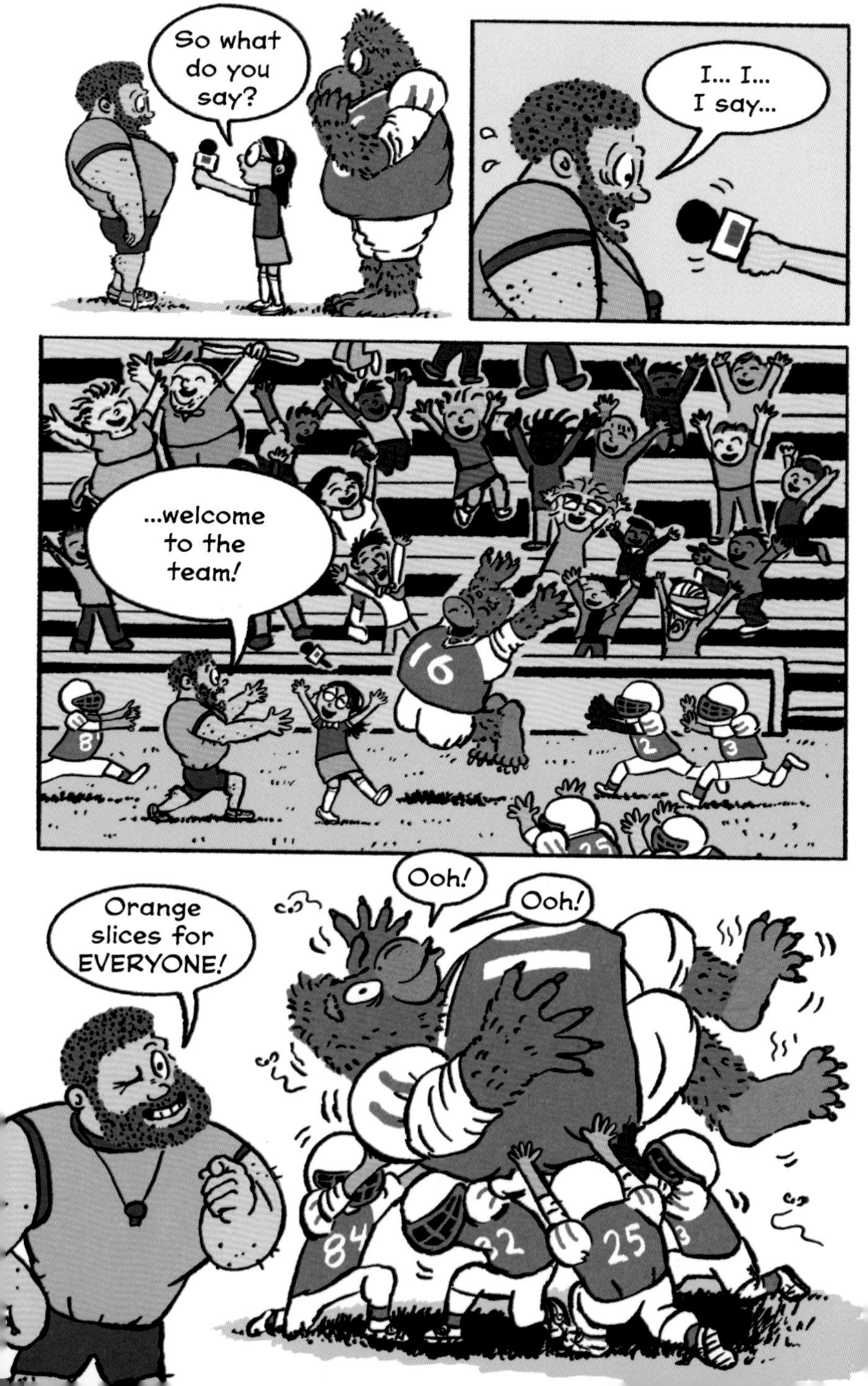
So what do you say?
I... I... I say...
...welcome to the team!
Orange slices for EVERYONE!
Ooh!
Ooh!

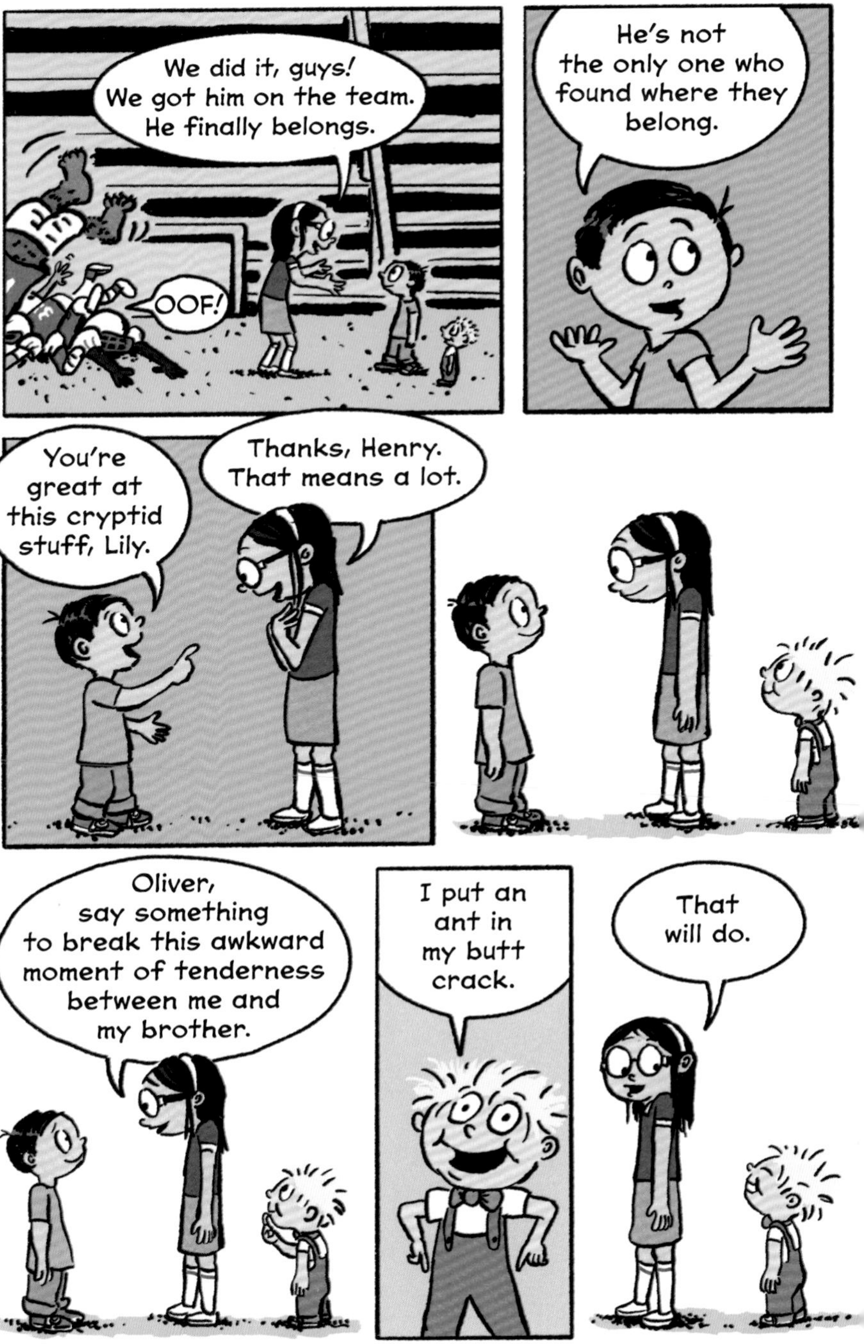
We did it, guys! We got him on the team. He finally belongs.
OOF!
He's not the only one who found where they belong.
You're great at this cryptid stuff, Lily.
Thanks, Henry. That means a lot.
Oliver, say something to break this awkward moment of tenderness between me and my brother.
I put an ant in my butt crack.
That will do.

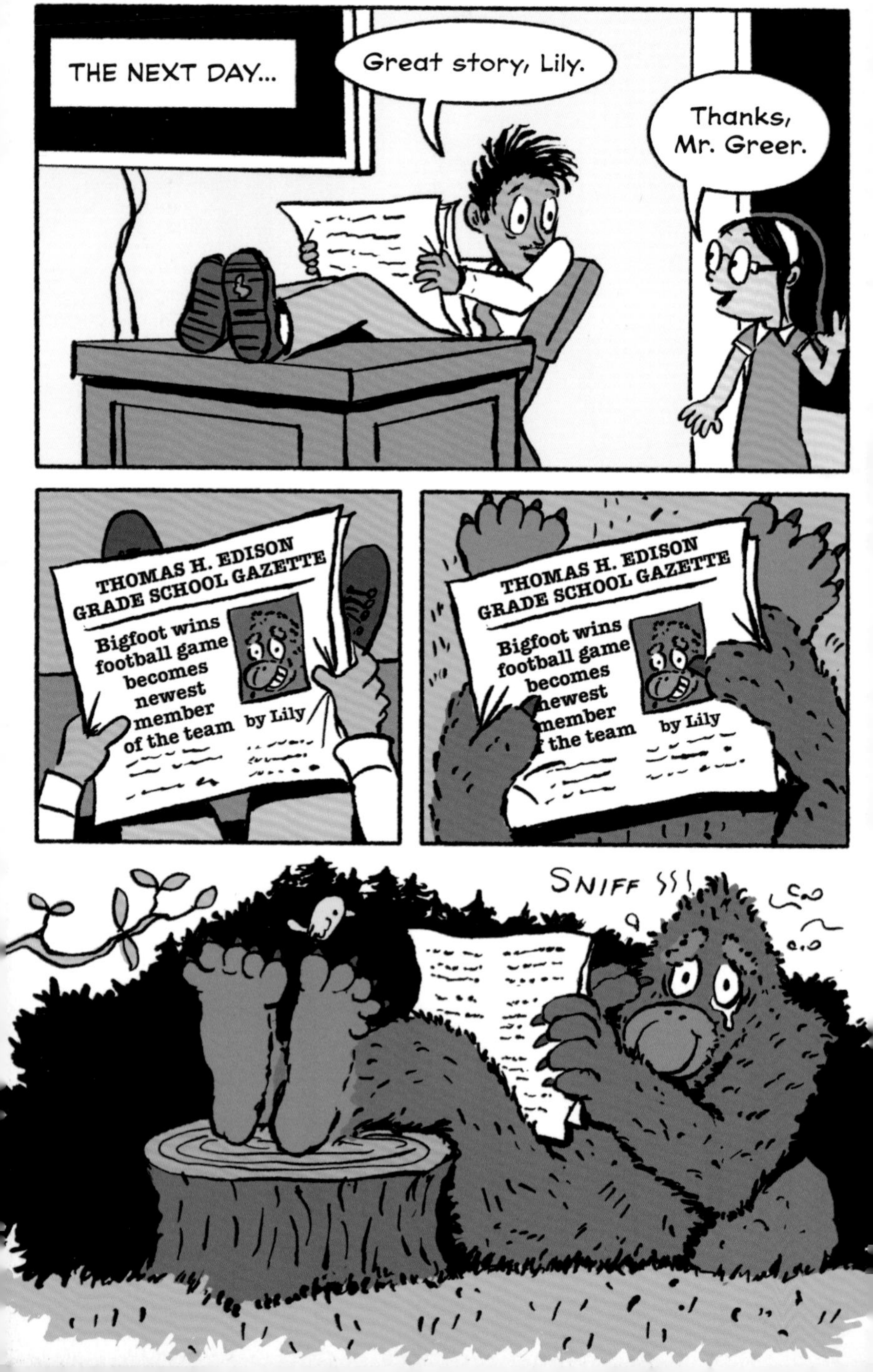
THE NEXT DAY...
Great story, Lily.
Thanks, Mr. Greer.
THOMAS H. EDISON GRADE SCHOOL GAZETTE
Bigfoot wins football game becomes newest member of the team
by Lily
THOMAS H. EDISON GRADE SCHOOL GAZETTE
Bigfoot wins football game becomes newest member of the team
by Lily
SNIFF

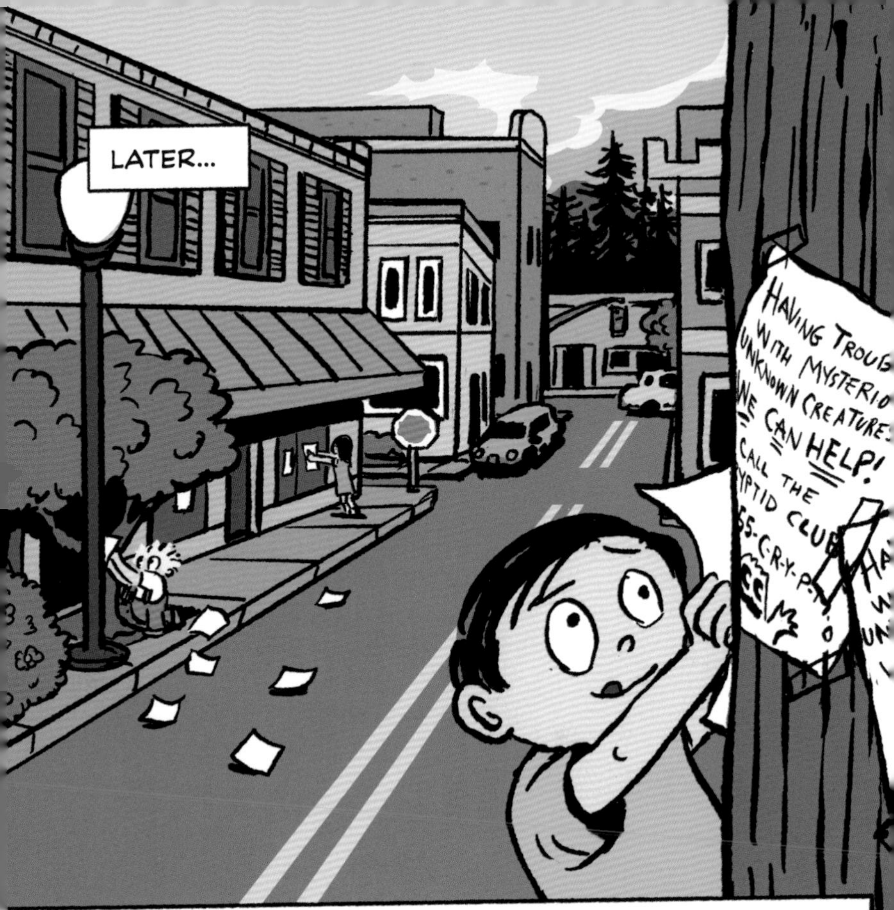

LATER...

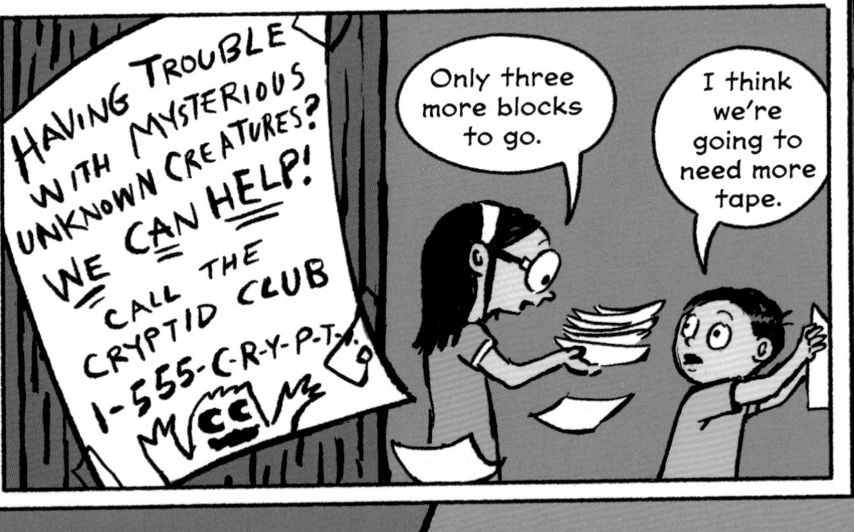

HAVING TROUBLE WITH MYSTERIOUS UNKNOWN CREATURES? WE CAN HELP! CALL THE CRYPTID CLUB 1-555-C-R-Y-P-T
CC
Only three more blocks to go.
I think we're going to need more tape.

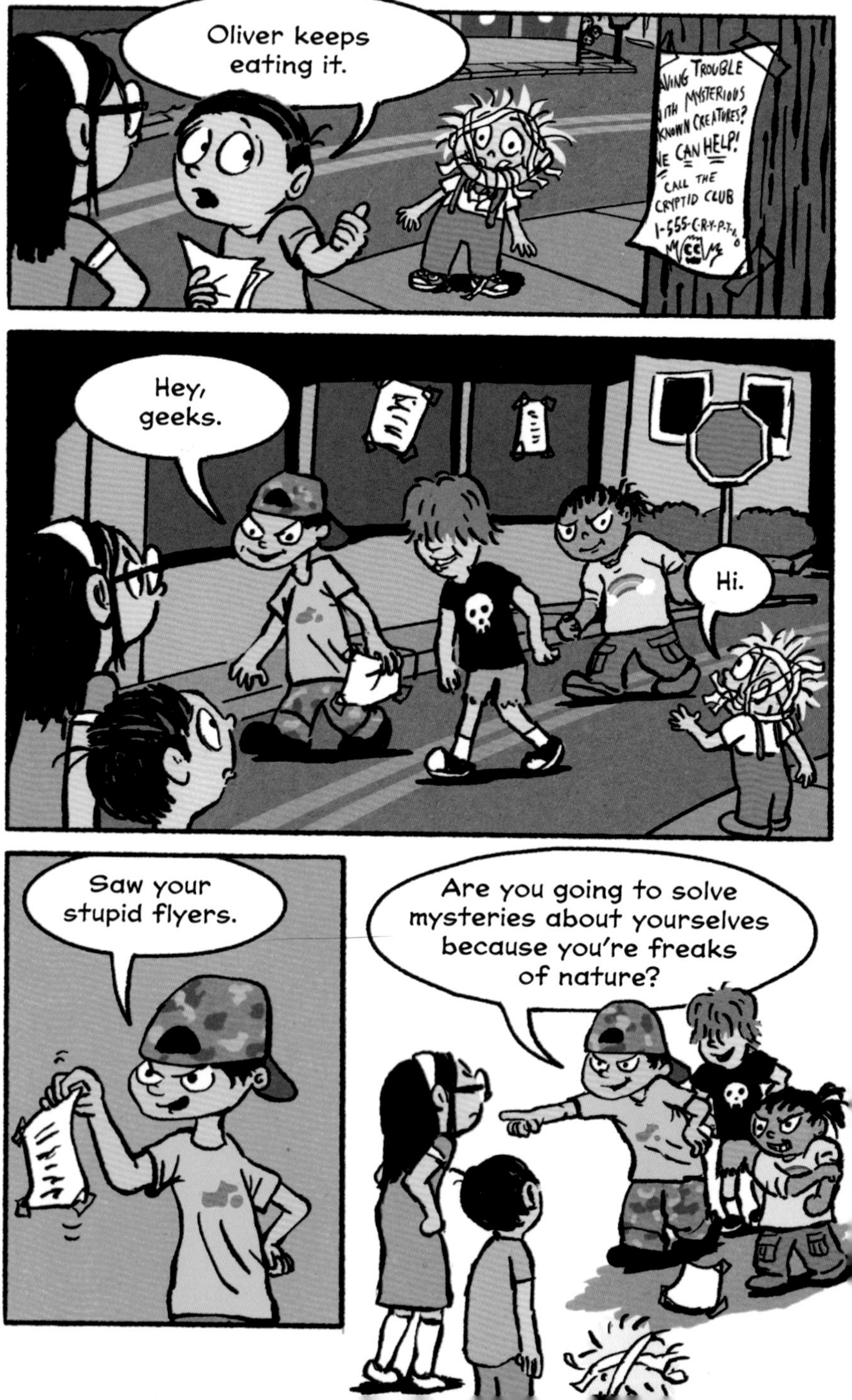
Oliver keeps eating it.
TROUBLE
MYSTERIOUS
CREATURES?
CAN HELP!
CALL THE
CRYPTID CLUB
Hey, geeks.
Hi.
Saw your stupid flyers.
Are you going to solve mysteries about yourselves because you're freaks of nature?

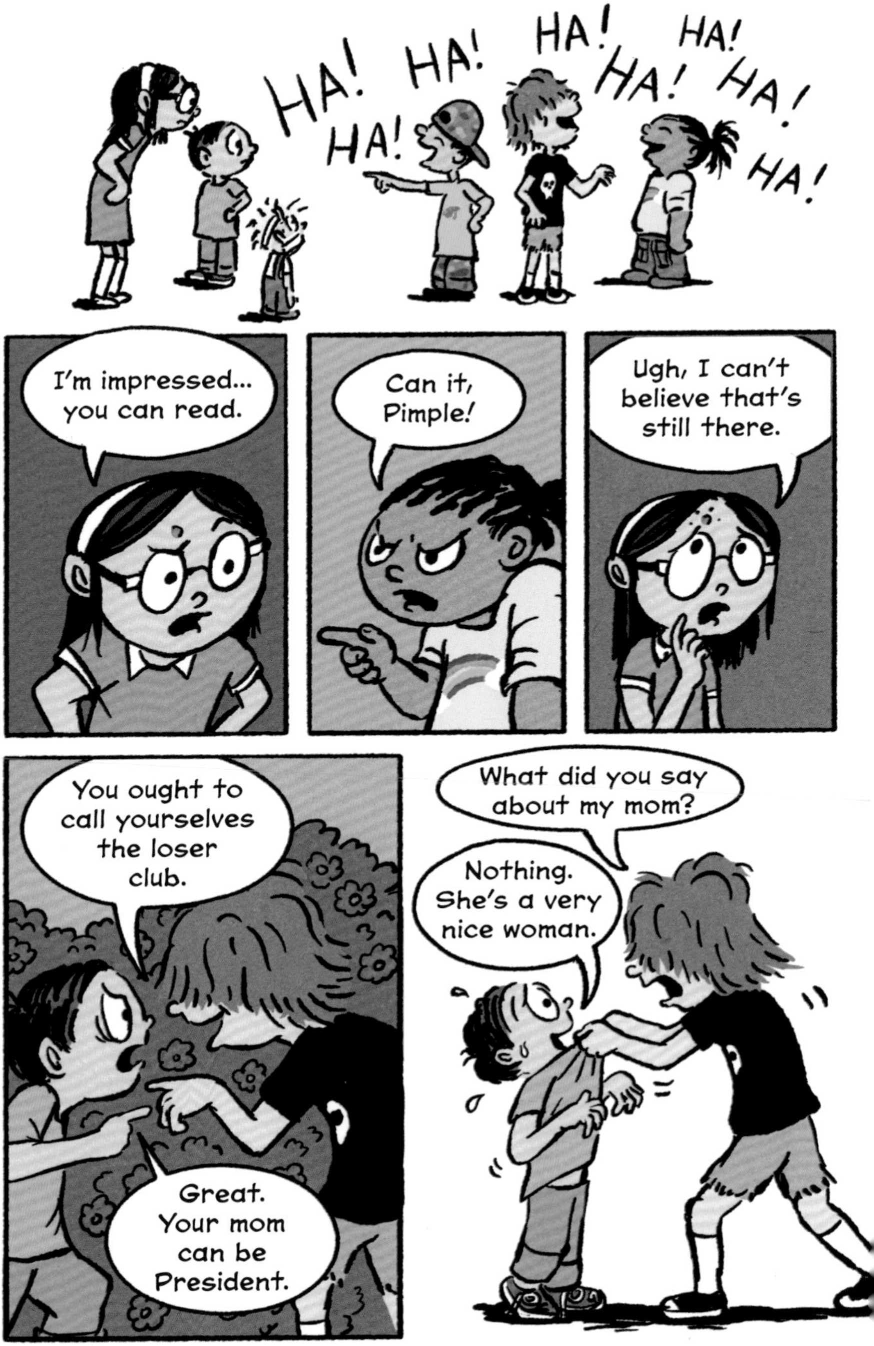
HA! HA! HA! HA! HA! HA! HA! HA!
I'm impressed... you can read.
Can it, Pimple!
Ugh, I can't believe that's still there.
You ought to call yourselves the loser club.
Great. Your mom can be President.
What did you say about my mom?
Nothing. She's a very nice woman.

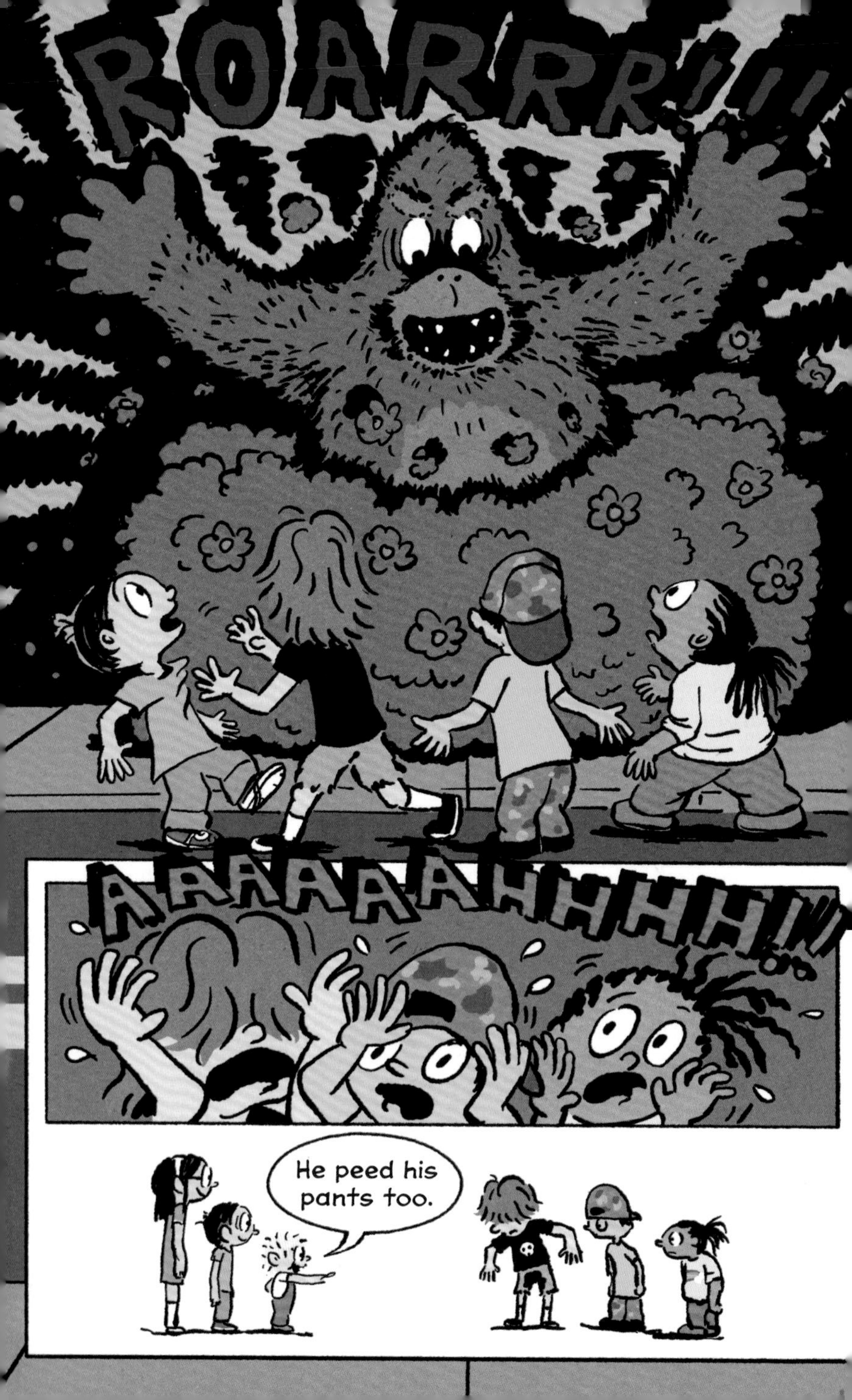
ROARRR!!!
AAAAAAHHHHH!!!
He peed his pants too.

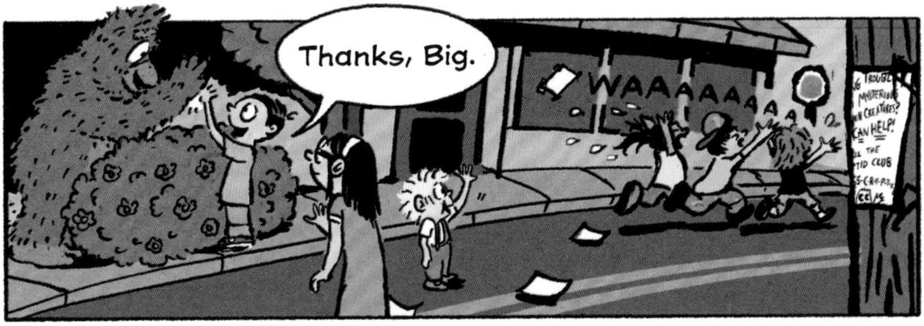
Thanks, Big.
WAAAAAAAA
CAN HELP!

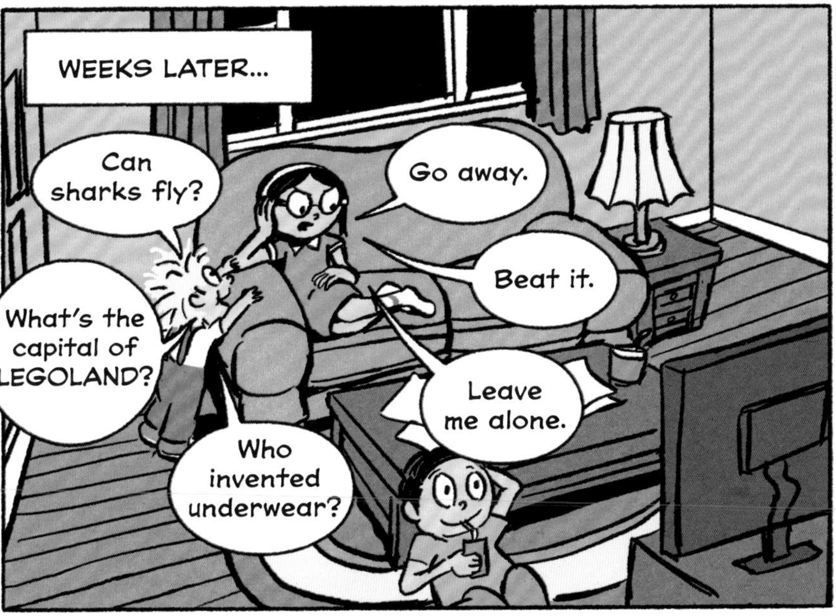
WEEKS LATER...
Can sharks fly?
Go away.
What's the capital of LEGOLAND?
Beat it.
Who invented underwear?
Leave me alone.

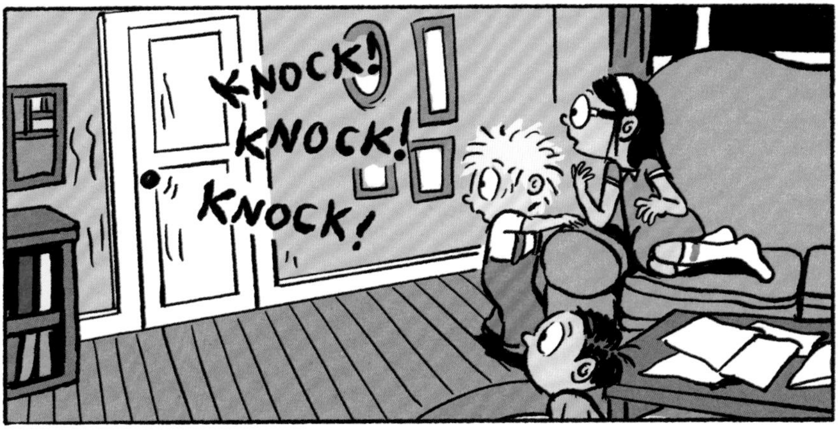
KNOCK! KNOCK! KNOCK!

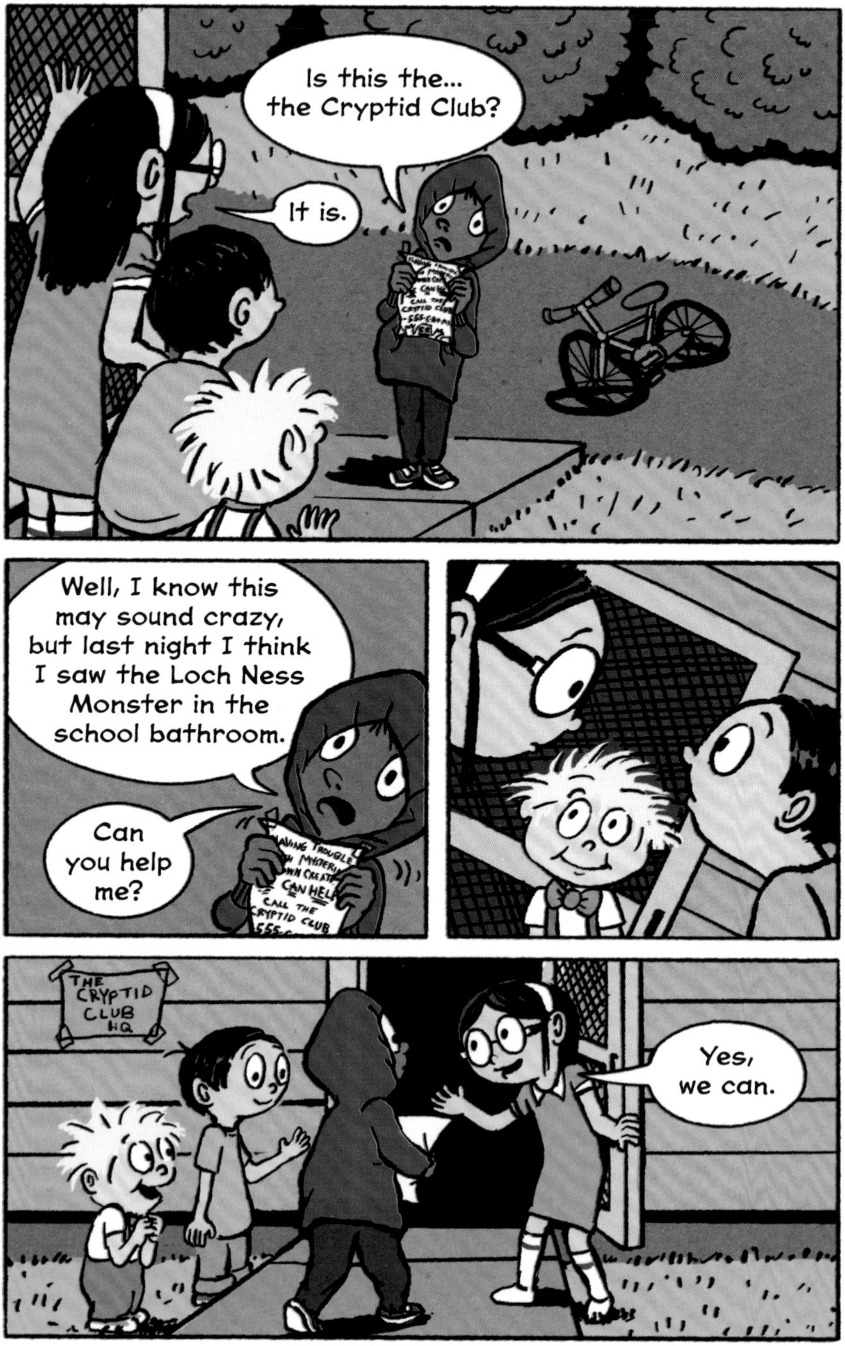
Is this the...
the Cryptid Club?
It is.
Well, I know this may sound crazy, but last night I think I saw the Loch Ness Monster in the school bathroom.
Can you help me?
CALL THE CRYPTID CLUB
THE CRYPTID CLUB HQ
Yes, we can.